REDSTONE MANOR

High Hopes

By

Mildred L. Burns

DEDICATION

To

Jeri

And

Larry

With joy for who you are
And hope that all your dreams
Come true

TABLE OF CONTENTS

REDSTONE MANOR
FAMILY MEMBERS

<u>Theodore & Margaret Randolph</u>
    Kingsley - 1865 -

    <u>Kingsley & Dorothy Gordon-Randolph</u>
        Kingsley, Jr. (1889-1895)
        Constance (1892--)
          Lawrence Tremblay
          Jeanette Tremblay
        Charles Kingsley Randolph (1896--)

        <u>Charles Kingsley Randolph & Isobel Graham</u>
          King (Charles Kingsley Randolph II)

        <u>King & Lehlia Orwell</u>
          Charles Kingsley Randolph III   1943
          (The Boy/ Little Rat)

<u>Other Major Characters</u>
        Charles Gordon
        Constance & Philippe
        Felicity Tremblay
        Dorothy Gordon
        Maria Elena Gordon-Orwell
        Lehlia Orwell
        Ernesto Chicachcio (Riata)

Servants:
Hubert, Joseph, Simon,
Martha, Hilda

CHAPTER ONE

Immigrants

Halifax – 1865-1870

Kingsley Randolph was born in Canada, but just barely. Theodorich and Margarethe Rudolf arrived in Halifax on February 25, 1865. They had planned to go on by river steamer to Montreal, but the stormy winter passage from Bremen to Liverpool, plus the Atlantic crossing brought on Kingsley's early arrival March 1. He was a tiny fragile baby, weak and fretful, so they took two rooms above an empty shop on Water Street while they considered what they should do.

They liked Halifax immediately. They were accustomed to the bustling, vibrant life of a port city. Here great shipyards built the sleek four-masters that sailed the world with cargo and with travellers venturing to new settlements. In fact Halifax seemed to Theodorich the hub of life connecting all of Europe and the New World.

Theodorich was a small man, not quite 5'9", but well-built

and trim. His broad flat face and wide brow, and his weskit and jacket of heavy brown wool proclaimed him a man of the working class. But his searching grey eyes suggested a spirited mind.

He had haunted the waterfront cafés of his native Bremen and listened to the tales of the vast land across the Atlantic. "We must go to Canada, Margarethe," he had said. "That is a land where one can grow. I do not mean to be the ordinary cobbler, which would be my fate here in Bremen. I wish to make high quality boots and shoes, create a business that can expand beyond repairs and shoes made to order. That I could do in this Canada."

Margarethe was a full two inches shorter than Theodorich but she towered over him, or seemed to at least. She had a huge and overpowering presence. Yet she admired her husband, saw him for what he could be. And she was a driver; she intended that her husband's dreams should be fulfilled. "You will succeed, my husband. It is good, this plan to go to Canada. This we must do."

Theodorich looked to a future of business and work, of making quality goods for people with money and taste. Margarethe imagined the people they would know and the social world they would fit into. So both saw their future in terms of "gentry," and to Margarethe that meant British gentry. That she would make clear.

"We must change the spelling of our names," Margarethe insisted. "This Canada is British, and we must join our proper social group."

"Names can't be that important in a big country like Canada," Theodorich protested. "We must be ourselves. We must be honest about ourselves."

"You are wrong, Theodore. (In her mind the change was already made.). Names, and clothes, and the way we speak will make a big difference in this country as everywhere. It is the same everywhere, you will see. And Randolph will be easy to get used to; it has a more dignified sound than Rudolf. We are now Theodore and Margaret Randolph, and we must learn to speak and dress and act properly. The Randolphs of Canada will become a name to count for something."

The baby cried suddenly and Margaret lifted him from the soft nest of comforters she had made on the bed. "We have so much to do, Theodore." She unbuttoned her dress and offered the full breast to the child. He suckled and whimpered, accepted the nipple, spit it out and whimpered again. "Here now, child, you must eat." Margaret squeezed the baby's cheeks and re-inserted the nipple. "Tomorrow, Theodore, you must make arrangements for the christening. The Anglican Church. That is the one most of the better class of people attend. We might as well get started there."

"But there is a small Lutheran church on Trent Street, Margarethe. Shouldn't we get the boy started in his own heritage?" Theodore liked the softer, familiar sound of his wife's name.

"Certainly not. That is just what I have been saying. We must fit into this new world, Mr. Randolph. We must create our Canadian identity. I have chosen the name for the boy: Kingsley. Kingsley Randolph, doesn't that sound right for him?" The baby had suckled weakly and had taken very little milk. Margaret shook the nipple free from his loose grasp and bundled him back into his blankets.

"Kingsley is a very British name, Theodore. It will make a difference for him as he gets older. Hilda was reading a novel by a British author, Charles Kingsley, on the ship. That's where I saw the name. Kingsley Randolph has a good sound."

Since Margaret was busy with the new baby, Theodore explored the city with Ernesto, a friend he had met on the crossing.

Their meeting had been partly by chance. Ernesto, scrubbing the deck, had accidentally pushed dirty water where Margaret was walking. He made profuse apologies, "Scuse, scuse, signora. The beautiful boots. I wipe them." He looked up at Theodore, "Very fine leather, these boots. My family make fine belts, shoes, jackets many generations," he added with pride. "In Canada I, Ernesto Chicachcio, will be leather craftsman."

The common interests immediately created a bond between the two men. Ernesto was working his passage to Canada, so was able to do many small favors to ease the rough passage for Margaret. This Italian worker was not of the social level Margaret aspired to, but she accepted his aid thankfully.

"Ernesto is a good-hearted man," she said to Theodore. "He speaks very fondly of Riata, his wife."

"Yes, she is a beautiful young woman. He showed me her picture. He plans to bring her over as soon as he can manage."

"You may do well to think of him working for you, Theodore. Italians have great skill with leather."

"I have thought of him. We have talked somewhat about the craft. He is a good man, and he knows much about working with leathers. He is now my friend. We will be partners in our new Canada."

Margaret shifted stiffly in her chair. "Friend" was not what she had meant, nor was "partner." Ernesto surely could

4

contribute to their business, but she thought of him as a hired worker. Partner implied a status she was not comfortable with; moreover, she was somewhat uneasy around Ernesto. He was admittedly handsome with his black curly hair, his bold blue Tuscany eyes and ready smile. He was a bit too handsome, too bold, too friendly. But Margaret knew her husband. She had a great deal of influence over Theodore, even in his business plans, but she knew the limits, too. She would deal with Ernesto and his place her own way, without confrontation.

Kingsley required constant attention. He slept poorly, often waking up gasping for breath, and he lost weight. Margaret became tired and she, too, lost weight. Theodore worried over them both, and fretted about the delay in completing their journey to Montreal. By mid-April they knew that their plans must change. They talked late into the night.

"I cannot make the trip, Theodore, and neither can the baby. We must stay here until Kingsley is stronger. Perhaps the summer will be enough."

"You are right, of course, my dear. The boat trip could take several weeks, and the accommodations are not suitable for you and the baby. It would be impossible. I have discussed this with Ernesto; we could start up something here in Halifax, I suppose. Ernesto wants to get busy immediately. He is anxious to bring Riata over."

Margaret spoke slowly, almost reluctantly, "Not start up, Theodore, not start up. If we stay - and we must stay - " she interrupted herself, "if we stay, we have to change our thinking, make new plans. It could be a good thing to start our business and our new life here in Halifax. We will make good friends and get a good start with the business. We can learn to speak the English better and take our place in society. We must stay three or four years to accomplish that. We have to change our plans."

"I think that is for the best after all," Theodore jumped to his feet and strode about the small room. "This Halifax is a good place. Many businesses, and growing, I think." He peered out the front window, "You see, the waterfront is still busy this evening." Turning back to the room he grew still, thoughtful, "There is that small shop downstairs which is empty. Ernesto and I looked at it through the windows. There is quite a large room at the front, and two smaller rooms at the back." Opening the bellied door of the room heater, he stirred the coals and stood looking into the fire.

"Yes, we will begin with or without Ernesto. We will see the shop tomorrow, find out what it needs." Margaret began to see that this plan would have advantages. They would make friends in the British community, and join St. Paul's Anglican Church on Barrington Street. Affiliating with St. Paul's would separate their lives socially from Ernesto who was Catholic. Margaret had already learned who were the influential people in Halifax, and she had learned where they shopped, where they dined, and most importantly who were the leaders in this community.

"Donalda Blackburn has good contacts, and she has told me much about this city." Margaret continued her own line of thought. They were like two balls at the ends of elastic threads, bounding off in separate directions, but tied to the same paddle - their future. "Thomas Blackburn has that contract to build the Sir James Wolfe Hotel in Montreal. And Knowlton Calvert's bank had a hand in that deal. They knew each other in Kent years ago. Serena Calvert was a Halliburton from

Edinburgh, and her family were in the investment business too, so they are good friends. You should make a point to meet Mr. Calvert soon. He will be a good contact for you, and I'm sure Thomas Blackburn would introduce you."

"Yes, yes, you are right," Theodore replied, his tone abstracted. "I think I will go find Ernesto and tell him what we have decided." He grabbed his heavy short coat from the rack in the hall, then turned back to Margaret. "You look tired, mein frau. This child is wearing you out. It is good that we will stay. You go on to bed, my dear. You need more rest."

"Yes, I must get to bed, Theodore. If I were stronger, I would make calls on Serena Calvert and Franga Macauley with Donalda. We must meet people, get involved in the community." She sighed, "By the time we move to Montreal we must be truly Canadian. And please, my good husband, remember we must now speak the English."

"Indeed, indeed," Theodore would not leave while his wife was talking, but he stomped his feet into the big galoshes and turned to go, "I will be back soon, Margaret. Ernesto will be very glad."

He hurried to the Thistle and Crown where he knew Ernesto would be eating and drinking with 'easy come' friends. He envied Ernesto's open friendliness with everyone he met, and knew it would be an asset in business. He strode to the table where Ernesto sat with four men. "Come with me, Ernesto, I must talk with you," he gripped his friend's arm. "We have decided. Come, I want to look at the shop."

"Lento, lento, my friend. First a beer," he waved to the waiter. "These are my friends, Roberto, Ashid, Frank, and Pierre. Sedersi, sedersi. Sit, sit. What have we decided? This is business, is it?"

In spite of himself Theodore smiled. Typical! What a crew; how did they talk to each other? He might as well join them and tell them all. By the time they had finished their pitcher of beer, Ernesto had whipped up the four who immediately set off to clean up "our shop," and they all followed him singing.

Theodore went upstairs to get a lamp and to warn Margaret so their noise would not frighten her. He found her nursing little Kingsley. "But you can't just go in there," she said.

"We'll speak to the landlord tomorrow. It will be all right. We won't harm anything." Theodore took the lamp, a candle and matches. A rear window let him in and he opened the door for Ernesto's crew. They began to plan. "That counter should face the door, not be off to the side." So the men shoved and shifted.

"We must clean, paint, fix very nice. Nice chairs for fine customers, beautiful sign. Your good lady, Margaret, will like that, no?"

They went from room to room talking about what was needed, what they would do. Ernesto said, "Maybe I will sleep in back room, OK? Cheap, I save money for Riata, be handy for work, you think?"

Finally the two men stopped and stood silently facing each other. They looked deeply into each other's eyes, and then, saying nothing, clasped hands, then arms, and then hugged, sealing their commitment to each other and to their work.

CHAPTER TWO

High Hopes

Halifax – 1870-1875

The next day rental was arranged, and Margaret was escorted through the rooms discussing and planning. "You make front like good drawing room, signora. Fine room for fine customers. Not so fine workers come to side door, OK?"

"Very good, Ernesto. That is wise. We do want to attract quality trade. We can serve tea in the front. But we will need the other trade too. I will do the accounts and books upstairs." Margaret had a head for business, and she also had a mind to keep charge of the finances. There were three partners in this enterprise: Theodore was the spear, and the arm was Ernesto's, but in some almost indefinable way, Margaret was the force.

They searched used goods shops for furnishings that would make the shop attractive and functional, submitting them for approval to La Signora. Margaret found a bolt of heavy yardage in rose and gold stripes on sale at Wright's

Mercantile. She cut and pleated drapes, which were hung on the windowless south wall of what they began to call the "tea room". She covered the seats and backs of three formal Edwardian chairs to match. With the two dark oak side tables and a fine used Axminster carpet, the front room began to take on an elegant, welcoming appearance. Dorothea Blackburn had decided that she did not want to cart her dark wine velvet side sofa to Montreal, and Margaret eagerly added it to the room.

Ernesto applauded, "Si, si! Signora. This is nice place." Margaret, too, was pleased with their work. Ernesto's crew did the painting (to Margaret's direction), cleaned, polished, and repaired all the while singing and laughing along with their "Italiano". Pierre designed and painted a large sign for the front:

Randolph & Chicachcio Cobblers
Fine Quality Leather Goods

The men accepted not a penny for their work and the shop quickly took shape. Business soon came to their door, at first the rough trade from the docks and the shops. But they prospered satisfactorily for a new business. The skills of the three partners complemented each other. Theodore was a searcher, always on the lookout for new forms, new ways to make footwear for special purposes, new customers they might serve. Could they make children's shoes, work boots, ladies bedroom slippers, shoes for sportsmen? Of course. He was alert for new markets, and for the ways people everywhere adapted footwear to climate and local conditions.

He became excited about native footwear. "Ernesto, we

must get some samples of these winter boots - and the moccasins, too. With the fur on the inside, the boots are very warm. Norwegians make their boots the same way." So they began to build a line of fur-lined dress boots with soft, supple leather outside, and warm sealskin linings. Ernesto shaped and fitted the boots to foot forms he had carved from mahogany. Ernesto was the leather craftsman. It was his art that made each pair of boots unique, styled to suit the pleasure of the customer.

Margaret was soon restless tied to the apartment and the baby. Life in Bremen had been dynamic, full of bustle - school, piano lessons, and church and family activities. From the age of seven she had worked in her father's merchandise store, growing through jobs suited to her age, but always dealing with people - customers and workers. By the time she was sixteen she managed the money of the business, keeping accounts, paying bills, dealing with agents. So cooking, cleaning, and caring for a baby did not satisfy her driving energy. She focused on her campaign to establish the family in the social life of Halifax.

She invited ladies from the church to tea in the shop's tearoom. This linking of business and social life was unusual, a new concept in the Halifax community. Margaret was a gracious hostess, so the ladies came and they regarded the elegant boots on display with interest.

Margaret was not entirely comfortable with the Anglican Church - it seemed somewhat popish from her Lutheran upbringing. But she was convinced that the church was an important entrée into the social world she aspired to, so she attended regularly. As soon as baby Kingsley grew stronger, she joined the ladies' society and baked, cooked and cleaned;

whatever was needed, Margaret pitched in willingly. She attended quilting bees and the sewing circle, and supported the church group's volunteer assistance at the hospital. Margaret missed her mother's piano. The church did not yet have a piano, but they did have an organ. She often arrived early to sit at the organ and try to learn the complications of pedals and organ stops. Occasionally she filled in for the regular organist.

Thus, because she had many skills and did not lift her skirts from any job no matter how demanding, she soon became an accepted member of this group of dedicated British matrons she admired. She hired Jennie, the daughter of a recently widowed member Sarah Hartley, to care for baby Kingsley and do light housecleaning. Jennie was a quick worker, so she frequently took little Kingsley downstairs and let him play with scraps of leather and blocks of wood while she swept and tidied the shop. Kingsley crept and toddled around the shop under Jennie's watchful eye and the easy friendliness of Ernesto and the young helpers.

Theodore attended the church services with Margaret although he was even less ready than she to accept this Anglican form of worship. He protested mildly, but was accustomed to letting Margaret lead the way in their community life. He was generally ill at ease with people except through work, did not enter into social conversations easily. Indeed his mind strayed off to business in the midst of conversations, and his blank, inattentive stare often made others quite uncomfortable.

"You must make more of an effort," Margaret insisted. "These are wives of the men you deal with, the men who will be important to us. The wives are very influential in the community. Just talk with them."

"They talk always about people, people I don't know. I cannot even remember their names. They are so formal, so...so...." He fumbled for words to express his discomfort.

He did begin to make solid business contacts, however. There was the banker, Knowlton Calvert who made much of the soft leather shoes Ernesto had designed for him. Calvert brought in his son Sammy, who had a twisted foot, and Ernesto built a special pair of boots with support in the arch and ankle. This eased the child's discomfort and made his limp less pronounced. The banker listened sympathetically to Theodore's plans to hire additional craftsmen, and to sell ready-made boots through the general store.

Johnathan Wright, owner of the prosperous Wright's Mercantile Establishment was friendly too; he displayed a few pairs of Randolph and Chicachcio winter boots and began to send customers to Theodore.

Angus Macauley, the shipwright whose yard could hardly keep up with orders for his clean, sweet-lined square-rigger barks, was swept into their company with Ernesto's easy-going friendliness. But he had a business mind and business interests, so Theodore enjoyed his company too. Theodore and Angus talked long hours about what the future held for Halifax and of the country. "The ship-building industry will die with this new business of confederation," Angus growled. "People don't see what is going to happen to Halifax. Business will move west along with that railroad. Blast John A., the bastard."

"Well, we must move west with business, Angus. Margaret and I have always intended to settle finally in Montreal; we've given ourselves three or four more years here at the most. We have to find new outlets to expand into. I'm looking at plimsolls and sports equipment as one possibility - skates, snowshoes. I think there's a future there, but Ernesto is not keen on anything other than leathercraft. He has to have leather in his hands to be happy - has bits and pieces in his pockets all the time. He works and molds them like clay. He'd like us to go into jackets and belts - that line of goods."

"Yes, I've been thinking of what I might get into, too. I've seen a few of these new carriages that run by gasoline. Some people think they are going to take over. But I don't know, for long distances it's going to be that railroad that kills ships I think." He sighed and knocked his pipe against his heel. "I can understand how Ernesto feels about leather, I need to work with wood. There's something so beautiful about wood - smooth, polished, warm. Metal is cold, and gas carriages are ugly compared with our beautiful ships."

"Well, you do the cabinetry of your ships - maybe that's something you should think about. The rail tycoons will want expert woodwork to make their cars attractive to the clients. That should be a big market soon. If Confederation goes through - and it will, we might as well accept it - there's going to be growth, and quality goods will be in demand. That's why I think the future is in hard goods. Ernesto and I don't see eye-to-eye on some things. Montreal is already becoming the financial center, might even be the capitol. Montreal is the place to be."

"It's coming, you're right. Might as well get ahead of the change." So the two friends pondered the country's future, and how they could best fit their own futures into the change and growth they foresaw.

Just before Christmas 1867, Ernesto and his gang of friends heard about the game of hurley which the students at

King's Collegiate in Windsor played. He described what he had heard to Theodore, "The boys skate on the ice of Long Pond near this College. They say the game is very fast and rough. They use curved sticks to strike a small hard ball, and it's a real battle with those sticks. We will go to see this game, no?"

It was a five-hour trip to Windsor over the mountain on the B and Q Railroad. As they watched the game being played in the cold, clear December air, both men were intrigued and excited. The rough and tumble violence of the game appealed to Ernesto. He shouted and cheered, then put on skates and joined the battle. It was the idea of a game played on skates that caught Theodore's interest. This Canada certainly was a winter country. Skates could be a good business - they might even be fitted to boots. His mind took off; this was the direction he wanted to go.

On the long ride home Ernesto talked enthusiastically about the game. "We must get some men to play this game. These guys from the boatyard and the docks would fight like devils, I think. I will tell them how it is played."

Theodore asked, "Could you fasten the skates to boots, Ernesto? Make the boots and skates more solid so they don't come apart and trip the skaters up like we saw there. We could do that, I think, and sell these boot-skates for the game - maybe even for anyone who skates."

"Sure, sure. I could do that. But where we get the skates? Maybe we just make good boots, I think. Others make skates."

"I think we might get Franklin Bronson at the ironworks interested. If we worked out an agreement - we would make the boots and Franklin could make the skates without those toe clamps and the straps. They would have to be fastened to the boots some other way. They can't be uncomfortable. We'll have to think. And those sticks they used - they were just tree branches, all different. Angus knows wood. I'm going to ask him about those sticks. We'll get him to go over with us soon, so he can see the game." His mind whirled with ideas.

Theodore talked eagerly with Margaret, describing the game and explaining his ideas for a new direction for their business interests. "I think Angus might make some sticks that would work better for that game. If I could persuade him and Franklin to go in with us on all of the equipment for this game, I think Calvert would back us with money."

Margaret nodded thoughtfully, "This could be Canada's game, like cricket is in Britain. Use the long winter to build something special, something new, not just fight it to keep warm." So their plans looked to a new business future as Theodore pursued his ideas.

At four little Kingsley had become a healthy, sturdy youngster. Margaret involved herself in church and community activities, cultivating her Anglican friends and entering fully into the social life of Halifax matrons. She had acquired a quick eye for style from her mercantile experience in Bremen, from the agents who brought in new materials and sketches of the latest fashions from Paris and Venice. She and her mother had sold the styles to Bremen ladies, cleverly fitting them to the stockier frames of those matrons. Now she avidly read the letters her mother wrote, and studied and copied the sketches of new models.

She was admired for her European knowledge of fashion, and was often invited as much to be observed as for the pleasure of her company. More and more little Kingsley was left to

Jennie's care, and to the boisterous attention of Ernesto and his friends in the shop. He quickly picked up both his mother's disdain for Ernesto and Riata (who had joined her husband in the summer of 1867), and the rough language and manners of the shop crew.

He became cheeky, smartly aware that he could play off his father's absorption in business and his mother's busy social life. He swaggered and talked back to the men who laughed and called him Little Mr. Big Boss. He was proud of himself, and tried to be more like Ernesto to make the men laugh more. He began to act smart around Riata, trying to ape Ernesto's familiar banter.

He parroted words without understanding their meaning: bloody, titties, tarts, and he tried them out with Riata who was not pleased. She complained privately to Ernesto, "He should not be around the shop so much, Ernesto. You have heard the way he talks around the men - so common. When you are not around, he speaks rudely to me, too. He is too free."

"He's just a boy, cara mia. But I will speak to Theodore. He has a sharp mind, this little one, but he must show respect."

Theodore was appalled. He dragged Kingsley upstairs, cuffed him and scolded harshly, "Ernesto is my friend, and he is very important to our business. I wish this business to grow, to become important. Some day it will be your business, and you must act like a man, a gentleman. You must never speak rudely to a woman. Riata is a good woman. Go to your room now. Your mother will speak to you."

Shame turned to anger as the confusion of charges and orders poured over Kingsley. He stood defiantly in the doorway to his room, face red, hands balled into fists, screaming, "No! No! I won't! I won't!"

Theodore looked at him in consternation. He was a small, gentle, quiet man and he was helpless in the face of defiance. He turned to young Jennie, "Take him to his room until his mother comes, Jennie."

Kingsley shook off Jennie's hand, stomped his foot and screamed again. When she tried again to take hold of his arm, he kicked her leg and jerked away.

"I hate Riata," he screamed. "She is a tart. A tart with big titties."

"You are not a man," Theodore said sadly. He turned abruptly and left the room. Kingsley ran wildly about the room, screaming hysterically, threw himself face down banging his head on the floor and sobbing. When his father did not return, Kingsley grew quiet. He did not mean those things he had said about Raita. He loved her. She was always kind, and she loved Ernesto. He wanted her to love him too. But he would not submit to Jennie; stubbornly he refused her pleas to obey his father's order. He lay on the floor and kicked his heels whenever the girl spoke to him.

Margaret returned late from her afternoon tea with Franga Macauley and Serena Calvert. They had been making serious plans to start a welcome center for new immigrants. They would help new families get settled, find homes and furnishings, get involved in the church, find out about services they needed such as doctors, and settle into their proper niche in the life of the community. She was happy, eager to talk about their plans.

Theodore met her in the front hall and followed her into their bedroom, talking angrily. "He must learn to behave like a man, Margaret. I will not have him stir up trouble with Ernesto. The business depends on him, and Riata is his wife.

He must show respect."

Margaret removed her gloves and hat slowly. She nodded soothingly as Theodore argued. "I will see to Kingsley now." We must change some things, she thought as she stepped into the sitting room where Kingsley still sprawled on the floor. "Stand up!" she commanded coldly.

"Father hates me! He hit me!" Kingsley burst into dramatic tears.

"Stop!" Margaret's voice was icy. "Stand up and straighten yourself. Jennie, take him to the kitchen and wash his face, and then bring him back here to me." Kingsley knew when to follow orders, and he went with head down, jerking angrily from Jennie's hand. When they returned, Margaret straightened his jacket and collar, and took his face in her hands, forcing him to look at her. "You will not go into the shop again. You will begin to learn your letters, and you will accompany me when I go out. You must learn the manners of a gentleman. Jennie, take him to his room now, and see to it that he takes a nap."

Kingsley's eyes brimmed. That was not what he wanted. He loved the shop and he loved the way Ernesto always laughed and sang, and the way there were always people talking. And Riata was soft and gentle; she was kind to everyone. They had fun. Mother and Father were always busy. It was Jennie's fault for getting him into trouble. He threw a wicked glance at her.

The next day Margaret met with Ernesto in the shop. "Kingsley is not to come into the shop any more. I will begin lessons with him; I believe he is old enough to learn his letters and his numbers. It is time he learns the skills and the manners of a gentleman. It is time he learns what it means to take his place in our future. I regret that he was rude to Riata, and he will apologize to her."

"Si, signora, if you wish it. He is very clever, he will learn quickly. If the signora would permit, the boy has a sense for the leathers. He knows them with his hands and his nose. It is a gift. One must help such a gift to grow."

"Perhaps. Thank you for your interest, Ernesto. For now he must learn to read and write. I will bring him to Riata to apologize after tea."

The apology was given stiffly to Riata with Ernesto standing near. The childish lips trembled, but anger lurked behind the gray eyes, in the tight small shoulders, and in the defiant spread of small legs. Riata sighed afterwards, "That was not good, Ernesto. The boy has been shamed; he will not forget. The signora does not want love or friendship. We must loosen the ties."

Ernesto pulled her to him and brushed his hand down the curve of her back. "You are right, cara mia. They will move to Montreal soon. Theodore speaks of it often lately; he has many big plans. We shall stay here in Halifax and keep this shop. It is a good business for us. We can remain partners with Theodore, but he can go on to the new things he thinks of."

CHAPTER THREE

Becoming Canadian

Halifax to Montreal – 1875

"Margaret, I want to talk with you about our plans." Theodore stood with his back to the glowing pot-bellied stove that heated the large front room. They still lived above the cobbler shop in the flat they had first rented ten years before. Little had changed in their style of living, but they had prospered. The business under Theodore's management and Ernesto's craftsmanship had grown steadily.

"Yes, Theodore?" Margaret glanced up, but her hands stayed busy with the quilt spread over her knees, her third this winter. It would go into the church bazaar next fall and compete with the many traditional designs. She was sure her Dresden Plate would draw its own admirers. Log cabin patterns look so primitive, she thought, and the stitching is so… ordinary. She leaned over the quilt, smiling with satisfaction at her own tiny, precise stitches, "Yes, Theodore?" she murmured again.

"I believe it is time we opened a separate business for our hockey line." Theodore opened the stove's front door and poked at the embers. Earnestly he began to explain, "I believe that our real future will lie in the hockey skates. I'm more sure of it now than ever. Our teams here are becoming very competitive and we got that good review in the Boston Evening Gazette, The strongest teams all want our new skates. Bronson's clip-on design is the best on the market; everyone wants them. I think we should put everything into this business now. There is a building on Lower Water Street that would be a perfect site. This is the time to do it." He rapped the poker twice against the hod and thrust it into the tool stand.

Margaret laid aside the heavy quilt and focused her attention on Theodore. "Yes, my dear," she said emphatically. "Yes, now is the right time to make the break." If Theodore had listened carefully he might have recognized in Margaret's words a very different agenda. The break she wanted was with all vestiges of their immigrant status, and that included Ernesto and Riata - and the image of herself as a shoemaker's wife. To rid herself of that image was what drove her in every choice she made. I have always known that our future should be in Montreal, she thought; it is there we can build our proper place in society. But she must go carefully, "Would Ernesto give up the shop?"

"Oh no! Ernesto is not interested in the skates - except to play the game, of course." Theodore chuckled to himself, "That guy's a wildcat. He loves nothing better than a real bang-on with those Mi'kmac devils!" He shook his head and stood silent for a minute. Margaret knew he admired this in Ernesto, envied him even. All the more reason to make the break. She did not want her son to grow up under Ernesto's influence. "But he would make the boots, I think." Theodore sounded a bit unsure, and this gave Margaret another opening.

"What kind of sales would we have to make for the business to pay, Theodore? Skates, boots, sticks? Could Bronson supply enough skates, and Ernesto the boots?" Margaret's own assessment was that Ernesto would be bored with making only hockey boots. He was proud of himself as a craftsman and artist. He would not be interested in mass - producing anything. Fitting women's fancy boots was Ernesto's style, especially flirting with them, she thought angrily.

Theodore shook his head uncertainly, "We would have to hire more men for both the metal work and the boots. Luckily we can get all the hockey sticks we need from the Mi'kmac wood carvers. But we will need to borrow from the bank."

Margaret knew that money was the major issue in Theodore's mind. She dismissed his concern lightly, "I'm sure Knowlton would put the bank behind you."

This was another small nudge in the direction she wanted to go. Knowlton Calvert was being transferred to Montreal. The Bank of Nova Scotia was opening new branches in Montreal and Toronto. Knowlton would be manager of the central region and his support there would be very important. Margaret's strategy was to drop little facts on her side of the scale one-by-one. Soon Theodore would believe that he had weighed all of the factors himself and made his own decision.

Sometimes I just wish I didn't have to beat around the bush so to make him see what we should do, she thought. She swallowed her impatience, got up and began to fold the heavy quilt, "I'm sure it will all work out, my dear. You will make the right decisions, I know." Then seeming to change the subject she dropped another small pebble on her side of the scale. "Did I tell you I received a letter from Amanda Creighton this morning? They are very pleased about their move to Montreal. She says they built with some kind of stone that Angus brings back from England. Apparently the architects model the homes after those impressive British mansions, though smaller, of course. I think they call it greystone. She says they are quite grand."

"Yes, Angus brings that stone back from Britain as ballast sometimes, limestone. There is some red, too, I believe."

"Hm-m-m! Red might be very nice - warm. But you would be more interested, I think in what James says about the game. Apparently he has trained some McGill University football players and they are going up against a team of rink skaters. They are going to play on an indoor rink, as I understand it. That is something new, isn't it?"

"Indeed it is, Margaret. Indoor rinks could turn hockey into a winter spectator sport. Could make quite a difference. But we do have a good reputation here. That's important, too." He turned to the fire again, but just stood staring absently at the coals through the glass window.

I won't say anything more tonight, Margaret thought. He'll stew about all of this for a few days, but he can't hold back. Underneath he is just as eager to make a change as I am. "I'm off to bed, dear. Would you like a hot chocolate?"

"No, no. Not right now. I'll be along. Have to bank the fire and be sure we're locked up. It is snowing again," he added as Margaret gathered her sewing. She would check on Kingsley before she readied herself for bed.

Slowly Theodore banked the fires in the kitchen range and the heater, checked the wind-stopper by the front door, and then stood gazing out the window at the blowing snow. Across the street he saw Ernesto come out of the Thistle and Crown, his arm around the waist of a young woman in a bright green coat. Theodore watched them head off toward town. He turned away from the window with a sigh.

As he unbuttoned his heavy union suit and slipped into the flannel nightshirt, he said regretfully, "Ernesto's off with that young French girl Therese again. Poor Riata. She doesn't deserve that."

Poor Riata, my foot, Margaret said to herself. Any woman can't keep her man in her own bed deserves what she gets. She fluffed up Theodore's pillow, and answered smugly, "You can't make a silk purse out of a sow's ear, my dear. You've been very good to him - to the whole family." She turned toward her husband and brushed back the lock of black hair that always fell out of place. Theodore reached out to his wife and stroked the curve of her breast through the heavy flannel nightgown, buttoned to the neck.

Margaret shifted restlessly, and the image of Ernesto's laughing blue eyes and shock of curly black hair flashed in her mind. Theodore reached under her gown and caressed her nipples as they began to harden.

"Not tonight, Theodore."

But he was a patient lover. He knew that hers was a slow rhythm, so his hands were gentle and persistent as they followed the curves of her stomach toward the brush of hair. Margaret's inner sex began to tremble. She opened her legs slightly as Theodore's fingers touched the curves of her thighs and sought her fragrant wetness. His fingers probed, and Margaret's pelvis twitched in response.

"Not tonight" now far from her thoughts, she opened

fully, and Theodore brought his heat to hers. Slowly she began to press under him, her body stroking his as they moved together. He teased, testing, but she was eager now, and her legs reached out clasping his firm buttocks, grasping him into her.

Now they slowed, each aching with the pleasure of the building sex. Margaret climaxed in gasping release. But still Theodore moved inside her, slowly circling, stroking all of the swollen softness, and feeling her relax completely to him.

Then he thrust, and thrust again deeply, and came with a harsh groan of abandon, "Liebchen, Liebchen."

They lay together for a long moment, Margaret touching the curve of his jaw, kissing the lobe of his ear, holding herself tight against his thigh, murmuring, "Theodore." Abruptly she roused to go clean herself and bring a warm washcloth and towel. "You must go to Montreal to see what James Creighton has arranged, Mr. Randolph. It could be important." He grunted sleepily as they settled.

It was still snowing in the morning. Theodore and Margaret looked out amazed. The door and windows of the tavern across the street were not visible. The street itself was smoothly white as far as they could see. Their own doors would be buried too; they were snowbound.

Kingsley came prancing out of his bedroom shouting. "Look at the snow! Look at the snow! No school today, I bet! Me and Zack can make a snow fort."

"Nothing to shout about," Margaret said crossly. "No customers either. And you may not be able to get out at all. The snow is as high as our heads! Theodore, go down to the shop and try the door, see if everything is alright. We must find out what is happening. At least we have plenty of lamp oil and wood. Kingsley you get the candles out, and check the lamps are full just in case." Margaret lifted the lid of the cookstove, shook the damper, and stirred the coals. She added splits to hasten the fire, then two small chopped blocks laid carefully on top. She dipped water out of the warming tank on the side of the stove, and handed the pitcher to Kingsley, still in his nightshirt. "Take this to your father for his shave, and get yourself washed and dressed, son. There will be work to do after breakfast."

They were just finishing their breakfast of oatmeal, beaten biscuits, and thick slices of ham when they heard a loud, "Hal-o-o-o, up there!" Margaret rose and looked out the front window. Ernesto was on his snowshoes, his eyes snapping, a big grin showing his teeth, stained brown from the constant chaw of tobacco he held in his mouth. "You fellas, you should be out in this. Some little snowstorm, eh? Five-six feet and I think more coming. We're all gonna be buried alive. Get your bearpaws and climb out the back window - only a little drop, maybe few feet and nice soft snow to catch you, eh? We get front door open, yes?" Ernesto waved his snow shovel and started digging away near the entry.

"Riata and the boys all right?" Margaret asked.

"Oh, sure, sure. They fine. Riata good today. That one in the oven not ready to say 'Hello world' today, eh!" Ernesto patted his stomach and let go his booming laugh. "Riata clear our walk. I say I must clear walk for shop. Riata good worker."

Margaret turned angrily to Theodore, "If he thinks I am going to jump out the window and shovel snow, he has another think coming. Riata is a fool. She works like a man and she produces those babies one after the other. They will never be anything but low class immigrants, Theodore!" Gone was last night's resolve to go carefully. This was the most she had ever said.

"The boy, Margaret. The boy!" Theodore reached out to touch her arm, to soothe her. But Margaret turned sharply and hurried into the kitchen, not heeding Kingsley's sudden stillness, his frozen face. I'm glad it's said, she thought. We must get away from here.

Theodore wiped the remaining grease from his plate with a biscuit crust, drank the last of his strong black coffee, and stood up. "Come boy. Get the shovels and bearpaws from the mudroom. We can't let Ernesto and Dino do all this clearing."

"I don't want to. I don't like Dino." Kingsley was defiant with his father. Often enough he got away with it because he knew his mother's prejudices. "Me'n Zack want to build a fort."

"We have work to do. Have to get the shop open. Don't forget your toque and gloves." Theodore ignored his son's foray. "Dino is younger than you, but he's a good worker - always helps his father."

The admiring reference to Dino angered Margaret. That was just what she did not want - fraternizing with Ernesto and his sons. "Let the boy stay and help me, Theodore. I want him to run errands for me." She smiled grimly as her husband shrugged and climbed out the window onto the snow bank. Theodore was aggressive in the business, but he always gave in to her demands. He would give in about moving to Montreal too. Margaret quickly wrote a note to Franga about the scheduled hospital meeting. "Take this to Mrs. Macauley and come back right away, son. I have chores for you. Don't dawdle."

Kingsley had succeeded. Freed of both parents he had no

intention of returning to work. He went in search of Zack. They began a labyrinth of passages behind the Water Street shops, watching for passers-by and pelting them with snowballs.

"You boys should be helping, not making trouble," Angus Macauley scolded, standing tall above them. "Go on home now, Kingsley Randolph. You should be helping your father."

Kingsley ducked and ran down the narrow passage they had cleared. "Old man Magillicooly thinks he's the king of Water Street," Kingsley muttered to Zack. He wanted to shout his defiance, but he knew that his mother would not favour rudeness to Mr. Macauley. "Let's get the I-ties, Zack. Them I-talians think they're so big shot."

"Sure, let's make a pile of snowballs. They'll be around here pretty soon."

"I want that Dino," Kingsley was still smarting from his father's earlier praise of Ernesto's son. "Let's get the snowballs wet and let them freeze. We'll get those dirty meegrants good."

Soon Pietro and Lorenzo came by on their way to the waterfront, "Hey Kingsley, what you doing?"

Zack shouted, "Dirty meegrants, Wops! Stay away from our place." Startled, Pietro quickly scooped up a handful of snow and fired it off at Kingsley and Zack. But the icy snowballs soon drove them off.

When Kingsley saw Dino trudging home for lunch, he quickly got set. He pounded the unsuspecting younger boy with hard blows of the icy balls. Dino, hampered by snowshoes and tiredness, tried to get away but stumbled and fell. "Dirty Wop! Dirty meegrant!" Kingsley shouted again and again as he pelted Dino with ice balls.

"Come on, Kingsley, let's quit." Zack pulled at Kingsley's sleeve. "Come on, let's get out of here. He's bleeding."

Kingsley, panting, stared down at the boy, lying still and quiet on the snow. A sense of terrible loss filled him. He really loved to be around Ernesto and Riata; they sang funny songs, and laughed and teased each other. But he always got in bad with his father or his mother because of them. He would always hate them now. He would get them sometime. He looked down at Dino again, "Dirty meegrant!" he muttered and kicked the boy's head, then turned and ran.

Kingsley returned late for dinner. At 6:00 PM it had been dark for two hours and he was met by a pair of angry parents.

"Where have you been? I told you to come right back. Did you even take my note to Mrs. Macauley?" Margaret forgot that she had worried all day because of the deep snow. "Theodore, speak to this boy. He does not mind me."

Theodore spoke heavily, slowly, "Where were you, son? Dino was badly hurt. Were you with that gang that threw ice balls at him and Pietro? Dino has a bad cut over his eye - had to have stitches, Margaret."

"Not me, Papa," Kingsley lied boldly. "I wasn't any where near the market today."

"You are not telling the truth, Kingsley. I did not say the market." He turned to Margaret, "The boys attacked Dino and Pietro at the market, Margaret. Angus Macauley saw them. They threw ice balls and shouted, 'Dirty meegrants!' and 'Wops!' I am ashamed, my son. Ernesto is my partner and my friend. Don't forget that we are immigrants, too." Theodore slumped in his chair, and looked pleadingly at Margaret.

"We are not immigrants in the same way, Theodore. We

30

are now Canadians. Ernesto and Riata will always be Italians."
She turned to her son, "But that is no way for a gentleman to
talk, Kingsley. Go to your room. You will have only bread and
milk for supper. You must learn to speak always as a gentleman,
not a roughneck."

"Speak as a gentleman! Speak as a gentleman!" Kingsley
muttered in his bedroom. Shame and regret were buried under
anger. "Dirty meegrants." Ernesto and his house full of boys
always laughed. They were making fun of him. "I'm glad I got
Dino a good one. When I get big enough, I'll get Ernesto,
too."

CHAPTER FOUR

Appetites

Montreal – 1875-1884

Margaret had her way, of course. Theodore eagerly arranged to go to Montreal for the indoor hockey game James Creighton had organized. He came home boiling with enthusiasm and plans. "You are right, Margaret, Montreal is the place to be. You should see the city - hotels, the exchange, two universities, electric trolley cars. And the streets in the centre of the city are paved with cobblestones. But the best for us is Creighton. He's a real promoter; has backing for two teams. One was from McGill University. Got a good turnout for that game."

Margaret looked up from the socks she was darning and nodded, "That should be good advertising."

"You're right. I talked with Knowlton yesterday. They move to Montreal March first. The bank will open by the fifteenth, and he promised to support us if we put the headquarters there. He says Montreal has become the financial heart of Canada. It's growing rapidly; close to ten thousand already."

"Ernesto?"

"Well, yes, Ernesto. We have to work out an agreement. He is determined to stay here in Halifax, stay with the shop. I don't know if he will make the hockey boots. Every time I mention it, he just shrugs it off." Theodore was pacing the room, shooting out his thoughts in short bursts.

Margaret smiled. She loved his aggressiveness in business, admired his restless urge to expand, to try new ideas. Only Ernesto held him back. He had led them to hockey that was true. But his interest was in personal pleasure, in having fun, in the moment - not in the future. Theodore's loyalty to Ernesto is not good, she thought, we must break free of this partnership. "We should be able to find good boot makers in Montreal. Ernesto is not a good partner for expansion, and you know it. He is weak."

She didn't like weakness; it irritated her, made her impatient. Her own clear-headedness was strength, she believed. Maybe she had few really intimate friends, but people respected her. They looked to her to get things done, even Theodore. She was only vaguely aware that most people skirted around her warily, but she would have said that was because they couldn't keep up, had no imagination.

She would see to it that Kingsley was not weak. She brought her mind back to Theodore. He was still talking about Montreal. "I put a bid down on an acreage on the western edge of the mountain," he said. "Creighton put me onto it; he's in the market."

"We would build before we move?" This was a surprise;

Margaret had not expected such ready or complete commitment. But that was like Theodore. Once a decision was taken, a direction chosen, he moved rapidly. He would always be in the forefront.

"No, we can take a town house for now; there are some very good ones, good locations. I looked at a couple - stone, and glazed windows. High ceilings. Wood panelling. Felt like home." He pulled her up and whirled her around the room, scattering darning wool, socks, and basket. His arm around her they stopped at the big window, looking out but seeing, not the snowy Water Street and the harbour, but the hills, and mansions, and bustle of Montreal.

"You will like them, Liebchen. Those mountain lots are going to be at a premium soon. We were lucky to get one. We'll build once the business takes off." The move had become Theodore's idea, his plan. Margaret kissed him smiling, and stooped to gather up the scattered work.

Nine years later Margaret and Serena Calvert stood on the raised steps at the entry to a grand ballroom. Fredrich and Freida Buchler's Christmas ball was the event of the 1884 season. A twenty-foot fir, flaming with lighted candles, stood near the French doors, a pile of tiny gold and silver wrapped packages under it. Freida Buchler had the tradition of offering a gift to each person invited to the ball. Whispered guesses of what the gifts would be provided much of the excitement of the occasion each year. And exchanges between young women and men were tokens of real or fancied bonds.

The ballroom extended the full length of the house, well over fifty feet, and was at least half as wide. The orchestra sat on a balcony high above the floor at the far end, fenced by delicate iron work in white. Marble pillars ranked the two sides; jardinières (real Chinese porcelain, Margaret had heard) holding large ficus and palm trees provided conversation spots near the pillars. White iron benches and chairs padded with red or gold velvet were arranged around the walls.

Margaret spoke behind her fan, "Who are those two striking red-headed women there, Serena? Kingsley is certainly ogling them. They don't look like twins, but those forest green velvet gowns set them off beautifully, such creamy skin."

"They are the Gordon girls from Toronto. See, that is their father Charles Gordon over by Fredrich. William's cousin. You know. McGill. You could pick him out without knowing - the same red hair and green eyes. Charles is President of Laurentian Industries. Fredrich Buchler is on the board."

"Laurentian - that was Gordon Tobacco before they took over the winery, wasn't it?"

"Yes, and newspapers, too. Those Gordon girls will be very wealthy women some day. Knowlton has met them several times. He says the older girl, Felicity is the mainstay of the family. Very independent though, and never married. Felicity runs the household, and has pretty much raised Dorothy. Their mother passed away nearly fifteen years ago."

"The family is well established then?" Chatting and plotting, the two women moved down the steps toward Theodore and Knowlton waiting for them near the entrance. They accepted the glass of champagne offered by a young waiter, and continued their conversation.

"Yes, I believe they are related to the Redpaths. You know, the sugar family. And by marriage to Lord and Lady Hampton-Smythe. She was a Redpath."

Margaret nodded, "Minister of the Interior. How old are the girls?" Every young woman was a potential daughter-in-law, and Margaret was determined to have a hand in Kingsley's choice. He was twenty-one now and it was high time he found a wife.

"They are beauties, aren't they? The Gordons are Scots; that's where they get their red hair. Felicity doesn't look her age of course, though she must be thirty-five. The younger girl Dorothy is probably about twenty." Serena knew why Margaret was asking these questions. Making the right match was very important. "Dorothy might be a good match for Kingsley."

"Indeed. But young Kingsley will have to step lively if he wants his name on one of their cards! Their cards are always full, even Felicity's," Serena laughed indulgently.

He is a good looking young man, with his black hair and chiseled features, she thought. Mentally she ticked off Kingsley's attributes. His ears are really a bit too prominent, oddly pointed, and his mouth is small. He should wear sideburns and a beard - maybe he wouldn't look quite so hard, so arrogant. There's a streak of cruelty there, I think. I'm glad my two girls are safely married.

He will have full control of that business in no time, I'm sure. Theodore will be no match for him, and Margaret supports him in everything he does. "He will be a good catch for some young woman," she commented. "He is very young to be where he is in the business. I could invite the Gordons to our Twelfth Night party, if you like. It will be a small group, more intimate."

Montreal society was tight knit; old money families were mainly British from the Isles - Scottish or English. Margaret and Serena were acceptable, but they were still new. The nearly ten years as outsiders since they had moved from Halifax had strengthened the bonds of their friendship, and they readily supported each other's endeavors.

"Good. We will see how Kingsley fares here. Theodore must make contacts with Charles Gordon." Margaret and Serena nodded to each other, strategies agreed, and slowly moved with Theodore and Knowlton to pay their respects to the hosts and greet other friends. Dancing would start soon.

"Surely, Miss Gordon, you have one number free on your card for a good dancer like myself." Kingsley reached for the card swinging from Felicity's wrist, but she snapped her fan closed and tapped it on her lips.

Her green eyes flicked from his face and grazed his hand; he jerked it back quickly. "I find that Montreal has many good dancers to choose from, Mr. Randolph." She shifted back slightly, making distance clear.

Kingsley flushed, "Perhaps your younger sister will be more kind to a forlorn newcomer." With a faint emphasis on younger, he turned his back to Felicity. "Miss Dorothy, would you do me the honour?"

Dorothy nodded graciously, and placed her gloved hand on his arm. That shadow of a smile - was it triumph? Mischief? Complicity? He was uncertain. They moved toward the ballroom floor.

"Do you favor the waltz, Miss Gordon?"

"Yes, indeed. We met Herr Strauss several years ago in Vienna. It was so exciting. He was quite old even then, but very vibrant. He was taken with my sister Felicity, kept her on his arm most of the evening. I was only a child, but he danced one waltz with me. Felicity is very beautiful, don't you think?"

"Yes, she is quite attractive." Kingsley still smarted from the rebuff. "But if you will not think me too bold, Miss Dorothy, she is not so beautiful as you."

Dorothy's half-closed fan brushing her left cheek, and her faint smile stirred him. The orchestra on the balcony above the floor settled their chairs and instruments, the leader tapped the music stand, and Kingsley and Dorothy took their places on the floor.

He felt a brush of skirts against his leg. Startled, he looked around to see Felicity near them on the floor, held lightly by her father, that shadowy half-smile in her eyes again. And again Kingsley flushed; he was slightly off-balance as the music started.

"Please forgive me, Miss Dorothy. I missed the first beat. I am not usually so clumsy."

"I think Felicity bumped you on purpose. She is sometimes very wicked."

Unnerved as much by Dorothy's frankness as by Felicity's boldness, Kingsley made a poor showing on the waltz. Hurriedly he returned Dorothy to her sister as the music ended; he stumbled through stiffly polite phrases and mumbled a brief acknowledgement of the introduction to Charles Gordon. Absurdly conscious that the sisters had again exchanged secret glances, he excused himself to dance with his mother.

Margaret took his arm and led him through the French doors to the balcony overlooking the winter whiteness of the garden. Kingsley drew a deep breath of the sharp air and shook himself, angry now.

"What happened? You looked upset, and you danced very

poorly. You know who the Gordons are, don't you?"

"Yes, of course I know who Charles Gordon is. But that Felicity Gordon is too full of herself."

"Felicity? But I don't understand. You were dancing with the younger sister, Dorothy?"

"Dorothy might be all right, but she couldn't keep to the beat. Her sister lords it over her; that threw her off." I'll take that Felicity down a peg one of these days, he promised himself.

"You must dance with Miss Felicity, Kingsley. It would have been more proper for you to ask her first."

"She's much older," he grumbled, startled to realize that he was eager to do as his mother commanded, but stubbornly unwilling to tell her he had done so and been smartly put down.

As midnight drew near, couples and family groups clustered together around the dance floor. The music changed to traditional holiday songs and the Buchler family gathered at the tree. Guests joined the family in Silent Night and O Tannenbaum in English and German, then Adeste Fidelis in Latin.

Freidrich Buchler beckoned for attention and the music softened. "We give you most pleasant welcome to our home at this happy time of year. The year 1884 has been very good to us - a new grandson, who sadly could not join us tonight." The guests laughed dutifully. "And the year has seen much growth in our Krystalwerks Industry in Bonn. We have grown from..."

Frieda stepped forward and tugged at his arm. "Oh, ja, my Frieda has said I must not talk of business tonight. So we push our happiness onto you with these small dinge, these small things. Now it is time for the St. Nicholas I think." He motioned to the orchestra and an ornately robed St. Nicholas descended the stairway behind the balcony to the music of Jingle Bells. The Buchler family picked up the gifts and began to distribute them - gold wrapped packages to the women, silver to the men.

Sporadically, individuals still sang choruses of Jingle Bells, but excited whispers and exclamations of delight broke into the music. Each woman found a tiny, delicate crystal butterfly lapel pin, shaded with iridescent colours - violet, rose, mauve. The gift for the men was a pair of cuff links entirely fashioned from crystal.

Kingsley had tried to maneuver himself near Felicity and Dorothy Gordon. He wanted to be asked to pin a brooch to a green velvet gown. But Felicity was kissing her Father's cheek, thanking him for the honour, and Dorothy's pin was in the hands of her cousin Linell.

"What a fop he is! No one wears lace cuffs these days."

"Hush, my son. They will hear you. You must try to get the last dance with Miss Dorothy. Or perhaps Miss Felicity; she has much influence over her sister. We will see them again at the Calvert's Twelfth Night party."

Kingsley looked over at Dorothy, but she was already moving toward the dance floor on the arm of her cousin. He turned to her sister, "May I have the pleasure of the last waltz, Miss Felicity?" He was rather more hesitant in his approach this time.

Felicity touched her Father's hand, exchanged a glance with him, and nodded to Kingsley. They stepped into place as the lovely Tales from Vienna Woods began. "Will you be in Montreal for some time, Miss Felicity?"

"For the season, yes."

"I believe we will see you at Knowlton's Twelfth Night?"

"The Calvert's, yes. They are very kind."

"Miss Dorothy said you met Herr Strauss in Vienna and he favoured you as a waltz partner. You must have been very flattered."

"Perhaps it did not feel like flattery. He was very gracious, a true gentleman."

Kingsley's face grew stiff and flared redly. He did not understand her abruptness, though he was somehow titillated by it. Desperately he tried to think of some appropriate remark that would receive a favourable response. Felicity did not seem disturbed by silence; clearly she loved the waltz. Her absorption in the music and dance was transmitted to Kingsley and they whirled and dipped and swayed with the music. The other dancers made room for them and they became the centre of attention. A light spattering of applause greeted them as the music ended. Felicity, that mocking smile in her eyes, said, "Very nice, Mr. Randolph. You are, as you say, a good dancer."

Flustered again, not knowing whether to be flattered or hurt, Kingsley returned her to where Dorothy stood with her father and cousin. "My pleasure, indeed, Miss Felicity. Thank you." Then to all four, "I will be eagerly looking forward to Twelfth Night. Miss Dorothy. Sir. Mr. Hampton-Smythe. Good evening."

CHAPTER FIVE

Felicity And Dorothy

Montreal Twelfth Night – 1885

The Calvert's large grey stone home sat high on the western slope of the mountain. A sweeping driveway led from the gateposts on Simpson Street up the steep slope to the wide ornately railed steps and the heavy oak door. Leaded windows marched away in either direction toward two copper-clad towers rising high above the third story. Narrow windows there surveyed the city and the river far below.

"You see, Margaret, what an excellent site this is. We are lucky to have that location just west." Theodore made the same remark each time they visited their friends. Now he added, "We must build this summer."

"Yes, my dear, you are right. Look. There are the Gordons just ahead. How fortunate, we will be just in time to meet them in the entry. Have Jacques bring my things in, Theodore. Kingsley, you help me on the steps." In the customary orderly bustle, guests greeted each other in the entry and dispersed to separate withdrawing rooms where they were helped to shed coats, boots, scarves, hats and gloves. They would freshen their toilettes and prepare to join their hosts in the salon.

The main drawing room was large but comfortable. Chairs and small tables provided easy arrangements. Settees were not cluttered with lace doilies and tables were not crowded with bric-a-brac or pictures. On one a small vase, on another, a delicate porcelain dish with mints. The walls, covered with soft rose coloured silk, displayed a painting by Caravaggio.

Elegant, Margaret thought as she moved to join the Gordons. Kingsley stood near Dorothy, but his eyes flicked to Felicity. "Are you enjoying Montreal society, Miss Felicity, Miss Dorothy?"

"It is indeed a beautiful city. Fascinating with its two languages, two peoples. Do you speak French, Mr. Randolph?" Felicity seemed always to throw out a challenge.

"Only a few words. Of course we have many French customers. They are great sportsmen - hockey, hunting, boxing. But our employees, many of whom are French or Italian, must all speak English. The French spoken here is a patois, uneducated, and rough, I believe."

"But would you not find it exciting to understand another language, sir? To know a different way of thinking? A different culture?"

"The French here are hardly a cultured people, Miss Felicity. They are mostly farmers, hunters, and labourers. And of course they are Catholic."

"That is a strange comment, sir."

Dorothy interrupted, "We have found that there are many cultural activities in the city, Mr. Randolph. We were able to attend a concert this past week - the Hallelujah Chorus. A wonderful tenor, Marc LeBlanc. Have you heard him?"

"No, I have not had an opportunity. We seem to have our time absorbed by business and sports activities, especially with the growing interest in hockey, and the university hockey teams. Are you interested in hockey, Miss Dorothy?"

"I think Felicity would have played, had she been a boy." Dorothy grinned at her older sister, and Felicity nodded positively.

"Yes, indeed. I should have been a boy. Sports, studies, business - they are all to my liking. This world is a wonderful place, for men anyway. So much to see and do." Felicity's green eyes looked far off. "But we have heard that McGill is now admitting women students, the Donaldas[1] they are called. How wonderful."

"Would you really enter the academic world, Miss Felicity? Would that be practical? Are there areas of interest to you?"

"I would study anything - history, literature, politics, medical developments. I would find it difficult to choose. There is so much to learn."

"And you, Miss Dorothy, would you also wish to go into academic studies?"

"I am yet too young. But I will tell you a secret, Mr. Randolph. Felicity plans to apply to become a Donalda. She is more eager than she admits. Our father encourages her. He has contacted Mr. Crampton at the University on her behalf. Right now I have a private tutor for my music, and that gives me much happiness."

44

The discussion continued through dinner. Felicity's eagerness to become a Donalda was received with amazed interest.

"Is it true that you are thinking of entering McGill formally as a student?" Serena exclaimed. "How wonderful."

"Yes, I hope it will be possible. Father has generously encouraged me to take that step. I do worry somewhat, for I will not be able to help him as I have in the past." She reached her hand fully toward her father and smiled with happiness.

Charles returned the gesture and the glow of affection. "Felicity has been my rock for these many years. However, Dorothy is quite capable of taking over the household duties, and Felicity has the mind of a seeker. This will be right for her."

"What will you study, child?" Knowlton was curious.

"Literature, history, natural sciences: all are included in the programme. The programme originated with the lectures offered to the Montreal Ladies' Educational Association. I believe that Madame Molson was instrumental in that programme. One of the lecturers was William Dawson, who was so impressed by the quality of achievement by those students that he and other lecturers began to plan for a formal admission programme at the university. The programme opened just last year - separate classes of course. This serious study will be most invigorating."

"William Dawson is a colourful person. I often see him racing across the campus, coattails flying," Knowlton chuckled.

"Are such studies useful for a woman, Miss Felicity? Are there opportunities for women to use such studies? Positions?" Margaret found the idea hard to accept.

"Useful. Perhaps that is not an essential concept to be

applied to studies, Mrs. Randolph. Does one not study primarily for pleasure?"

Kingsley felt embarrassed for his mother. He was angry that she was made to appear ignorant or unsophisticated. He turned his back to Felicity, "You say that music is your great interest, Miss Dorothy. I would be delighted to hear you play sometime."

"If you wish. Of course."

The conversation turned to seasonal events, the Christmas ball, a recent presentation of The Nutcracker, and an upcoming Mozart programme, "Symphony 40" and the "Requiem".

"When do you start construction on your home, Theodore?" Knowlton asked. "We are eager to have you as our neighbours."

"We were hoping for next spring, but the expansion of the business has taken so much of our attention, we are facing delays. And Angus was not able to get the red sandstone for his next trip. Margaret has her heart set on the red."

"Yes, it is so warm looking. Theodore is looking at Frank Courtney to do the work. He built the Morton's house and also the hotel on lower Peel. We have looked forward to this for many years."

As the evening continued, Kingsley became more attentive to Dorothy. He was intrigued by her forthright good sense, her simplicity, and was excited by unexpected flashes of humour. "I hope I may be permitted to call on you soon, Miss Dorothy."

His pleasure at her agreement was tinged with something else, a need to prove himself to Felicity. Did he feel acceptance? Victory? Loss? He was not accustomed to these jumbled emotions. He should focus on Dorothy; she was more womanly, easier to understand.

CHAPTER SIX

Choices

Montreal – 1885-1886

"Theodore, I want us to go to Toronto for Thanksgiving. The Chandlers have asked us. We can go up on the first and stay over for the opera on the fourteenth; they are doing the "Figaro" and Marc LeBlanc is the tenor. We can go with the Gordons and the Chandlers."

Margaret turned slightly to allow Anna to serve the thick wedge of apple pie and coffee They had dined alone since Kingsley was at the theatre with friends, but they sat at opposite ends of the heavily carved dark oak refectory table. Margaret had placed a low bowl of burgundy chrysanthemums at the centre of the table between a pair of burnt orange candles in their mahogany bases.

The room had high ceilings; a crystal chandelier highlighted the rich dark woodwork and was reflected in bevelled windows. Though the dining room was large for a townhouse, the six high-backed chairs with red leather seats crowded against the two buffets, high and low. The set was too large for this room, but they had broken ground for their new home on Bishop, and should be able to move in by next fall. The set had been a good purchase.

"I don't see how we can go, Margaret. We're really busy right now negotiating that equipment order for the new arena in Toronto. That could lead to an important contract."

"That's exactly why we should go. Charles Gordon is on the City Council. His support would be very important. And if Kingsley marries Dorothy…"

"Kingsley? Is he planning to marry?" Theodore looked up, his fork stopped in mid-air.

"At least hoping, I'm sure. There is her cousin Linell, of course, but that would not be a wise match. You could put in a good word for Kingsley with Charles."

"She is a lovely young woman, but I thought Felicity…. I think she has a head for business, might help him go far. She's like you, my dear, clever and independent."

"Felicity. She's much too old for him, Theodore. And she has strange interests for a woman. University indeed! She would not be a suitable wife - too self-centered, too opinionated." Margaret rang impatiently for Anna to clear the dishes and bring tea and mint biscuits. Theodore had to have his coffee with dessert, but Margaret's ceaseless campaign to appear British was emphasized in after dinner tea.

"If you say so, Margaret. Ties with the Gordon Institute and Foundation would be good, and Charles is an admirable man. I would be pleased to have him as a friend." As always, Theodore acceded to Margaret in family matters.

"Which should I wear, Fizzy? The pink or the green? Is the pink too bright for October? I can't decide."

"Corded silk is heavy enough for fall, and the Empress waistline suits you, but either one, child. I'm wearing my black bombazine. And I want you to put my hair up. Very sophisticated, don't you...?"

"Don't call me child! I'm almost twenty; I'm not a child." Dorothy's cheeks reddened with frustration. "I have to decide." She threw the dress down on the slipper chair between the high windows and twitched at the green velvet. "We wore green last Christmas. Maybe everyone would notice."

"Everyone! What is this? It's only the Randolphs. Wear what you like, Dot."

"Why do you say 'Only the Randolphs?' Don't you like the Randolphs?"

"Well, I like Mr. Randolph well enough. He's honest and straightforward. And Mrs. Randolph is quite pleasant."

"You really don't like them, do you?" Dorothy's face looked pinched, her chin trembled.

"We only met them last Christmas. It's hard to say. But what has that got to do with which dress you wear? You look good in either."

"But what do you think, Fizzy? Which one would...?"

"Ah! Kingsley! Well, if you want my opinion about Master Kingsley's preferences, I'd say pink. It's unexpected with your red hair, and it makes you look soft and sweet. Is that what you want, Dotty? Soft and sweet?"

"You're mean!" Dorothy flung herself down on the satin comforter, weeping, crushing the green velvet dress beneath her. "You don't like him, do you?"

Felicity sat down beside her, pulled her up and held her

close. "I'm sorry. It's just…. He seems a little arrogant, that's all. But come on, it's just a dinner party. We'll see them lots of times."

Felicity was becoming increasingly worried about Dorothy's attraction to Kingsley. She knocked on her father's study door, determined to raise the issue with him. Charles Gordon looked up from the Star. He had been reading about the progress on the locks, pleased that the reporter had given a very favourable picture of the project. "You must read this article, my dear, very well done."

But Felicity was not in the mood to talk business. "Father, have you noticed that Dorothy seems smitten by Kingsley Randolph? Do you think that's wise? Have you spoken to him?"

"Smitten, Felicity?" Charles smiled as he folded his paper and laid it aside. "He's a fine young man - well-mannered and attentive. But smitten? She's still a child. They are just friends, aren't they?"

"It's more than that, I think, Father. And she is twenty - not a child, and neither is he. What is your opinion of him? What kind of man is he? Should we see so much of them?"

Charles laughed indulgently, "Sometimes you are more like a mother to Dorothy than a sister. You're really the only mother she knows, and I never cease to be thankful for the way you've cared for her. So you think I should take this more seriously, do you?"

"Yes, I do, Father. Dotty is somewhat impressionable. She sees his manners, and she likes the family - and I do too, for that matter. But Kingsley worries me. His manners seem somewhat forced, not from the heart. I wonder how deep he is."

"You may be more worried than you need be, my dear. He is very astute in business - has a sharp mind. He will be able to take over after Theodore. I think he'll go far."

Felicity sighed. "Yes," she said hesitantly, determined to chaperone her sister, to make sure that Kingsley's visits were in company.

Kingsley stood at the curve of the grand piano as Dorothy played the last notes of the Chopin étude. She nodded acknowledgement of the smiles and applause from friends and family seated around the music room. Then with a grin she turned back to the piano and pounded out a rollicking polka. Everyone laughed and clapped the beat, sending the gaiety out the open French doors into the still October air.

The weather was holding well: chrysanthemums, petunias, and Shasta daisies still brightened the borders. Maples and birches at the lower garden near the pond were just beginning to turn. The feel of Indian summer was in the air with a bit of sharpness, the mustiness of soil turned and mulched for winter, and smoke from burning leaves. Toronto is later than Montreal, Kingsley thought.

The Thanksgiving party at the Chandler's had been a great success. He had been seated next to Dorothy at dinner. She was exquisite; he could not keep his eyes away from the soft curve of her breasts above the high Empress waistline. They had talked animatedly throughout the meal, about the two cities, about the tenor to be featured in the Figaro they were all planning to attend on Friday, and about the show of Rembrants scheduled for early 1886 at the Montreal Art Association. And they had shared a secret smile as Alice Foster from Boston repeated for the third time, "How strange it feels to celebrate Thanksgiving in early October!"

The Gordons' invitation to tea had been a compromise between Felicity and her father. Charles had insisted that they return the Chandler's hospitality while the Randolphs were still in Toronto. He liked and admired Theodore and was prepared to support his interests with the sports arena committee. But Felicity had persuaded him to be cautious about too easy familiarity. He had agreed to keep a watchful eye on Kingsley, and she had agreed to the afternoon salon.

Kingsley now gazed admiringly at Dorothy's shining red hair pulled back from her face and falling from an intricate arrangement in the back. Today she was wearing a lustrous pale brown taffeta with tight bodice and full crinolines. Her creamy skin gleamed. She looks like a golden maple leaf, he thought, his imagination waxing awkwardly poetic. Her loose ringlets bounced with the rhythm of the polka, laughing face turning from him to Linell who was standing close to turn pages for her.

Dorothy's relationship to her cousin puzzled and irritated Kingsley. He yearned to take that place near Dorothy, but he could not claim it. After the Thanksgiving dinner, as they had walked in the garden, he had come close to expressing his strong attraction to her. But glancing up he had seen Felicity and her father watching him closely. He felt startled and uncertain, retreated into formality, and avoided making any declaration. Now he welcomed the opportunity to see Dorothy again, hear her play, and perhaps to talk privately with her.

She stood as the group applauded and began to move toward the wide veranda overlooking the garden. Trays of delicate sandwiches and tiny tarts - sugar and raisin, pecan, and pumpkin were set out on the long table covered with a fine white damask cloth. Roses molded of pink ice floated in the large crystal punch bowl. Linell bowed and took Dorothy's hand to accompany her. She smiled toward Kingsley, "Come, Mr. Randolph, will you join us in the garden?"

Just then Felicity stepped near, "Would you escort me, Mr. Randolph? I am interested to hear how your plans with the sports arena committee are proceeding."

Startled, but unable to refuse, Kingsley offered his arm and they strolled together through the French doors. "I am always surprised at your interest in business affairs, Miss Felicity. Although, in truth, I don't know why I should be. My mother has always taken an active interest in our business, and she is on our Board."

"Yes, I have observed that about Mrs. Randolph. She has a keen mind for advancement. My father tells me that Mr. Randolph puts great faith in her judgment."

"Mother has always looked to the future. That has been a great asset for Father." Kingsley was not sure where this conversation was going, and he was slightly uneasy with it. He was not quite sure whether Felicity was complimenting his mother or criticizing her. And he was frustrated at having been so smoothly removed from Dorothy's side.

"Father tells me that you are also a great asset to your business, Mr. Randolph. He says you have a good eye for opportunities."

Flattered, but again with the sense of subtle meanings, Kingsley said, "I am pleased that you have been interested in my progress, Miss Felicity. I do have many ideas for possible future developments. Did you know we have proposed a roller rink for one section of the new sports arena? We have added a line of roller skates to our production, including designs for ladies. Have you tried this new sport?"

"Yes, many of my friends have tried the new skates. We have always ice skated of course, but I find that the techniques are quite different. I fear that roller skating will never be very popular. The skates are too rigid; one cannot turn or swing easily. One has more control with ice skates."

"I believe we've solved that problem with our new design, Miss Felicity. We have mounted the front wheels on a spring plate that both bends and turns with the skater. That gives the flexibility one needs. I would be pleased to send you a pair to try if you are interested." Kingsley had almost forgotten Dorothy. Business was where he was most comfortable, and Felicity's interest stimulated and excited him.

"That would be most kind of you, Mr. Randolph. That design sounds very interesting; it might make a real difference. Shall we join the others?" They returned to the group around the tables, and moved toward Dorothy who was now chatting with Margaret.

Felicity was captured by her aunt Lady Hampton-Smythe and Kingsley took the opportunity to speak to Dorothy, "I have not had the chance to tell you how much I enjoyed your music, Miss Dorothy. You play extremely well. Do you have plans to make music a serious career?"

"Oh, no, but music is such a joy. I do study with Josef Trankowitz here in Toronto and with Mme. Langlois at McGill whenever I have the opportunity. I get so much pleasure out of my music."

They continued talking easily as they had at the Thanksgiving dinner. Gathering courage, Kingsley asked, "If I wrote to you, would you reply?" Dorothy nodded, blushing faintly.

"Miss Felicity, what a pleasant surprise. Are you in Montreal for Easter?" Kingsley knew that the Gordons were to visit the Hampton-Smythes. He and Dorothy had corresponded, but he wasn't sure if Felicity knew that. They had all met again during the Christmas festivities, and plans had been laid for this spring, choral concerts, and the Rembrandt exhibit at least. "Is Miss Dorothy with you?"

"Dorothy is at the conservatory. She takes every opportunity to have a piano lesson with Mme. Langlois. I am on my way to Morgan's for a pair of gloves. I'm eager to see their new store. They say it is magnificent."

"Indeed it is. May I escort you? These wooden sidewalks are a great improvement, but they are sometimes difficult to walk on." He offered his arm and she took it gladly. Her shoes, though their toes were only slightly pointed, did make walking hazardous on the planks. She held her long beige wool skirt away from the muddy walkway with her left hand. It was styled like a sports skirt, slim and straight in the front, gathered toward the back. Her short Persian lamb jacket and black satin hat with its brim drooped to the left and trimmed with silk mums created a casual but striking outfit. Kingsley was proud to be seen escorting her.

Felicity admired the elegance of Morgan's new store. "It is huge, isn't it, Mr. Randolph, but warm and inviting. It's so open - with the low counters you can see clear through to Burnside. Makes you want to browse, and the chandeliers are magnificent."

"Yes, our friend Angus brought them over from France.

He said it was a miracle they came through without damage; the voyage was particularly rough. I'm told they were fashioned especially for Morgan's, patterned after some in the palace at Versailles."

Felicity moved toward the glove counter. "I thank you for helping me, Mr. Randolph, but I mustn't keep you from your own affairs. Were you shopping, too?"

"I was just going into Birks'. I wanted to get my mother a brooch for her birthday next week." That was a sudden inspiration and he hoped it would impress Felicity. "Would you be kind enough to help me select something, Miss Felicity? I'm quite hopeless with such things, and you have exquisite taste."

Felicity groaned mentally; she had left herself open for this invitation. But he had been kind; perhaps he was sincere. She made her purchase of gloves and they crossed Ste. Catherine Street to Birks Jewelery.

In the small booth they debated over the pieces brought out. Felicity watched him linger over a delicate platinum spray resting on a circlet of diamonds, each slim branch tipped with a lustrous cabochon emerald. Perfect for Dorothy, she thought, but not the thing for Mrs. Randolph. Margaret needs something bolder, more dramatic.

Felicity had an unerring sense of design and style, and she judged instinctively what would suit Margaret. She was impatient with herself for getting drawn in, but felt compelled to express her opinion. She said, "Do you like this rose, Mr. Randolph? It would complement your mother's colouring, I believe." The large single rose was formed by a series of baguette-cut garnets laid to shape the petals, its heart three tiny gleaming topaz stones. It was set on a short stem with one gold leaf, finely traced with black veins, strikingly bold without being ostentatious.

"You are right, Miss Felicity. My mother would surely like that." Glowing with undefined pleasure, Kingsley arranged the purchase on the family account. His father would not question the charge; he would appreciate the thoughtfulness. "Could I suggest a cup of tea at The Portico?"

"Thank you, Mr. Randolph, but I must get back to meet Dorothy. She will have finished her lesson by now."

"May I escort you, then? I would be pleased to greet Miss Dorothy." He seized on the opportunity to learn what plans could be made for the coming weeks. At the same time he indulged the strange titillation inspired by Felicity's nearness.

Felicity hesitated, but took his arm. As they walked the few blocks to Strathcona Hall on Sherbrooke street, Felicity became very formal again, and Kingsley stumbled to make conversation, about the University, her interest in studies, the chilly spring weather. Felicity responded shortly to any effort, "Yes." "No." "Fine."

Kingsley became more ill at ease, as though he had done something improper, had forced himself into her company. Dorothy might take his appearance with Felicity wrongly. He greeted Dorothy awkwardly, stammering a rather fanciful version of their meeting. "Miss Felicity spotted me going into Birks' to purchase a gift for my mother, and she was most helpful in making my choice." He laughed hollowly and shrugged. At his obvious discomfort Dorothy glanced sharply from Kingsley to Felicity. She flushed and withdrew the hand she had offered. Kingsley cursed himself; he should have explained to Dorothy privately. But it was almost the truth: the meeting had been by chance, and Felicity had helped him with the gift. He would clear it up with Dorothy later. He hurried to make amends, "May I call on you this evening, Miss Dorothy? Perhaps you would play for me?"

Dorothy glanced uncertainly at Felicity. "I am not sure what plans have been made by our hosts, the Hampton-Smythes. Perhaps you should call to find out if we are to be at home."

Thoroughly disgruntled with himself and the ambivalence of his interests in the two young women, Kingsley took refuge in formality. "I shall hand in my card this evening and hope you are free to receive me. Miss Dorothy. Miss Felicity." He bowed and left hurriedly.

CHAPTER SEVEN

Growth

Montreal and Toronto – 1886-1888

The weeks and months of 1886 passed quickly. Kingsley Industries won the lucrative contract to provide equipment for the Toronto arena. Their new ice maintenance machine was the deciding factor in negotiations for the contract. It was Theodore's design; it operated somewhat like the automobiles being suggested, powered by a battery, and it scraped and buffed the ice base much more rapidly than had been possible by hand finishing.

Kingsley sat with Charles and the two sisters in the Folly on their lower garden. He was now Vice-President of the company, in charge of the Toronto work, and of promoting the new machine across Canada. "Your support really made the difference in gaining the contract, Charles. My Father and I are most grateful. This means that I will be spending a great deal of time in Toronto."

"Perhaps you should rent a city apartment here in Toronto, Kingsley. Those new flats on Yonge Street are very nice, and a perfect location. Close to the station, to the university, and right in the heart of the business community." Charles was delighted to have Kingsley in Toronto. He had always secretly longed for a son, and in spite of Felicity's reservations he was beginning to look on Kingsley as a future son-in-law, a member of the family.

Increasingly Kingsley's thoughts involved Dorothy. He became a frequent visitor to the Gordon's magnificent estate. He and Dorothy, accompanied always by Felicity, walked often in Bletchley Park, or picnicked near Lake Ontario to watch the heavily laden barges pulled up from Hamilton by teams of dray horses. Under Dorothy and Felicity's tutelage, he began to appreciate symphony, opera, and ballet - none of which had held much interest for him previously. And to his delight, all three Gordons became more enthusiastic hockey fans.

Felicity realized that she could not dampen Dorothy's growing affection for Kingsley. In Charles's view the two families were bound together by thriving business interests, and he regarded Kingsley with favor, almost, she could see, with affection. In fact, Felicity herself found Kingsley's constant presence more acceptable. He was attentive to her also, and obviously admired her knowledge of business and her interest in many sports. Since her father had been one of the few men who accepted her wide range of interests unquestioningly, she warmed toward Kingsley, and noted his favourable qualities more than the flaws that had previously concerned her.

Charles and Theodore were becoming good friends despite their different personalities. Charles was out-going and gregarious. He loved the social life of a wealthy businessman, and encouraged Felicity and Dorothy to fill the house with friends, as well as to act as hostesses for his business entertaining.

Theodore was much more reserved, a watcher and listener rather than a mixer, although he enjoyed being among company. What drew the two men together was what they had in common: thoughtful common sense, fundamental honesty, and a dedication to build - to build a business, a good life, and the country they so admired. They were innovators in business, but conservative in personal life and in politics. Their tastes were simple, though they were indulgent with their families.

Margaret was deeply unhappy that Kingsley was spending so much time in Toronto. She would not admit it even to herself, but the fact was that her fulfilment was her belief that she was the guiding force in Randolph life, and especially in Kingsley's. She was shocked and hurt when she learned that Kingsley had rented the Toronto flat. "Why in the world did you do that, my son? And without discussing it with...."

"It was a business decision, Mother. We've talked many times about extending the business westward. And with the new contract. You know I'll have to be in Toronto a lot. Father and I agreed that it was a good move."

"So you discussed it with your father? And you, Theodore? You didn't see fit to make me a part of the choice? You have your 'team' - I guess you don't need my opinions any more!" Margaret set her cup down with a crash, stood and stalked to the door.

"My dear! My dear! Of course we need your opinions! This was a sudden opportunity..." Theodore's voice trailed off.

"Come on, Mother!" The childishness Kingsley had

always felt in his mother's presence was now impatience. "Don't get all emotional about this!"

"I'm not emotional! You go ahead. It's those Gordon girls that have twisted your thinking! They don't like me, I know. I've tried to be helpful to them, but they are too fond of themselves. Don't want advice; well, I won't offer my help any more!"

"Margaret, Margaret." Theodore went to her, touching her lightly on the arm, then the cheek. He nodded to Kingsley to leave it to him, and Kingsley shrugged and left. "Please, Margaret, please. Come, let's have a glass of wine." He touched her again, lightly, suggesting, urging her back to their chairs. "Liebchen, Liebchen, you are my strength, my heart, my life. I am sorry we did not discuss this move with you. I have thought you are so involved in your Women's Auxiliary work, and the Royal Victoria group. You are so much in demand."

"The Women's Auxiliary! The Royal Victoria Women's Aid Society!" She dragged the titles out scathingly. "You know how hard I've worked for them! But have they ever elected me to an office? No, of course not! I'm just fit to do the accounts, the scheduling, the organizing! Am I a part of their society? No!" Suddenly the drive to be accepted into this Montreal society had become a desperate fear that it would never be. Not unless we build our home on the mountain, she thought. We must get away from this townhouse down here on Mackay Street. We must!

Margaret joined Theodore and Kingsley with a tot of brandy after dinner on Friday. This was an hour they frequently spent together. Margaret would work on a sampler or a block of her latest Dresden Plate quilt; they always brought in satisfying sums at the fall Auxiliary raffle. Theodore and Kingsley relaxed with a fragrant cigar. Sometimes they tested each other with a game of chess. But always there was quiet talk, review of the events of the past week, community activities, and plans for the future.

Tonight Margaret had an agenda. "Theodore, I want us to get the new home built; I don't want any more delays. This has been a good place, but we always said it was temporary. We need a larger home now; Kingsley is an adult and we need the space."

Theodore spoke thoughtfully, "Yes, probably you are right, Margaret." He hesitated, took a slow sip of his brandy. He had been thinking of an alternate possibility, but he hesitated to suggest it. "These three townhouses here are well made and a good location. What would you think of buying the other two and tying them together as one? That would give us….."

"Absolutely not!" Margaret was trembling. "Mr. Randolph, you promised we would build next to the Calverts. What would we do with our lot, then, I ask you?" She could not sit still; she stood and walked shakily to the desk, then turned to Theodore, more angry than he had ever seen her.

"I was just thinking, my dear. I had a very good offer for…."

"Of course you had a very good offer," Margaret's shoulders jerked. She picked up the silver letter opener and stabbed angrily at the green desk blotter. "Our lot is one of the finest locations left. I do not want a knocked-together place down here. I want us to have the home we planned on all along. Please, Theodore." Her voice shook, and tears welled.

Kingsley stood up and looked uneasily from mother to

father. He did not want to be seeing this. Violent anger, it had been impressed on him, was low class, unacceptable. But he was not, it appeared, the only one to harbour violent passions, to vent them on someone loved. Vague thoughts about anger and punishment surged through his head. He felt exposed in some profound sense, exposed to passions in himself. He took a step toward Margaret, looked desperately to his father, started to say something, anything, "I...I..." Neither parent looked at him. His shoulders slumped and he slipped silently out of the room.

Breakfast Saturday morning was a quiet affair. Kingsley kept his head down, but there did not seem to be any tension in the air. He could never have imagined that Theodore and Margaret had resolved their anger and had gone to bed soothing each other and re-affirming their bond lovingly and assuredly in that very normal human way, through sex.

Kingsley was astonished, shocked when Theodore said, "We must talk to Angus on Monday, son, and pin down the contract for that shipment of red sandstone he is bringing back this trip. We should break ground as early as possible next spring."

"The...the house?"

"Yes, yes, of course the house. We should get it ready to move in before Thanksgiving. Your mother wants to have the Calverts and the Gordons in our own home next year." As always for Theodore, when a decision was made, there was no hesitation, no second-guessing.

Kingsley shot a look at his mother, but she was calmly spooning scrambled eggs onto their plates and laying several strips of crisp bacon on each. She said, "I believe we can get Frank Courtney if we approach him right away. We've always planned to get him, and I read that he has finished the new hotel, so now is a perfect time."

"Yes, I'll talk with him this week. Kingsley, you see Angus about the sandstone."

Well, the thing was done it seemed. Kingsley was pleased enough, though slightly unsettled. He was just being told what to do; he felt left out, like a child again for a moment, but soon began to dream of his own vision of the house. He would see to it that he worked with the architect. Father would make the contact, but he would leave the day-to-day planning with Kingsley. That would mean the house would really be his. Even his mother would not override his ideas.

Kingsley rushed upstairs to write Dorothy the news and make plans to see her the following week. He wanted to call her on their new telephone, but hesitated. There had been much talk about possible dangers from the electrical impulses sent over wires to make speaking connections by telephone. Mr. Ingram had warned Charles not to permit his daughters to speak on the machine. "There may be dangers to females whose systems are delicate," he had said pompously.

Felicity had laughed impatiently, "Oh, for goodness sakes, Mr. Ingram. Surely you don't believe such a tale."

Nevertheless there were many concerns about these instruments. Kingsley had heard that the waves of power coming through the wires could very well cause serious harm to women's private organs. He would not put Dorothy in jeopardy. He wrote quickly:

Saturday evening, July 10

My Dear Dorothy,

I have good news and I am eager to meet with you next week to tell you all about it.

Father and Mother have made the decision to begin our family home on Grosvenor Street. This has been discussed for so long I had begun to believe it would never come to be. But Mother rather put her foot down last evening and so we are under way.

Father hopes to get Frank Courtney as the architect, and will speak with him this week. One must give Father much credit. Once he begins something, he goes at it with great enthusiasm.

I will be put in charge of the design and construction, which pleases me greatly. Of course, Mother will have much to say; she has been longing for this home for many years.

I have many ideas about the house, dreams perhaps, and do want it to be notable. I am beginning to scratch ideas already.

I hope you will not think me too forward if I discuss these plans with you. Perhaps your father would listen to my ideas too. He has given me guidance and advice on many things, and I respect his judgment so much.

Please give my sincere regards to your father and to your sister. May I see you next week when I am to be in Toronto? Looking forward to your early reply.

Yours in true friendship,
Kingsley

He finished the letter and prepared it for the post, then sat jotting sketchy ideas about the design of the house he wanted.

In Toronto the following week Kingsley found it hard to keep his mind on business. He signed contracts with construction firms, with suppliers, checked finances with accountants, met with Knowlton Calvert, their old friend from Halifax who was now head of the Central Division of the Bank of Nova Scotia. But he ran the business with half a mind. In his thoughts he kept designing layouts for the new house. And always he saw Dorothy in the rooms he imagined - sitting at a wide marble fireplace in the evening, lighting candles on the long refectory table that would go to the new house, descending a broad sweep of stairs to greet a party of guests. He imagined the large bedroom with windows opening to the view of the river below the mountain. But his mind blurred the vision of the bedroom. He was uneasy with that dream, reticent about imagining Dorothy in that intimate setting.

He called on the Gordons, walked in the garden with Dorothy, talked of business, the weather, the opera. For three weeks he buried his hopes in trivialities, thinking alternatively of the quick certainty with which his father acted on an idea, and the heavy burden of his mother's driving ambition. Would Dorothy's gentleness enable him to satisfy his mother? Or should he seek someone more like her, more ambitious, more aggressive? Always the image of Felicity flickered through the back of his mind, bringing resentment at the sense of inadequacy she aroused, and something like jealousy at her perfect self-assurance.

Finally, near the end of August in a restless session of chess with Charles he made a foolish move that left his queen unprotected. He shrugged, "I'm sorry, Charles. I don't seem to be able to concentrate. May I be excused, sir? May we join Miss Dorothy and Miss Felicity on the verandah?"

"Of course, of course, young man." Charles swallowed a small chuckle. He was quite sure he knew the cause of Kingsley's restlessness. "Come. Perhaps my girls have fresh lemonade waiting. Then I must get to some work if you will excuse me."

They joined the girls and talked quietly for a while, enjoying the evening breeze, warm from the heat of the day, but already teasing with the loamy smell of autumn ahead. Soon Charles excused himself and turned to Felicity, "Would you mind joining me in the study for a short while, my dear? I would appreciate your reaction to the proposal as I have written it." He explained to Kingsley, "We are hoping to preserve the Barratt Swamp area for a natural habitat. We believe that it would be a criminal mistake to drain the area and build there. It is home to a thousand species of wildlife, and could be a magnificent viewing area if properly designed. We have been pushing City Council, and want to present our proposal before the area gets snapped up by developers. I hope you will excuse us for a while."

Pleased and relieved, Kingsley stood and bowed. Then, his voice shaking slightly, he asked, "Would you care to walk in the lower garden, Miss Dorothy?" They walked to the pond where Kingsley threw a couple of stones, making them skip across the quiet water. He was nervous and excited; he felt like running or jumping into the pond to swim madly across. He skipped from topic to topic: the wonderful fall weather, the new coach of the Montreal hockey team, the work on the arena, that amusing American fellow who called himself Mark Twain. His readings at University Hall were drawing huge crowds - a bit naughty perhaps, but wickedly funny about their president Cleveland. They had tickets for Friday. He heard himself babbling on and

Dorothy responding quietly.

"Please, would you sit for a minute, Dorothy?" He did not want to say Miss Dorothy. He led her to the white wrought iron bench under the willow; he was trembling. "May...may I ask you something?"

Dorothy only nodded; she glanced at him quickly, then ducked her head shyly.

"If...would...could...." he stammered; he had never been so nervous and at the same time so gloriously eager. "If I asked you...your father I mean... would you consider me too forward to ask you to be my wife?" He had said it; he was shaking, and suddenly kneeling by the bench, he took her hand in his and looked up, knowing that he would beg if he had to.

Dorothy's eyes brimmed and she reached her other hand to cover his. She whispered, "Yes, yes." Then she turned and, with the directness that so surprised and delighted him, she said, "Kingsley Randolph, I would be proud and honoured to be your wife."

Kingsley gaped for a minute, then jumped to his feet grabbing both her hands and pulling her up. "My dear, my very dear Dorothy. You...I...we.... You have made me so happy. You are so very dear to me." He bent and kissed her softly. "May we go speak to your father?"

Again Dorothy answered directly, "Yes!" Her face broke into a happy smile. "Let's run! Come!" And they did run, and broke panting to stop at the door of Charles's study.

"You are sure?" he asked.

"I'm sure."

They knocked and burst into the study hand in hand.

"Well," Charles looked up, a half smile on his face. "It

seems something is afoot! Methinks we may have need of a glass of bubbles."

'Sir, Miss Felicity. I have...she has...Miss Dorothy has done me the honour to accept me...I have asked her...Honestly, Sir, I am too happy to talk straight!"

They all laughed, and Charles rang for a bottle of champagne and glasses; they toasted the couple and their future. Charles shook Kingsley's hand, then pulled him close to throw a strong arm around the younger man's shoulder. "I am very pleased, my boy. Dorothy's happiness means much to me, and I place her in your care happily." Only Kingsley noted the shadow that crossed Felicity's face, and he felt a light twinge of uncertainty. Could he live up to the faith that Charles Gordon felt in him?

Theodore and Margaret were delighted with the news. Margaret, in fact, was openly gratified. This formal tie with the Gordons would ensure her place in the social world of Montreal. "You see, Theodore," she said, "how necessary it is to get our home built. We must allow for Kingsley's new family, and for a more active social life."

Life became increasingly hectic as 1886 came to an end. Holiday parties took on added gaiety and meaning as the young couple were feted. Plans for the new home were drawn and re-drawn. They would break ground by mid-April unless the city should be hit by late winter storms. Angus would be in harbour by then, and the coveted red sandstone would be on site soon after.

They held many Friday night debates about the design. Should it have square towers or round? And how many? Should it front on Bishop Street looking out over the city, or on Pine Avenue looking up toward the mountain? Should the servants quarters be in the house or over the carriage house? How far back from the street should it be set? Should the main staircase sweep from right to left, or from left to right? How many rooms should have fireplaces? The pleasure of debating and deciding all of these questions involved not only the three Randolphs, but all of their friends as well.

Kingsley was kept busy between Montreal and Toronto, and he made one trip west to Edmonton to promote the ice machine. He was overwhelmed by the grandeur of the Rockies. "We could spend our honeymoon at the Banff Springs Lodge, Dorothy. It is the newest of the Canadian Pacific chateau-style hotels. It is rustic as compared with the Laurier, but the service is excellent, and you have never seen such beautiful country. And the wildlife - I can't begin to tell you all of the animals I saw: bear, deer, mountain goats, elk, wild cats. You can see all of them quite near the Lodge. I did not visit the glaciers, but I was told that the ice falls are truly spectacular."

Margaret was appalled. "It sounds so dangerous, Kingsley. Do you really think it is wise? Why don't you spend your holiday at Niagara Falls?"

Dorothy was interested, "It sounds splendid, Kingsley. The Falls are indeed wonderful, Margaret, but we have seen them, and we can go there often. Jasper Park would be the trip of a lifetime. Even the train trip should be an adventure."

"An adventure, perhaps," Margaret tightened her lips, "but much of that land out there is still untamed wilderness, child. Wildlife is all very well at a distance, but you couldn't explore much. There would not be many activities, I should think."

She turned to Theodore to seek his support, but Dorothy interrupted. "It is very good of you to think of our safety, Mrs. Randolph. But you know we have your example of courage to inspire us. After all, setting off across the ocean to a new land when you were a young bride was dangerous too, probably more dangerous than a train trip to Banff. I do so admire you for your spirit."

Margaret opened her mouth to continue the argument, then stopped, catching her breath uncertainly. It had not occurred to her to draw this parallel with her own life. She blushed faintly and felt a warm glow of gratitude at Dorothy's praise. It was not often that she received such an expression of appreciation. It would be very pleasant to have this young woman in the family.

Theodore spoke up at last, "Why don't you go to Halifax, Kingsley? Dorothy? There is a good hotel there, not a chateau, but good accommodations. The harbour is beautiful with the tall ships. There are many interesting places within a reasonable ride. And you could check on the shoe shop, Kingsley. We do need to think about the future in regards to the shop."

This argument swayed Kingsley, "That is a good point, Father." He turned uncertainly to Dorothy. "What do you think?"

Dorothy nodded and admitted to herself that Margaret's arguments were valid, too. There would be a greater variety of interests at Halifax. "Halifax would be very interesting, Kingsley. As your mother suggests, there would be no bears to worry about. And I have an aunt and cousins there. It would be good to see them."

So it was decided; plans would be made.

Life moved smoothly toward 1890. Montreal was growing rapidly; it was becoming a sports and arts center for North America as well as the financial heart of Canada. Boat races, hockey matches, tennis, lawn bowling, and ice skating were increasingly popular both for participants and for spectators. Young men trained for long distance swim meets by battling the St. Lawrence currents from the lower shore to the river islands. A Gilbert and Sullivan company came to present their amusing librettos, and a fad for all things Japanese followed in the wake of Madama Butterfly.

The Montreal Stock Exchange on St. Francis Xavier Street listed all Canadian and many US companies. Kingsley Industries went public in the fall of 1886 and showed strong results. Work kept Kingsley busy promoting and overseeing the various sectors of the company. Theodore more and more distanced himself from daily affairs of the company. He now served on the Boards of several local companies, was actively involved in Chamber of Commerce committees focused on enhancing Montreal's position in the financial affairs of Canada.

With the business growing and expanding into new markets, the increasing social demands of the young engaged couple, plus the work on the new house demanding attention, the days and weeks passed quickly.

The new house on Bishop Street began to take shape and was the focus of much attention. Red sandstone was relatively rare in the city, and many questions were debated: did it look too garish? Would it look unsuitable in the neighbourhood where grey stone predominated? Would it weather well in Montreal's severe climate? But Margaret and Theodore both found it especially pleasing, as did Kingsley and Dorothy. They were already calling it "Redstone Manor" or "the Red House", viewing it as home.

As the work progressed, all cheered each step completed. The red sandstone had its effect; it began to look gracious and yet comfortable. The broad sweep of the driveway led up from Bishop through what would be lawn and gardens. The driveway continued around to the carriage house giving the appearance of a wing of the house. Living quarters above would accommodate Herbert and Martha privately, as well as Jacques the coachman, and perhaps a gardener and yard boy. The front staircase rose to a stone slab entry with a glass-enclosed sunroom off to the right, and a large open receiving room through the main doors.

Dorothy glowed. Her happiness shone out and was reflected back in the smiles of everyone around her. With plans, parties, rendezvous with Kingsley, consultations with caterers, florists, musicians, bridesmaids, with fittings, choices, and the pre-nuptial classes required by Reverend Wilson, life at the Gordons ebbed and flowed around Dorothy.

Increasingly Dorothy seemed to be moving into a new orbit, a new life that would take her away from the quiet, rather formal, family life in Toronto. Increasingly she appeared to withdraw into some quiet corner within herself. Charles was not given to introspection, but he was struck suddenly one January evening by an odd, disquieting thought. 'She has a Janus look about her,' he thought, 'the fresh buoyancy of the child she was, and the expectant wonder of the woman she will be.' He reached out and took her hand, "Don't ever leave us, child," he said, his voice thick. "You are very dear to us."

"Of course, Papa. You and Fizzy are my rock, my

heartland." Then she grew pensive. She moved to the soft leather hassock at Charles's feet and leaned against his knees. Hesitantly, she reached for his blunt-fingered hand and clutched it nervously as the child she had been had always clung to it. "You and our Mother were very much in love, weren't you? You were happy, weren't you, Papa?"

Thus Charles suddenly realized what Dorothy needed. She needed a mother to talk with her about marriage and what it could bring - its great joy and its great demands. "Your Mother, my Ernestine, was my heart and soul, my dearest, best friend. That is what I believe a good marriage can be - the truest, most intimate friendship." He did not know how these words were coming to him. He was not one to talk of the personal life of love. But Dorothy's need made these words suddenly simple and easy.

"I know, I am very sure, that my Ernestine got great pleasure from our loving, our sex. And, of course from the fruits of our love - Felicity and you, my dear. She did not live long enough to know you as I do, but she held you in her arms before she died, and she gave you to me to care for. If she were here today, I believe that she would tell you to look forward to this most intimate of unions. And she would tell you, also, that the rights and duties of love are the same - the right, and the duty, to accept, and the right and the duty to refuse. It is not always easy to know when to accept and when to refuse, but you will know when it comes time."

"Father…" Dorothy hesitated. "Reverend Wilson places much emphasis on the vows we take, 'love, honour, and obey.' He would not say we have a 'duty to refuse,' I think. He would say, does say in fact, that it is a wife's duty to obey her husband."

Charles did not respond immediately. He thought back to his own life with Ernestine. Had she felt it a duty to obey? No, they had had many heated debates about their personal lives, about the children, about social customs, about politics - big things and small. Always Ernestine had freely expressed her way of viewing the world, her beliefs about what life, their lives, should be. He smiled, remembering.

"Well, my dear, Reverend Wilson has been schooled in a very conservative tradition, you know. "Love and Honour and Obey" don't refer just to your relationship with Kingsley, your husband. I believe that they must also refer to your relationship to yourself. You must love your husband, of course, but you must also love yourself. And you must honour yourself equally, and obey your heart. I would not gladly give you to Kingsley if I did not believe that he understands and respects this. You are very precious to me, my love. You are worthy of honour and of true happiness." He pulled Dorothy's head to his chest, caressing her, and wiping the sudden tears from his eyes.

They sat quietly for several minutes, both lost in the moment of love and communion. These words would stay with Dorothy for a lifetime. Then Dorothy stood and moved with a quieter serenity to complete the evening chores. Charles sat long in his deep leather chair before the fire, remembering the child she had been and realizing how much he would miss her constant, loving presence.

Felicity withdrew her application to enroll in the fall Donalda group at McGill. She told Dorothy only after she had sent the letter cancelling her application.

"Why, Fizzy? Why did you withdraw? You've wanted that so much! It's because of the wedding, isn't it? We can cut down on everything. I don't need all this fuss and bother if it means you have to give up your plans. Please, Fizzy, please!"

"For heaven's sakes, child. Don't take on so. It's just for this fall. Anyway, you can't change everything now. The invitations are out and everything is decided - the church, the reception, the music. The contracts are signed; everything is arranged. I'll be fine. Don't take on so."

"I've been so selfish. I just never thought you'd do that, Fizzy. " Dorothy plopped down on the low slipper chair, her face showing her misery.

"You're not selfish, goosey. I decided it myself. I want everything to be perfect. I don't want my mind on some famous historical battle, or some political or philosophical treatise." Besides, she thought to herself, when I study, I want to be able to put my whole mind to it. I want to be a full-time student. "I'm the selfish one," she went on to Dorothy, "I want to be in on everything right here and now. It will be a beautiful wedding, Dotty, and I want to be a part of it, to help make it a success. I want you to be very happy." She paused for a minute, then continued, "You know that Papa would buy you a house here in Toronto if you would live here." Felicity and Charles had discussed this possibility; they really knew it would not happen, but Felicity wanted Dorothy to know that she had the option.

"I know, Fizzy, but Kingsley must stay with the head office. He'll be in charge soon enough, so he must be there. Theodore depends on him all the time."

So with a swirl of pre-wedding plans and holiday events 1887 became 1888, and the June wedding was before them. The wedding party assembled in Toronto and threw themselves into last minute activities.

CHAPTER EIGHT

The Wedding

Toronto – June 1988

Kingsley sang, quietly, he thought:

> "D...D...D...Dotty
> D...D...D...Dotty
> You're the
> ony...ony...ony...pony...tony...wony"

He snickered and hiccupped. "Sh-h-h!" he warned himself, and grinned as he tripped on the carpeted stair riser. "Oops! Mus' be qui't!" The bachelor party, at least his part in it, had gone on until well after midnight. He was tired. He stumbled again and lay down across the top step, then looked up to see a vision in a white night dress, red hair loose around a pale face. "D...Dotty?"

"No, of course not. Be quiet, you'll wake everyone." Felicity had heard the noise and stepped out of her room to make sure Kingsley didn't make a fool of himself - and Dorothy in the process. She tugged at his arm, "Stand up. You must get to your room."

Kingsley struggled to his feet and grabbed Felicity to support himself. "Ummm, soft," he mumbled.

With a moue of disgust, Felicity put her arm around his back steadying him, and headed down the long hall toward Kingsley's suite. They had all taken rooms in the Westin to be prepared for the wedding tomorrow. "You're drunk," she said, "You must get to bed, get some sleep." Why do men have to get drunk to handle their emotions, she thought. Like Father after Mother's death. At least Father was never crude, but they are so ridiculously childish. "You'll be embarrassed tomorrow, Kingsley. Give me your key."

Kingsley just tightened his hold and pulled Felicity closer, pinning her to him and running his hand down her back. "Um-m-m!" he groaned again..

Felicity whispered harshly, "Mr. Randolph. Stop! Don't be a fool!" She shoved his hand away and jerked back from him.

"Don' 'Mr. Randolph me', Fe'c'ty luv. Tha's nice." He pushed more forcefully at her and tugged at her robe. "Came to meet me, din' you. Not so hign'n mighty after all!"

Felicity twisted away and hissed, "Stop! Stop this at once! Think of Dorothy!"

Suddenly a strong hand yanked his head by the hair and another grabbed the collar of his shirt. He was pulled roughly back.. "You slimy scum! You arrogant little peacock!" The harsh voice was Ernesto's, the strong hands those of the cobbler, long-time friend and partner of his father Theodore. "Miss Felicity, I can handle this filth. I'll get him to his father and wake Mr. Gordon. They must decide what to do about this."

"No, no, Ernesto. Please. We mustn't make a scene of

this. Dorothy! We have to keep this from Dorothy. I'm all right. I'll be all right." Felicity was shaking and stammering. "Please, get him to bed. I'll be all right."

Ernesto hesitated, put his arm around Felicity's shoulder to comfort her and said quietly, "You go on. I'll knock on your door in a few minutes to see if you are well."

Felicity hurried out. Ernesto grabbed the cowering bravo and punched him viciously in the stomach. He opened the bathroom door, pushed Kingsley to his knees, and stuck his head into the porcelain commode. "You slimy rot. You are a disgrace to your father. You will not get away with this."

The blow to his stomach had a powerful effect. Kingsley vomited again and again, and lost control of his bladder. He was a sodden, filthy mess. And in the presence of this man who had been the idol of his early childhood he was afraid.

He was a small boy again, standing shamed under his mother's hand, forced to apologize to Riata without truly understanding. He had only tried to be like bold, laughing Ernesto, had only aped Ernesto's swagger, the colourful language. Angry and defiant, he had cringed under Ernesto's scornful glare, and hated his mother. Now Ernesto would not hesitate to haul him in front of his mother, his father, Charles Gordon, even in front of Dorothy. He could lose everything. "I'm sorry. I'm sorry," he whimpered.

"Sorry! You are a sorry excuse for a man. We'll make mighty sure you are sorry, my fine feathered peacock! If it weren't that Miss Felicity wanted to keep this quiet, I'd know how to deal with you." He grabbed Kingsley by the arm and jerked him over to the mahogany drop-front writing desk by the window. He slapped down a sheet of cream-coloured writing paper with the Westin monogram in the corner, and forced Kingsley to take up the quill pen. "You will write out exactly what you did and sign it right here and now. You write exactly what I say." As he dictated, Kingsley wrote shakily, the words staggering across the paper.

To Whom It May Concern:

This night I did get exceedingly drunk and I did force my attentions on Miss Felicity Gordon, sister of my fiancée Dorothy Gordon. I alone am responsible for my actions. Miss Felicity has in no way encouraged my advances. I sincerely regret my actions. Miss Felicity Gordon has my full permission to use this letter however and whenever she wishes.

Signed,
Kingsley Randolph
This 8th day of June 1888, Friday

Ernesto folded the letter and tucked it into his waistband. "Get yourself cleaned up and get some sleep. Do not shame yourself and your family any further." He left Kingsley's room and walked quietly down the hall to Felicity's door. He tapped softly and was admitted.

It was nearly 3:00 AM when he emerged and headed for his own room. He paused at Kingsley's door, but heard no sound. He did not notice that the door at the other end of the hall had opened and Theodore had caught a glimpse of him at his son's room.

The wedding took place Saturday at 1:00 in St. Edmund's

Anglican Church on Wellington Street.

The sun shone, pink vergilia and heavy boughs of spirea cascaded in well-tended beds on either side of the frontage. Soft strains of Mendelssohn's Scottish Suite could be heard through the open double doors. Handsome carriages drawn by perfectly groomed horses deposited guests at the slate-paved entryway.

Ladies created drama with the style and colour of their costumes. Straight-fronted waists were buttoned to the neckline, or laced tightly away from a fitted bodice. The back was shaped into the fashionable "S" curve by means of yards of fabric folded and tucked just below the waistline, or by strategic placement of a small bustle or tournure. Lavender was no longer the fashionable colour, so patterned silk in rose, ecru, or pastel green swayed in the sunshine.

Escorts wore frock coats buttoned high to a wide tie and wing collar, or cutaway dress coats with starched shirtfront and white bow tie. Silk top hats and ornate walking sticks added to refined airs. It could have been a painting by Cézanne: the iridescence, the stylized posing, the formal inevitability of a dance.

Inside the church the perfect June day was lost on Kingsley, waiting in the left antechamber with the men of the party. He stood looking out the window at the gathering crowd, imagining scenes of shame and embarrassment. Had Ernesto, had Felicity told anyone about last night - his father, Charles Gordon, that foppish Linell who stood now talking with Ernesto? Ernesto, stern-faced and silent by the door.

Ernesto was to be his best man - decided months ago after heated debate between Margaret and Theodore. He had agreed. He had been secretly pleased when Ernesto had accepted, had felt again the glow of childish admiration for

Ernesto's vibrant love of life. Why had he supported his father's insistence? Now nothing could be worse. His stomach cramped, and he felt an uncontrollable twitch at his left eye. The sun was too bright, the tableau of guests too glittering. A low groan escaped him.

"Easy, old man. Just bridegroom's nerves." Linell was at his side, his haughty voice jerking Kingsley to attention. "Do you have the ring?"

Kingsley's mind skittered frantically. "Uh, yes, I think…," his voice trailed off. "Ernesto…."

"Well, it's time to go, get into place. The organist just started the introduction."

Kingsley threw a desperate glance at Ernesto and stepped as close as he dared. Ernesto's face held no expression as he turned to usher Kingsley ahead of him to their place below the altar. Kingsley's mind was so frozen by fear that the crowd of family and friends was a blur. He did not see his mother's pleased smile, or his father's nod of support. He could not think what he was supposed to do.

The strains of the wedding march filtered into his consciousness. There was a rustle of movement as everyone turned to watch Dorothy on her father's arm start down the aisle toward him.

Dorothy was a gleaming vision in the white satin gown that fitted smoothly from an inset V-front to a pointed waist, emphasizing her slenderness. The edges of the "V" were embroidered with tiny pink rosebuds shaped from narrow satin ribbon. Her veil of Belgian lace fell below her bust in front and trailed down across slightly puffed sleeves almost to her fingertips. The train, falling from the soft bustle, was edged with the same small rosebuds tucked into ruffled lace. The two little girls who carried her train proudly wore their first small bustles.

It wasn't only the dress that made Dorothy beautiful. Her eyes glowed with happiness and a soft smile curved her lips. She walked proudly, seeming to hug her father's arm.

The picture registered in Kingsley's mind - but there was her father, ominously proper in his smartly fitted cutaway, stiffly starched wing collar and bow tie. And Felicity, slim and cold in an ice-green asymmetrical lace overskirt open on one side and adorned with a matching pale green riband on the other. The slight tournure accented her stately elegance. He saw no sign of last night's shame.

Kingsley's mind retreated from the scene. He walked through the vows and promises as though mesmerized. He knelt, he stood, he sipped the wine and opened his mouth to receive the host, quaking inwardly at the blasphemy. He fumbled the ring onto Dorothy's finger and repeated words.

Only when Dorothy lifted her face to him for his kiss did feelings return, mixed and confused. A pang of regret, a sense of triumph, and then a burst of anger at his humiliation coursed through him. As they turned to walk together as man and wife, Kingsley threw his head back, shaking off the fog of fear. His arrogant stride and bearing now cloaked determination to deny the bitterness and alienation he felt toward the two people whose admiration he had most desired.

The reception was held in the Gladstone Room of The Westin Hotel. The members of the wedding party stood just inside the wide double doors, receiving congratulations and best wishes. Since Ernesto was a stranger to everyone, Linell, as head usher and close friend of the family, made the necessary introductions. Kingsley shook hands automatically and his stiff words of welcome and thanks elicited puzzled glances and awkward silences.

When he stumbled over a name, or mumbled unintelligibly, Dorothy smiled to herself. 'He's so nervous. I never saw him like this,' she thought. But when he mispronounced Lord Haversham's name, she was sure there was something wrong. Kingsley was always conscious of propriety and this was almost rude. She touched his arm, giving the touch a slight pressure to ask for attention, and spoke to the guests, "Lord and Lady Haversham, we are so delighted that you are able to join us today. Your good wishes mean a great deal to us. And let us congratulate you, Lord Haversham on your election to the Order of Canada. A great honour, sir."

Kingsley, recalled to his duties, added, "Indeed, and a justly deserved honour, sir. You are recently returned from the trade conference to Australia are you not? Some very important developments there, sir. And how did you find Australia, Lady Haversham?"

"Sidney is quite comfortable, of course, but much of the land is truly desolate. Life there is very hard for most people, I fear. But Alban was greatly impressed by the potential for trade contracts, weren't you, dear?"

"Indeed, indeed. A big market."

"I hope we can hear more of your ventures, sir." Dorothy squeezed Kingsley's arm with thanks as he warmed to the company. "You know the Calverts, don't you, Lady Haversham? Why don't you visit with Serena and Knowlton; we'll join you soon." The line moved on into the grand dining room.

A magnificent wedding cake dominated a long buffet at the far end of the room near the doors to the kitchen. Five tiers, it had been baked for Dorothy by the hotel's famous pastry chef, Leonard Altman who had trained in Viareggio under his father. The signature initials, L.A. could be found if you looked carefully, formed by twisting stems of roses on the lower tier. A huge steamboat roast, sliced breast of turkey, cured ham, and medallions of pork were ready to be served by white-coated chefs. Waiters in black coats and bow ties, white shirts and gloves gleaming, took orders from the guests seated at tables around the room.

The two families faced the guests from the head table midway along the right wall. Kingsley and Dorothy were in the centre; Margaret sat to Kingsley's right, then Theodore and Ernesto. Charles, Felicity and Linell were to Dorothy's left. The centrepiece of their table was a small replica of the wedding cake, created by layers of white and pink rosebuds. And every table in the room had a similar centrepiece.

Felicity stopped beside Dorothy before she took her own place. She leaned over to kiss her sister and hold her close for a minute. "My beautiful sister," she whispered, "be happy, be strong."

Dorothy took the hand that held her and leaned her cheek against it. "Dearest Fizzy! You have made this a perfect day for me. My sister, my truest friend." She looked up at Felicity with such a glow of happiness that sudden tears flooded her sister's eyes. Felicity turned her face away and spoke a few brief words of good wishes to Kingsley. She glanced toward Ernesto and caught him looking at her with understanding and sympathy. Shaking her head slightly she sat down as her father held her chair.

The five-piece chamber group played quietly from the balcony to the right of the double entry. The flautist played the opening notes of Schubert's sonata for flute and violin, one of Dorothy's favourite pieces. She touched Kingsley's arm and smiled up at him. He smiled stiffly back and patted her hand, but then lowered his eyes to his plate.

He could not look at the family ranged around the table. They were too close. Their eyes felt threatening. Shrinking into himself, anger flared in his thoughts; his heart hardened. He would not let these people destroy him. He turned to Dorothy; her happiness softened his anger somewhat, but he had to force himself to touch her arm naturally. "You are very beautiful, my love," he whispered.

Theodore stood and rang his glass. "I want us to drink a toast to Dorothy, our beautiful bride and our new daughter. We are delighted to welcome you into our family, my dear. We look forward to many happy years with you. May love light all your days and years."

All the men of the company rose to the toast, and there was a chorus of Hear! Hear! Cheers! Long life! Happiness! around the room. Dorothy nodded happily to everyone. Felicity raised her glass, anguish in her eyes; tears welled again, but she would not let them flow.

Then Charles rose, "Let me propose a toast to the happy couple. To my daughter Dorothy who has been a joy to me as a child and as a young woman, with her sister, my life's happiness. And to my new son, Kingsley, whom I have learned to respect and love these past few years. I give you Mr. and Mrs. Kingsley Randolph, our future."

Kingsley's face crumpled; he hid his eyes behind his hand. Only pride drove him to stand, raising Dorothy beside him, to acknowledge the enthusiastic applause and cheers. Surely Charles did not know, he sounded honestly happy for them.

Felicity and Ernesto only touched their lips with the champagne flutes; they did not drink. Kingsley's eyes flashed anger, quickly hidden. He would not bow down to them.

Margaret, too, noted that Ernesto did not drink to the couple. She spoke to her husband, "Ernesto should have offered a toast to Kingsley, Theodore. It is improper of him not to do it. I could have told you he wouldn't fit in. He has embarrassed Kingsley. See how uncomfortable he is."

"Never mind, my dear. Ernesto is a good man in many ways. A good friend and a good partner over the years." Margaret would not be pacified. She turned to Kingsley and repeated her complaint. Kingsley shuddered, "Just drop it, Mother. I'll take care of him."

The dinner progressed through its several courses, conversation flowing from the beauty of the wedding, the plans for the honeymoon, business, politics, the bounteous feast, the perfect weather, to gowns, gossip, and coming social events. Only at the head table did there appear to be some stiffness, a strained formality that grew more noticeable as the meal continued.

Finally after dessert and coffee, Charles called for their attention, "It has been a wonderful day, but the evening is ahead. Now the hotel staff would like to clear the tables and set up for the dance. You will all be joining us about 7:30, I hope, but you must wish time to rest and refresh yourselves." Slowly the dining room emptied as guests withdrew to their rooms to prepare for the evening.

The wedding party assembled in the MacDonald Room

for the official photos. By the time everyone was satisfied, all were ready to go to their rooms for a needed break.

The family parted at the elevators. Margaret and Theodore went to their suite at the eastern end of the long corridor, Charles and Felicity to their adjoining suites at the opposite end. Dorothy would rest and refresh herself in Felicity's rooms; she and Kingsley lingered for a moment at the open door. Dorothy waited for something, uncertain what to expect, but expecting some expression of their love and their new status.

Kingsley, too, hesitated indecisively. He could not look directly at Dorothy while the open door shrieked of Felicity's presence. As always when uncertain, he resorted to formality, kissed her briefly on the cheek, said, "I will call for you at 7:30," and winced at the hurt, faltering expression in Dorothy's eyes. "I do love you," he said gruffly as she turned to go in. "I'm sorry," he added to himself, and he walked heavily to the suite he and Dorothy would share that night. Talk would have to wait.

To Kingsley the dance was another quagmire to flounder through. If he could only get back to Montreal, get clear of this confusion of fear, shame, and anger. He had a flask in his luggage; he drank heavily and sat, head in hands, for a long time. The picture of himself hanging over the commode vomiting and weeping under Ernesto's hands filled his mind.

A knock at the door startled him, his heart pounded and he felt nauseated. It would be Charles come to charge him. "Who is it?" he stammered.

"Father," Theodore answered. "May I come in?" Kingsley opened the door and turned back to sit on the bed. "Your

Mother was worried about you, son. Is something troubling you?"

"I'm all right, I'm fine." Kingsley waved his hand in front of his face, brushing away cobwebby thoughts.

"Do you need anything?" Theodore persisted. "You have your tickets?"

"Yes, there on the desk. Charles's man Terrance has taken the main luggage down to the station and checked it for tomorrow morning. We have the smaller bags for the train:"

Theodore tried again, "Your mother thought Ernesto was behaving peculiarly. You haven't had a falling-out with him, have you? Ernesto's a good man."

"Good man!" Kingsley cautioned himself to be careful. "He's your friend, Father. You can call him a good man if you want."

"Well, the thing is," Theodore continued, "I didn't tell your Mother, but I saw him stop by your door last night - about 3:00 this morning, in fact. He didn't knock, so I wondered what he was doing by your room at that time of night?" His voice made a question of this statement.

"How would I know what he was doing at 3:00 AM?" Kingsley growled. "He certainly didn't knock, so I have no idea." That's no lie, Kingsley thought; he didn't knock - at any time! In fact, what was he doing at 3:00 AM? I'm sure he left me by 1:30. But relief flooded him and his rapid heartbeat slowed. So the mighty Ernesto was still prowling at 3:00. What was he doing for so long? Was he sniffing after Felicity? These rapid thoughts chased themselves across Kingsley's mind, revealing themselves in a clash of emotions on his face.

Theodore noted, but was not able to interpret these signals. He too would be glad when they were back in Montreal and settled into a quieter routine. "Well, we will all go with you to the train in the morning. The carriages will be here early." He hesitated, never finding it easy to express his feelings. "Your Mother is very proud of you, son. Dorothy is a beautiful young woman, beautiful and gracious. We are very happy for you."

Kingsley let his father pull him close, and some of the misery washed away. At home in Montreal he would be free of Felicity and Ernesto. All this would be past; he could put it out of his mind.

The crowd of friends ringing the grand ballroom applauded lightly as Kingsley and Dorothy, followed by the two families, stood for a moment at the top of the three broad steps leading to the dance floor. Plush burgundy carpeting in the foyer behind them, gold gleaming from picture frames and sconces, shimmering crystal chandeliers, floral printed silk wallpaper, velvet-covered chairs near potted plants at strategic spots around the floor. The Westin had been built in the early days of Toronto's growth, and nothing had been spared.

More photos were taken as Kingsley and Dorothy descended the stairs and led the way into the ballroom.

The orchestra, now prepared to play waltzes, mazurkas, reels, or a sprightly two-step were opening with a soft medley of lieder while waiters carried trays of champagne to the guests. Groups gathered and conversation flowed. Charles signalled the orchestra and it moved into the popular "Tales" as Kingsley and Dorothy stepped to centre floor to start the dancing. Again a flutter of applause saluted them. Dorothy held the train of her wedding gown lightly with her left hand and they circled the room, nodding and smiling to their friends. As they whirled past each group, couples fell in behind them and soon the floor was a kaleidoscope of colour.

Felicity, her ice-green moiré silk framing her red hair piled high and pulled back to hang in curls, danced with Linell, brilliant in his red and black velvet waistcoat. Charles, more conventional in black tie and tails, led Margaret to the floor. Margaret, the senior woman of the family party had allowed herself to shine. Her soft golden taffeta showed the faintest pattern of bamboo shoots. Her dressmaker had assured her that this hint of Japanese was the very latest fashion. And she was pleased that it was being noticed with interest and perhaps a bit of envy. She was still at heart the fashion-conscious young woman who had grown up in the garment industry of Bremen.

Theodore was dancing with Serena Calvert. "They are a lovely couple," Serena said, smiling to herself as she remembered that her Twelfth Night dinner back in 1884 had set the stage for this romance. Knowlton and Theodore were friends and allies in business, as she and Margaret were in their social life. Of course she was not quite as slim as she had once been, but she was still a striking woman. Her greying blonde hair was pulled up and away from her face in the popular style of the day that many of the women present followed. The rose silk of her gown complimented her creamy complexion. The soft bodice fitted snugly, and the full drape of the skirt was tucked up under a small bustle at the rear. She smiled knowingly at Margaret as they crossed paths with her and Charles.

Ernesto escorted Franga Macaulay to the floor. Angus and Franga had made the trip from Halifax, delighted to renew their friendship with the Randolphs, and to toast the young couple. Angus would use the opportunity to test out the waters for his foray into home construction. Franga was a sedate matron in her deep lavender cut silk. The sleeves were a little too full and there was a little more fullness at the front of the skirt than was current in Toronto, but she was still a handsome woman.

The dancers changed partners as the music changed. Dorothy danced with her father, with Theodore, then with her cousin Linell. He whispered, "He is a very lucky man, my dearest cousin. Would that we were not cousins."

"I love you, Linell," Dorothy pleaded. "You are my dearest, truest friend. Do be happy for me."

"Yes, yes. With all my heart."

Ernesto danced three sets with Felicity. He cut a striking figure at forty-eight. His black curly hair was touched with grey, but his blue eyes sparkled with a love of life that could never be repressed. His full evening coat with long tails, the starched front shirt and black tie looked almost dandyish as he swirled around the floor.

Stomach clutching, Kingsley marked his every turn and dip. He held out his hand to his mother leading her to the floor. As they danced she admonished him, "You must dance with Felicity, son. It is beginning to become awkward. This is not like you."

"I will, Mother, I will. I have approached her, but each time she has taken the arm of some other partner." He had been relieved, but agonized because he knew it would be noticed.

Finally he grabbed another glass of champagne at the bar, drank it quickly, and approached Felicity. She, too, knew that this was necessary for Dorothy's sake. They took one stiff, awkward, turn around the floor. She asked to be returned to her father, and Kingsley, sweating, his heart pounding, was glad to oblige.

He danced once more with Dorothy, and by common consent they excused themselves to go to their suite. The dance would continue, but their friends saw them leave with sympathy and understanding.

"Isn't Felicity beautiful?" Dorothy smiled up at Kingsley as they waited for the elevator. "She and Ernesto made such a handsome couple - as if they have known each other for years!"

Her innocent chatter about the two people who so threatened him angered and frightened Kingsley. He slammed the button for the sixth floor, hardly waiting for Dorothy to arrange her train inside the elevator. "Not very proper. Danced three sets together. He's a married man. Much older!" He had drunk too much champagne; his words slurred, sentences chopped short. He was revealing too much.

Dorothy looked at him strangely. "It was just because neither one had a partner, Kingsley. They were good together. She knows he's a married man!"

"Sure. But maybe he's forgotten it himself," he mumbled as he reached for the door and dropped the key. He put his hand against the frame to balance himself and stooped to pick up the key. He stood uncertainly inside the room as the door closed behind them. All the loving words that had filled his heart and mind in the past months now seemed blocked.

He reached for Dorothy's hand and turned her toward him, "Forget them. You were the most beautiful woman there. You are mine, mine." He pulled her to him and kissed her hungrily. His hands slid down her back to her waist and he pulled her closer. He groaned as he felt the curve of her hips, then reached up to cup the soft breasts that curved against him.

"So beautiful, so beautiful!"

Dorothy pulled back slightly, "My love," she smiled into his eyes, "my dearest love. May I change? Would you unbutton the back for me?" She turned and Kingsley began to fumble with the row of tiny buttons. He kissed her neck, behind her ears, her shoulders, as the dress opened down the back. And again his hands found the curve of her hips, the flat of her stomach. Dorothy's face flushed and the heat of growing passion glowed in her eyes. "I will not be long, my love," she whispered and went to the other room where her night dress had been laid out.

Kingsley stumbled to his chest of drawers and reached for the flask he had carried with him. He took a long deep drink, shuddering with its bite. He turned to the night table, picked up the bottle of Dom Perignon from the ice cooler, and struggled with the wire and cork. The pop startled him and he jumped back, spilling champagne across the table. He poured two glasses, lifted one and quickly drank it down, then refilled it.

He turned as Dorothy came in, now in her negligee - blue satin cut low across her breasts, tiny ribbon straps, blue rosebud buttons of the same narrow ribbon from bust to waist.

"You...you're...please!" the broken words were clumsy as he tried to express his feelings. He held out a glass of champagne. They drank together, hesitantly moving toward each other. Kingsley emptied his glass and jerked at his jacket and shirt. He dropped the jacket and struggled with the buttons of his pants as he reached for Dorothy's hand.

Looking deeply into each other's eyes to read question and acceptance, they moved slowly to the bed. Kingsley's rough passion with Felicity was now hesitant, almost innocently naive.

They murmured their names, loving phrases, "Dorothy," "Kingsley," "so beautiful," "my dearest love," "want," "please," do you?" "yes, yes."

But Kingsley had drunk too much. The champagne sapped his strength. The guilty vision of Felicity struggling and crying, "No, no" filled his mind and he felt weak, lost. He groaned and turned away.

Dorothy lay troubled by his side. Had she displeased him in some way? Was something wrong? Hesitating, she said, "Kingsley?"

"Not now," he muttered. "Sorry." He got up and staggered into the other room of the suite, taking his flask with him.

Dorothy lay quietly for several minutes, then got up and followed her husband. "Kingsley?" she asked again. "Is something wrong? Are you sorry we…?"

"No, no!" his voice was harsh. "No, never. Just sorry I…"

"We're tired, love." Relief washed over Dorothy. "Come back to bed."

"Later. Later. You go back, get some sleep." He could only glance at her. The directness that had so delighted him now made him uneasy.

She put one hand on his arm and he faced her with such a look of unhappiness that she turned quietly and returned to bed, to sleep restlessly through the night.

CHAPTER NINE

Bittersweet

Quebec City / Montreal – 1888-1895

When the train reached Quebec City, the young couple took the carrier up the steep slope to the Hotel Frontenac. Hardly daring to look out, Dorothy said, "This must be the pathway General Wolfe took when he surprised the French army and won the city for Canada.

At the top they looked back out over the tracks and river far below. "No wonder the French thought they were safe," Kingsley said. "General Wolfe would have been considered foolhardy if he had not won." They turned and followed the porter into the elegant lobby.

Kingsley signed, then looked at the page almost in surprise. He turned to Dorothy with a look of wonder, an uncertain question. She reddened slightly and her face glowed as she realized he had signed, 'Mr. and Mrs. Kingsley Randolph for the first time.

The days that followed were warm and happy. They did not rush into passion, but moved slowly, each eager to learn the other. They ate in the grand dining hall or ordered room service, walked around the plaza in the early evening, talked of hopes and plans as well as of the history that was coming alive for them. Dorothy wrote thank you notes to Margaret and Theodore, and to her father. Her letter to Felicity overflowed.

Dearest Fizzy,

How happy I am! And how much I owe to you and Father! Your love enfolds me!

We reached Quebec City last evening and settled into our rooms at the Frontenac. This is a fascinating city. The hotel is on the upper flat – the Plains of Abraham. You remember that history. We have walked where those brave soldiers fought and won Quebec for Canada. Our cabriolet up from the train followed the path that General Wolfe and his men climbed – although it is more than a footpath now.

I believe that my worries of the past few days have been for nothing. We are at last united in our love. I did not know how deeply satisfying love could be. I feel whole, complete in an entirely new way. It puzzles me to remember things I have heard women say as they exchange confidences about the act of love. I have heard some speak of it as an unpleasant chore or duty. I confess that I was quite timid. Really, Fizzy, I cannot understand this. Surely it is the reality of what Reverend Wilson has said it should be – uniting Kingsley and me as one. I believe it is good.

You will no doubt think me fanciful, dear Fizzy, but I have an odd feeling about this place. The hotel is marvellous, good food, good service, beautiful in every way. But I feel cocooned in English here - in a glass bubble. I have the queer sense that there is another world outside our 'bubble' that is proceeding in a very different ambiance. Everyone speaks English to us, of course, but one hears, in the halls and in the city outside, only French. It is not just that they speak French, Fizzy, but that conversations are more relaxed, more alive. It is another world outside of the hotel, I think.

Well, enough introspection. We will be on our way to Halifax tomorrow. So good night, and my love, always.

Dorothy Randolph
There, I wrote it! Amazing!

The weeks in Halifax offered slow, lazy days, learning the intimacies of living together, the small habits of daily living - of tidiness or carelessness, of consideration or thoughtlessness. They began to find ways to live easily with each other.

Even when they went out they maintained an air of privacy strolling the beaches, wandering through small shops, and whiling away time watching ships at the harbor. There were new tastes for Dorothy to experience. Lobster and shrimp fresh from salt water to table delighted her. She hesitated over snails and clams in the shell, but quickly cultivated a taste for clam chowder. "We must add chowder to our menus at home."

"If you say so." Kingsley was not at all sure that his mother would be eager to experiment.

The Dalhousie Theatre group was presenting

Shakespeare's "As You Like It" and they were able to get good seats for Saturday evening. It was a rollicking good performance and Kingsley laughed heartily. He admitted that he enjoyed it.

Kingsley met with Ernesto as charged by his father. To disguise his nervousness he spoke brusquely. "Father says that he would offer you the opportunity to buy us out of the shoe-making business for $5000. Are you interested?"

"Ah, for sure, I would do that. But," he shrugged eloquently, "by golly, I don't have $5000. No money!" He laughed easily. "All money goes to university! Dino, he will be engineer. He does good. And Pietro soon, too, will go to Dalhousie. He, I think will be teacher, or maybe priest. Others too - that university gobbles up my pennies faster than they come. You tell Father I just stay like always. Keep business with my good friend Theodore!"

" Well, as you wish." Kingsley hesitated, still feeling like the small boy he had been, he offered his hand.

Ernesto shook it strongly and Kingsley turned away. Had he failed his father? Would Father have offered to negotiate? He would talk to Dorothy.

The month in Halifax ended and they settled into their suite on the second floor of Redstone Manor. Kingsley returned easily to his interests and duties at the firm. Dorothy tried to discover what her role in the household might become. The comfortable two-headed management that seemed so natural for her and Felicity in Toronto would never work in Margaret's home.

She spent hours reading and writing letters and thank-you

notes. But Dorothy chafed at these small chores. She wanted to be busy and useful. She wanted to create a full, meaningful life for herself and Kingsley. She wandered restlessly through the rooms of the suite, imagining changes she might make. The dark oak furniture, the paintings in their gilded frames, and the heavy velvet draperies overwhelmed her. She itched to bring in softer colors, to brighten the rooms. But most important, she missed her piano. She would ask Father to ship it to her.

At dinner that evening, she mentioned her plan. "Perhaps we could have a musical soirée," she suggested.

"We don't have a music room." Margaret dismissed the subject flatly. "There's no room for a piano."

"I...I..." Dorothy stammered uncertainly.

"We could put it in the small room at the end of our hall," Kingsley broke in, attempting to offer a solution.

"But....but ...music is for everyone, don't you think? For when we have guests? Could there not be room in the salon?"

Theodore glanced at Margaret's stiff back and pursed lips. He liked this spirited young woman. He would have to offer Margaret something, or someone important to bring this about. The Gordons and the Knowltons would not be enough, too familiar. Ways and means, ways and means, he thought; surely there is someone who would spark Margaret's interest. He would put his mind to it. "We'll think about it," he said, and an uneasy calm settled around the table.

Dorothy realized from this exchange that it was not going to be easy to make the changes she wanted in the suite. Kingsley is comfortable, she thought; he finds the furnishings and décor familiar. But if this is going to be our home, I must make it more to our liking; she was determined.

"We should move these heavy things upstairs," she suggested to Kingsley later. "Really, I cannot live with such dark colors, Kingsley. I can get a decorator who will help us change over to lighter, brighter tones so we can enjoy the sunlight."

The forthrightness that had seemed so attractive before now shocked and unsettled Kingsley. "Mother worked hard to....' Kingsley started.

"You know these things can be used in another area. We need our own style of furnishings, Kingsley. Blue, and green and sand - the colors of the harbor, the sea - that would be beautiful, wouldn't it!"

Kingsley shrugged without conviction. He will not want to confront Margaret, she thought. Maybe we should have taken our own place, those townhouses on Fort Street, or maybe Toronto. Kingsley has to spend time in Toronto for business.

In early November Dorothy received word that her piano had arrived. Theodore and Kingsley supervised its transfer and placement in the salon. Margaret bustled around, acting as if all this were her own idea. She had decided (at least she believed she had decided it) that a Christmas musical evening on December fifth would serve two purposes. It would introduce Kingsley and Dorothy to Montreal society as a couple, and suggest that music would be the focus of interest in their lives. Theodore engaged Laurence Franks, a gifted young cellist who sat first chair in the Toronto Symphony Orchestra as guest artist. Dorothy would accompany him on some concertos and each would also present solo selections.

December arrived with a heavy snowfall, but by the fifth it

was cold and clear. Theodore and Margaret, with Kingsley at their side welcomed the guests as they arrived rosy cheeked to shed boots, hats, gloves, and coats, laughing, ready to celebrate their good luck at outwitting 'typical Montreal weather.' Dorothy and Mr. Franks rested in their rooms, relaxing and preparing for their program. Felicity and her father Charles Gordon circulated among guests as they returned to the salon. Chatting and greeting, they introduced one guest to another, made sure everyone was seated comfortably among companions.

The evening went smoothly. The cello was not commonly a solo attraction so interest was high. Mr. Franks easily won enthusiastic applause with concertos from Bach, Handel, and Elgar. Dorothy presented her own favorites from Mendelssohn, Chopin, and Mozart as well.

When the program ended, champagne appeared. Theodore gave the formal words of thanks to the musicians and proposed a toast to the season. Guests moved to congratulate Mr. Franks and Dorothy, and to speak to the hosts. Small tables were set in convenient spots. Felicity circulated, chatting with Toronto and Montreal guests and making introductions.

Margaret motioned to waiters with trays of delicacies, crisp cucumber sandwiches, and thin toast triangles topped with fresh shrimp or lobster bits. Spicy ham, beef or turkey, crisp bacon crumbles, cheese and egg sandwiches were offered. Then came trays of sweets, bite-sized tarts and slices of rich dark Christmas cake so thin they were almost translucent.

Theodore brought Mr. Franks to introduce him to Mr. and Mrs. Buchler, who stood a bit apart as other guests came up to greet them. Mr. Buchler might become a helpful contact for this gifted cellist. Felicity moved around speaking to friends and helping Margaret keep food plentiful and conversations vibrant.

As the evening ended, guests began to re-robe in their winter coats and sent for their surreys or cabs as they slowly departed. Mr. Franks excused himself and Kingsley ushered him to his room to see that all was comfortable.

In a quiet corner Dorothy spoke to Theodore. "I know that it was through your intervention that all this has come about. I am very grateful; this means so much to me."

"Not at all, child. Only business in a way - making things happen. What I do!" He laughed at himself.

"Well, I want you to know how much I admire your tact and resourcefulness. And I love you for your kindness, for this gift to me."

After guests had departed and the servants had cleared the salon, the family realized that they really were quite tired. They congratulated each other one final time, said goodnight, and slowly went off to their own rooms.

Kingsley held Dorothy close and she rested against his chest. "You were wonderful," he said. "You are so beautiful." He touched her cheek, her neck, and slid his hand down past the curve of her waist.

Dorothy murmured softly, then pulled back and looked into Kingsley's face. "I have something to tell you." She looked deep into his eyes, questioning, seeking an answer even before she spoke. "I am with child." She caressed her stomach. "We shall have a child."

Kingsley's hand jumped to her shoulder and he pushed her slightly away. "Are you sure?" he asked hesitantly.

"Yes, I'm sure. I got the answer from Dr. Michaels

yesterday."

"Oh!" he gulped. "I'll be a father! I'll have a son!" he said in an awed voice. He lifted her and sat in the big sofa chair holding her close.

Dorothy rested contentedly against him. She had her answer.

The news set off a flurry of activity. The nursery had to be prepared, walls re-painted, suitable pictures hung. There was baby furniture to be bought or brought from family storage. Dorothy would need maternity clothes so a seamstress moved into a room upstairs. Every woman in the family began furiously to knit, stitch, and embroider. Dorothy took advantage of the excitement to make some of the changes that she wanted in their own rooms; she commissioned new drapes and wall covering. Whatever she expressed a longing for, someone was ready to provide it. The first grandchild! It was not just this child who would be the spoiled darling of the family; even Margaret became lavish. Kingsley's son! Dorothy must take care of herself.

Kingsley Randolph II was born August 11, a husky eight pounds with Kingsley's solid countenance and Dorothy's flaming red hair. Theodore said, "He looks just like you, son. Has the Randolph chin, and pointed ears!"

Kingsley said dubiously, "But that red hair! He should have black hair!"

Dorothy smiled impishly, "Well, he had to have something from me! Else everyone might forget I was involved. Do you want to hold him?"

"Oh! Uh...maybe later." He didn't know how to hold a

baby! He didn't know anything about a baby! He was embarrassed in front of the crowd of family.

Kingsley Junior was quickly awarded the role of spoiled darling. Margaret made the christening gown of finest lawn, trimmed with her own tatted lace and delicate schwalm embroidery. He was held, rocked, talked to endlessly. Still, he was a good child, sleeping through the night at an early age, smiling and burbling happily. He did everything with gusto - ate heartily, cried lustily, cooed and babbled earnestly. When Kingsley was home in the late afternoon, he spent time with Kingsley Jr., watching him play and discussing his day with Dorothy or the nanny. Since he had never really learned to play as a child, he treated the child much as Margaret had treated him; he talked about him, not really to him.

Constance Margaret was born almost two years later. Dorothy told Kingsley, "I would like her to be named after my mother, Constance"

"Well, I guess. But Mother said she hoped we would name her Margaret." Kingsley was caught between the two women.

"Would you like Constance Margaret?" Dorothy asked. Privately she thought that was a heavy name for a girl to bear, but did want Margaret to be pleased. So it was decided.

Constance was a thin, restless baby, kicked covers off, twisted and wriggled in Dorothy's arms. She sucked greedily at the nipple, spit it out impatiently after a few minutes, but was hungry again an hour later so she absorbed much of Dorothy's time. "If she would only nurse longer, maybe she would feel more satisfied and would not be colicky so often," Dorothy sighed.

"She seems always on the move," Dorothy laughed to

Nanny. "Almost as if she has something important to do and can't wait to get at it!"

When she began to pull herself up against the side of the bassinet, it frightened Dorothy. "She could tip the bassinet over, Kingsley. We have to bring the crib down again." And Constance was standing up against the sides of the crib within a few weeks. For a change, Dorothy put her on a blanket on the floor. She soon had the blanket bunched into a twisted ball, rolled off it to explore the room. She began to crawl when she was a little over six months old. But she didn't crawl in the ordinary way, on hands and knees. She ran on all fours, arms and legs unbent.

Margaret was aghast, "you can't let her do that! It is not ladylike!"

Dorothy ignored that, thinking she is not yet a lady. But Kingsley, too, was uneasy with the picture the baby made,. "Should we let her do that? It looks...uh...odd. It isn't normal, is it?"

Dorothy described it in a letter to Felicity, "You should see her, Fizzy. She runs around like a little kitten. So fast! Much faster than if she went on hands and knees. She tries to keep up with Young Kingsley, and gets so frustrated when she trips on her dress and falls! She sets up a howl they can hear in the kitchen, and then is up and off again. She's so funny!"

The two children absorbed Dorothy's attention. She read to them and played simple games with Young Kingsley - rolling a ball or stacking blocks, but the nanny moved into the small room next to the nursery and began to take over more responsibility for the boy as he grew.

When Young Kingsley was presented with his two-year birthday cake, Dorothy said, "See, two candles. One. Two.

Two candles for Kingsley II."

"Kingsley two?" He said hesitantly. "Me two? Papa Kingsley two?"

Dorothy tried to explain it, but got hopelessly confused. She gave up and laughingly told Kingsley what the boy had said. So Young Kingsley was often called Kingsley Two in an admiring tone around the house. He grew rapidly and began to run Nanny ragged. He ran for the big stairs and Nanny only saved him because she grabbed his arm tightly before he fell headlong. "Your legs are not long enough to go down these stairs by yourself, young man. Wait for me." Kingsley tried to pull away, but she held firmly and let him try one step. When he stumbled, she said, "You see! You need to let me hold your arm."

Kingsley Two took one step down, then flipped around and scooted down backwards, landing at the bottom before Nanny could reach him. He grinned triumphantly at her.

By the time he was three it was clear that he had a mind of his own. On a beautiful October afternoon Kingsley took his son for a walk down to the park. Young Kingsley held the black spaniel's leash and they walked slowly, giving the dog time to sniff the bushes and trees.

It was color weekend and there were many neighbors out to enjoy the maple leaves. They met Mr. Fisk, a dapper old gentleman with a Van Dyke beard striding up the hill, wielding a shiny black cane. He had just sold his two grocery stores to the young Mr. Steinberg, so Kingsley stopped to congratulate him.

"Yes, yes. Time, don't you know. Noreen has been after me to sell for some time. Wants to see something of the world, she says."

"So will you travel?"

"We took a place in the south of France for two months, may stay on another month. Depends on how much snow you get here, I guess. Noreen says we should buy, but I don't know. Canada!" He touched his heart. "Hard to give up home," he hemmed a throaty chuckle. "And who, may I ask is this young man here?"

Kingsley started to reply, but the boy broke in. "I am Kingsley Three," he announced.

Mr. Fisk looked at Kingsley, a bit startled. "Kingsley Three?"

"Yes," Kingsley shrugged. "It's a family thing, Sir. When he was two his birthday cake had two candles. We thought we could begin numbers, said, 'One, two, you are two now.' He said 'I am Kingsley.' Dorothy said, 'Yes, Papa is Kingsley and you are Kingsley II' I guess that stuck with him because when he saw his birthday cake this year…"

"Oh, yes, I understand. Three candles, Kingsley Three! Clever boy! So who is Kingsley Two now?" he asked.

"Jojo is Kingsley Two. I am Kingsley Three" the boy said determined to set matters straight for this old man.

Kingsley shrugged with resignation. "He'll understand it when he gets older, I guess."

"No doubt! No doubt! I believe there's a daughter too? Is she…?" He pointed at the boy, then at Jojo.

"No, thank goodness! Don't even mention a number! He'd catch on in a trice!" That would really put the cat among the pigeons, Kingsley thought. If the boy started calling her…. Dorothy is touchy enough about Constance as it is.

He and Mr. Fisk wished each other a good season, and

Mr. Fisk strode off up the hill, "Need to get my legs prepared for the hills of South France." He was shaking his head, laughing to himself, "Kingsley three! Have to tell Noreen about that!"

They laughed about the name among the family, but the boy did respond differently to 'Kingsley Two', 'Young Man' and 'Master Kingsley.' Even at four and five he stood up straighter and looked at the speaker with more confidence when he was not addressed as 'Young Man' or 'Junior.' He accepted Constance's 'Ki-to' indulgently, however, as she ran after him, trying to keep up. Sometimes he said, "I'm going to hide where you can't find me," and he ran off laughing.

But Constance was too impatient to look very long. She knew how to entice him out of hiding. She sat down by the window and said, I am writing a very good story, and it might be about Ki-to. Or it might be about some other brave boy."

Kingsley always came running back, "It's about me, isn't it, Constance? It' is me, please?"

Over time Kingsley had settled on a man-to-man style of fathering his son, but he had no idea how to act with Constance. If she had been a 'sweet baby girl,' he might have adapted, but she resisted cuddling, even twisted away from being held after a few minutes. She seemed to be looking at him questioningly. "I don't know what she wants," he told Dorothy.

"She is just trying to understand, I think. Babies must find the world pretty confusing at first." He hadn't noticed when the boy was little, Dorothy thought. He was so wrapped up in soaking up every move Little Kingsley made he just thought everything he did was natural.

Young Kingsley soon began to talk in more complete sentences and to understand numbers, "I want two strawberries," or "I want three cookies." Dorothy suggested, "We should look for a good tutor for him soon."

"Later, maybe. He's only four. He is smart, even recognizes his name when we print it. He needs to learn to skate. Maybe I'll get a hockey stick his size. Want to get him on a horse too - let him learn how to handle himself first."

As always Christmas morning was special. Young Kingsley woke early. He had not slept well, had been up once in the night to use the chamber pot. He felt hot and a bit dizzy but jumped out of bed and soon had the whole establishment on the move. Nanny joined the family for breakfast in the dining room where the crèche was set up on the low buffet. After breakfast, the servants came in to listen solemnly as Theodore read the story of the First Christmas. Then Margaret sang "Silent Night" in her rich contralto with all joining in on the last chorus. Both children were old enough to feel more deeply the spirit that enfolded them, and they sat quietly for a few minutes. Dorothy and Kingsley exchanged a secret glance. Dorothy had told Kingsley that she was pregnant again, and they silently blessed their two 'babies', now seven and five, and the new child to come.

Then the thought of the tree with its pile of beautifully wrapped gifts stirred the two youngsters and they adjourned, laughing, to the salon. Kingsley and Dorothy had never stressed the St. Nicholas legend except to suggest that the Christmas stockings were filled somehow by the magical visitor. Gifts came from family members. Both Young Kingsley and

Constance received skates - Kingsley his first boot skates, and Constance a pair of trainers. Kingsley gave his son a bright red fire engine that produced a satisfyingly loud siren. It had a tank and pump for spraying water, much to the distress of Nanny who would be the one to clean up any mess. Margaret had made two new outfits for Constance. "Oh Grandma! Thank you. The nightdress is so pretty and warm and cuddly. And now I will be really cozy when we go out riding," she held the white sweater with pink rosebuds that Margaret had knitted to her cheek, smiling.

But it was a small box about ten inches long and three inches wide that triggered Constance's excited imagination. Inside stood six tiny porcelain dolls, no more than two inches tall. "Oh Look! They are china dolls! They look exactly alike! And they are so pretty! They have yellow hair and blue eyes, and their arms and legs move. They have to have names." She thought for a minute, touching each doll lightly. "They are The Six Beautiful Sisters of Loving Family." And she began to tell a story.

"The Six Beautiful Sisters of Loving Family have been taken prisoners by the horrible China hating monster in the house next door. They have to be rescued and the only one who can do it is their brave brother King Sly."

Kingsley II shouted, "The brave brother King Sly is me, isn't it, Constance. That's me, isn't it! I'll rescue them." Constance always made up stories about everything and her brother loved them. He was always the hero in Constance's stories.

Kingsley interrupted, "That's enough nonsense, Constance. It's Christmas. Let's think about Christmas. You have your new skates, why don't we all go try them out."

An unexpected thought flashed through Dorothy's mind. 'He's jealous! He loves the boy so much.' She said, "We will have to dress very warmly. The children are excited. Kingsley's cheeks are flushed; he may be over heated."

The cook prepared a basket of sandwiches and hot cocoa, Nanny dressed the children, Joseph sent Tom for the sleigh and the group was off, well bundled and clutching skates. There were already a number of skaters at the pond, and a good fire was glowing in the pit. Young Kingsley was already a good skater and he raced off to join a friend.

Kingsley was solicitous of Dorothy, "Are you all right to skate, Love?"

I'll take it easy," Dorothy replied, touching his arm. "You go on. Watch the boy and get a good skate in. Nanny and I will get Constance started."

Constance was convinced she could manage. "I don't want those keepers on my skates. I can do it!" But they led her out onto the pond, helping her control her balance as she learned to keep her ankles firm. She did learn quickly and they soon let her try a few tentative pushes without the trainers.

Time passed quickly, but suddenly Dorothy realized that Young Kingsley was huddled down by the fire. "Are you all right, son?"

"I don't feel so good. I don't want to skate anymore."

That was such an unusual statement that Dorothy immediately called Kingsley. "We have to get the boy home and in bed. He seems to have a fever. Get everyone." Kingsley saw that she was serious so he hurried off to round up their group and get the sleigh ready.

They rushed home. By then Young Kingsley was breathing harshly, his cheeks were flushed, and his eyes were bright with fever. Kingsley called Tom, "Get the surrey and go get Dr. Michaels. And hurry." But it was Christmas Day.

"The doctor is out," explained his footman. "The family is at their country place."

When Tom rushed back with the message, Kingsley, worried and angry, was flustered, "I'll have to go get him. I'll go faster on the horse."

"But to bring him back? Won't you want the surrey?"

"Yes! Yes! I guess you are right. Bring it back around, Tom."

Precious hours were lost before Dr. Michaels examined the boy. Dorothy and Nanny had set up a steamer tent. Water laced with vinegar was boiling under the tent but the child was clearly worse. He gasped for each breath and would not swallow the broth they offered. "Hurts!" he whispered.

Dr. Michaels listened to his chest and shook his head. "I'll have to bleed him." He prepared his equipment.

Dorothy touched Kingsley's arm, "Do you think that is good, Kingsley? I have read..."

Kingsley shook her off angrily, "Stay out of it, Dorothy. He's the doctor!"

They stood back near the window, hovering anxiously as the doctor proceeded. "Well, that should take care of it. It's all I can do right now." Dr. Michaels repacked his bag and snapped it closed with a frighteningly loud click.

"But... but...? Will he be all right? What do we do?" Dorothy turned to Kingsley. They were both close to tears; they wanted reassurance, more help, but were afraid to ask the dreaded question.

"The best you can do is just keep him warn and quiet and

keep the tent going. Try to get him to take some broth. Now, can your man get me back to my family? I'll stop by tomorrow to check on him."

Kingsley looked at Dorothy, shocked. He turned to Theodore and Margaret who were standing quietly by the window, worried and uneasy. "This does not seem right, Father. He can't just leave like this. There must be something..."

"I have done all I can do today, Mr. Randolph," Dr. Michaels interrupted gruffly. "I will check on the boy tomorrow, I promise. Please, I need to get back to my other business."

Unhappily, Kingsley ushered the doctor to the surrey, his helpless frustration spilling over onto young Tom, "See to it that you make good time, and get yourself back here to wipe down Homer and clean the rig before your dinner."

As the days passed, Young Kingsley's breathing became heavier. The house grew silent. Pots and pans were moved about with great care. Doors were shut silently. Constance huddled on Nanny's lap. She resumed sucking her thumb as she had when she was a baby.

A nurse came. She, Dorothy, and Margaret kept a constant vigil by the boy's bedside. Charles and Felicity appeared unannounced.

Dr. Michaels came and bled the child a second time. When he suggested it a third time, Dorothy protested. "It's not working, Kingsley. He looks worse each time. I don't think..." She looked uncertainly from Felicity to Charles.

Kingsley snapped, "You are not a doctor. If he says that is best, don't keep trying to tell him his business!"

Dr. Michaels said, "We can try kerosene in the steam. It is a stronger de-congestive. And I want you to thump him on the back several times a day to keep the congestion loose."

He demonstrated and the boy whimpered softly, "Papa! Hurts!" Kingsley hurried to the bed, ducked under the tent and gathered the child in his arms, refusing to leave.

When the child died three days later, Kingsley swore passionately, "There is no God!" He slammed out of the room, flinging chairs aside and knocking over anything in his path.

The others, too stunned even to weep, shrunk silently where they stood. Until at last they began slowly and silently to undertake the terrible chores of caring for the child.

The funeral was held Sunday afternoon in Christ Church Cathedral on St. Catherine Street. Kingsley swore he would not attend. "I won't listen to those useless words. You can't tell me he is in a better world! At God's side! I want him at my side! I want him alive." And he turned away, tears streaming.

Theodore urged, "You should be there for Dorothy's sake."

Margaret said bluntly, "You have to, for the family."

Dorothy whispered, "Please, Kingsley."

He brushed them all off waving a hand as though to wipe away buzzing gnats.

It was only Charles Gordon's quiet voice that penetrated. "You must go, my boy. For the boy's sake. And for your own sake. You must tell your son goodbye. We will be with you."

So Kingsley was there, stony faced and silent, wincing from every expression of sympathy. They sat through the simple service, stood silently at the graveside, tears welling to hear the child committed into God's arms. Charles pressed a small mound of dirt into Kingsley's hand, insisting that he complete the ritual. They hurried away, not wanting to see the closure of the site.

In the weeks that followed, Kingsley isolated himself. Dorothy tried to break through his icy barrier, and grew paler and more listless as the months passed. Charles and Felicity stayed for a month, but realized that their presence only emphasized the rift. Kingsley appeared at mealtime but ate little. He watched Constance like a hawk, criticized every tiny flaw. "Haven't you learned how to fold your serviette?" "Don't you know how to use your knife?" "You are so clumsy!" "What a stupid question" "Go to your room if you don't know how to behave at table!"

Dorothy asked Nanny, "Would you mind taking your meals with Constance in the kitchen or in the nursery? She is getting so nervous I am afraid she will be ill."

"Not at all, Madame. The child needs time to do her own grieving. It might be good for her to be in the kitchen, around Cook and the others. Not so lonely as the nursery, maybe."

Dorothy spent more time with Constance, reading to her, helping her struggle through nursery rhymes and fairy tales, or getting her started on simple embroidery tasks. The child did seem to grow less restless, her eyes less haunted.

Summer was hot and humid, and Dorothy, heavy with child, could not counteract the lassitude that had settled over the family.

The absence penetrated the house.

Charles Kingsley Randolph was born September 30th.

Kingsley looked down at the boy in Dorothy's arms, "Well. At least he has dark hair. No more of those foppish red curls."

"I think he looks a lot like you, Kingsley. Would you like Charles, after my father for his name?"

"Whatever you want. Any name will do."

"Charles Kingsley Randolph then," Dorothy knew that Theodore and Margaret wanted to keep the name alive. And Kingsley's anger was not about the name. It was the unfairness of their loss he would not accept, the cruelty that life itself had inexplicably offered. He would be secretly pleased by the name.

CHAPTER TEN

Forging A Life

Montreal – 1896-1910

Constance stood by the bassinet absorbed in every tiny essence of the baby - the sucking lips, the wiggling fingers, the blinking eyelids, and the tiny nostrils. "You are our baby," she whispered. "You are my brother!! I will love you forever." She reached out a tentative finger and the baby grasped it. "Look, Mama! He is holding my hand. He loves me!"

"He will always love you, Constance dear. You are his big sister. You will be his best friend."

"Charles Kingsley Randolph," Constance said soberly to the child, "I will be a good big sister. I will make you happy! You are so beautiful, baby brother."

Dorothy picked up the child and prepared to nurse him, laying a soft cloth over her breast.

"Look, Mama! He knows so much! He knows how to get his dinner!"

Dorothy smiled, but thought, 'It really is quite amazing, even if it is so natural.' As the child finished with a big gaping yawn, she said, "Now we must let little Charles sleep. Babies have a lot of growing to do in the first few weeks of their lives."

At dinner that evening Constance was fairly bubbling, "He is so beautiful, Papa. He has toenails and fingernails. They are so tiny, but they are just perfect. And he knows how to get milk from Mama's breast!"

"Don't be stupid! Of course he knows how to nurse. All babies know how to nurse!"

"But how do they know, Papa? Who teaches them?"

"You ask the stupidest questions. Eat your dinner and be quiet."

"I just want to know, Papa. I was a little sister for so long, now I'm a big sister and I need to know."

Kingsley slammed his fist down on the heavy oak table making the dishes rattle, shoved his chair back violently, and rushed out of the room.

Tears welled in Constance's eyes, "What did I do wrong, Mama?" Her voice trailed off to a whisper. "I just want to know."

Dorothy felt the lump of tears in her throat too. "You did not do anything wrong, dear Constance. Papa is just still terribly unhappy about Kingsley's death. We all are, but your Papa feels the pain so deeply. He loved little Kingsley so much." She sighed, thinking, 'He is angry with all of us for being alive, but he is most angry at Constance. She gave a small shake of her head and, trying to lighten the mood, asked, "Have you written any new stories lately? Have you written about the Six Beautiful Sisters?"

"Oh yes, Mama! I am writing such a good story, and about King Sly, too. I will read it to you when it is finished."

Constance's days were full. Nanny taught her simple embroidery, she read often - to herself or aloud to Baby Charles. She did simple sums, and she wrote fanciful stories, tall tales of her brother Kingsley's wonderful adventures. Sometimes she was at her brother's side in the story, and now sometimes, they saved Baby Charles from disaster. Although she seldom mentioned the lost Kingsley, he was never far from her thoughts. She had many questions. But Mama was busy and worried. It was easier to talk about him to Martha, the cook.

Martha was a big, soft woman, and she seemed just to absorb everything. She was like a big basket; you could put anything in and it would never spill over, so Constance asked her the questions that bothered her.

One Friday morning, Constance swarmed into the kitchen. "Oh, Martha! I could smell the bread way upstairs. It's baking day, isn't it! I just love the smell of baking bread!"

"I knew you would be down just as soon as you smelled the bread."

There was a long silence, so long Martha glanced up at the child. At last Constance, her face lowered, asked, "Do you think Kingsley knows how much I miss him, Martha? Do you think he knows what we are doing?"

"Child, child! The things you worry about! That is something we must accept because we believe it. It is part of our faith in God. It is not a thing like knowing that Mama has red hair, or that the sun will rise tomorrow morning. It is something we know in our hearts, and we believe it because our hearts tell us it is true. But come, child, that is something you will understand better when you are older."

"Martha, I wrote such a good story about Kingsley. I wish I could read it to him."

"You read it to Baby Charles, dear child. That way, he will grow up knowing about his brother, and loving him."

"Martha, I love you," Constance said. "Could I have a cookie?"

"Of course! Now go along with you! And come down later to have a hot crust." She turned away, banging the lid of the soup pot loudly and wiping her eyes with the corner of her apron. Constance flew out of the kitchen and ran into Theodore and Papa in the hall. "Oh Papa, Grandpa, isn't it a wonderful day. Baking day! Cook said I may have a hot crust when it is ready!"

"A hot crust and a cookie? You will be a little fatty one day!" Papa said lightly.

"I don't care if I am a fatty if I can be like Cook. She is so comfortable!" Constance tossed over her shoulder as she ran upstairs.

"That one is a caution," Theodore said with a shake of his head. And Kingsley felt the ice in his heart melt a bit.

Charles Kingsley was one of those good babies; he seldom cried, slept through the night at an early age, rolled over, stood up, walked and talked at all the expected ages. This was a blessing for Dorothy because Kingsley had become more demanding, petulant. He seemed not to know what he wanted, not to know how to make a decision. He looked uncertainly at any shirt Joseph offered. Every tie was examined and discarded. Which shoes should he wear with the dark blue suit? His querulous "What do you think, Dorothy?" kept her at his side.

Conversations at dinner grew stilted, guarded. Any hint of reference to Little Kingsley, however far-fetched, brought a strong reaction - unhappy, angry, desperate.

Theodore, anxious about business, broached the subject after dinner, "We need to line someone up for the B. C. sector, Kingsley. Have you finalized your discussions with Tom Allen?"

He was met with a blank stare and a grunted, "Not now!"

Margaret, impatient as always, said bluntly, "You need to get back to business, son. Get your mind on something positive." But she visibly wilted under his angry glare.

Dorothy, too, knew that Kingsley needed to be jolted out of his shell. She would not tell him what he should do, but she would not be silenced. The next morning, after nursing Charles, she said, "I have arranged for the baptism on Sunday, February 3, Kingsley. Here, hold the boy a minute so I can decide about the christening robe." She held the baby out insistently. When Kingsley folded his arms across his chest, Dorothy simply laid the boy in the nest of the folded arms and turned away. 'He has to accept the child,' she thought. 'It has been long enough.' She prayed he would not just drop his son, but continued, "I want us to have a family portrait. I have scheduled Frasers to come that afternoon so we can get it with everyone dressed for the christening." At last she turned back around, almost weeping with relief to see the child cradled, somewhat awkwardly, but carefully, in his father's arms.

"Mama you should see what Charles does." Dorothy smiled and sighed, Constance was always extolling Charles's every small accomplishment. "What has Charles done this time, dear?"

"I know you are laughing at me, Mama. But, really, this is important, I think. It was the other day; he was playing with that big wooden spoon Cook let him have from the kitchen. He kept banging it on a box. And when I really listened, I think he was playing a rhythm."

"Playing a rhythm? What do you mean?"

"Well, it sounded like 'bang, bang, pause - bang, bang, pause - bang, bang, pause - over and over."

"Yes?"

"Well, I thought I would try something. So I took a small block and I tapped it on the floor: 'tap, tap, tap, pause - tap, tap, tap, pause'. You know, three times. And Charles looked at me and then changed to three times, too. Don't you think that is important, Mama?"

Dorothy looked thoughtful, "I do. I certainly do. At least it is quite surprising. You were very good to recognize that and think about what it might mean, Constance dear." As soon as she could, Dorothy went to the nursery and tested the baby many times. She spoke to Margaret and brought her up to watch.

"Maybe he has the real talent, Dorothy. It wouldn't be too surprising; there is music on both sides of the family as we have often said." They looked at each other and nodded in silent agreement. They would not hurry into anything, but this was something both women would nurture.

It was almost two years before the family began to regain some balance. It was not the balance that had been developing before young Kingsley's death. And it was a balance that disturbed Dorothy greatly. Kingsley returned to work and spent more time in the evenings discussing business. The business prospered. They tried a brief foray into roller skates, but that fad did not develop. They began to focus on bicycles, and dreamed of developing a powered cycle.

In private Kingsley was affectionate and attentive, but Dorothy was seldom included in business discussions. And Kingsley never spoke of the children unless Dorothy initiated some issue. Constance, unsettled by the obvious displeasure Kingsley greeted any comment she made, now generally took her meals with baby Charles and Nanny in the nursery.

Dorothy grew increasingly restless and impatient with the limitations that were developing. Household affairs and care of the children could not satisfy her interests and enthusiasm. As was natural to her, she took action. Over coffee one evening she said, "I have told Joseph to remove the funeral wreath and the black ribbons from the front door tomorrow." She heard the sharp intake of Margaret's breath, but ignored it. 'This loss is ours,' she thought, 'mine and Kingsley's, not Margaret's. And the period of mourning must end. The house belongs to the parents, but Kingsley and I will decide about our personal affairs.' "I want Jennie to open the drapes slightly, too. It is time we begin to receive callers."

Dorothy asked Jennie to lay out her green taffeta with the high neckline and the gathering of the skirt in the back that gave only the slight hint of a bustle. It was simple and modest enough for the first step. She had no wish to create unpleasant talk.

She told Nanny, "I want you to put away Constance's black dresses. She can wear anything simple. Of course not too bright, but it is time we get some color back into our lives." Nanny breathed a sigh of satisfaction, and Constance's face lighted up when she saw her favorite blue dress laid out.

"I have begun sorting things to go into storage," Dorothy told Kingsley that evening. "Many of our darker things can be hung under dust covers in the attic closet." She knew that Kingsley had not the slightest interest in such details of the household business, but she was determined to emphasize that the period of mourning was ended. "Some of Kingsley's clothes and toys can be stored in the big trunk," she went on. I have been separating things we will want to keep from things that could go to a charity group. The Christmas fire engine may as well go into storage until Charles Kingsley is old enough to enjoy it." She glanced at Kingsley who was still sitting hunched over, arms on his knees, face in his hands.

But he was listening, so she went on, "We don't have many photographs of our son, Kingsley, but we should do something special with them, don't you think? I would like to have one or two framed so we can keep them with us, in our rooms. And I want to start a family album."

Again she ignored Kingsley's silence. 'We have to be able to talk about the boy,' she thought. 'We cannot just wipe him out of our lives. I will not pretend that he never existed.' So she chattered on, less nervous as Kingsley seemed to accept this talk. "There is that beautiful photograph of you and Kingsley in the park last summer. I am so glad we have that one; you both look so happy! I will get at least that one framed, and maybe others. What about this one with just Kingsley and Jojo? What would you like, Kingsley?"

Kingsley sat a little straighter. The anger had left his face; there was only sadness and resignation. "Yes, yes. Please."

Dorothy touched his arm and leaned over to kiss his

cheek. "I will get things started, Kingsley. I had a big trunk delivered and put in the attic. We can store quite a lot in that. Everything will always be there. I think that things are important, don't you, Kingsley? They have so many memories tied up in them. I think we need to keep those things close - the things that remind us of our love for him."

Kingsley scrubbed his face with his hands, "Yes, alright. Yes." He sighed deeply. "You decide." Slowly, wearily he got up, held Dorothy close for a few minutes, then went to the small bar and raised a questioning eyebrow, holding up a wine bottle and pointing to the brandy decanter.

So as the weeks, and months, and years followed, Dorothy did decide on the life they would have. She consulted Margaret, and often took her advice. But knowing that she had Kingsley's "Yes" and Theodore's tacit approval, she created her family and its life, within the household, but not ruled by it.

Dorothy paused by her piano, slowly removed the dust cover, folded it carefully, and laid it aside. She brushed the glistening wood lovingly, lifted the heavy lid and propped it open. It was fall, the season that Dorothy loved most - colorful and pleasant, with the hint of an ending - the end of the year, but with the joyous Christmas season ahead. She had not touched the piano since that Christmas Eve two years ago. She hesitated, then leaned over and played a simple chord. Sighing, she gathered the folds of her long silk skirt, sat down and ran through a few scales. Giving a shake of her shoulders, she sat up properly and began, almost hesitantly, one of her favorite Chopin etudes. But suddenly, gloriously relieved, she started over and played for Young Kingsley, the sadness and love singing. She did not see Margaret step to the salon door, handkerchief at her eyes. And she did not know that work stopped in the kitchen, that Constance put her hand over the page she had been reading aloud to Nanny, or that Kingsley and Theodore stood motionless in the hall where they were preparing to leave for work. She played on for an hour, from one favorite to another. The house relaxed, and life moved again.

Dorothy played daily now, often with seven-year-old Constance at her side watching the flashing fingers, and listening intently. In a break, the child asked questions, "How do you know which keys to play, Mama?" Or, "What do the numbers mean - 3/4 or 4/4?" Or, "Why do some of the flags go up and some go down?"

So Dorothy began with simple explanations of the symbols - staff, notes, tempo, and how they related to the keys on the piano. And she asked, "Would you like to learn to play the piano, Constance?"

"Oh Mama! Could I? Could I really? Is it very hard to learn?"

"Well, yes, in a way it is very hard. To play well takes years of study and practice. But to start it is quite simple. Then we could see how far you wanted to go. If you are really interested, I will speak to my own music teacher, Mme. Langlois. I want to talk to her anyway, and she will give us an idea of how to get you started."

"Mama?"

"Yes?"

"Could I try one key?"

"Of course. Climb up here beside me on the bench. Now

just touch this white key here. It is called 'middle C' and it is an important key." Constance did as she was told and looked up happily. So Dorothy continued. "The white keys all have names, letters of the alphabet from A to G, and the black keys have their own names, too. But that is enough for now. Most teachers have their own way of starting a pupil, so we will let your teacher tell you more about it." Constance ran off happily to tell Nanny her good news, and Cook, and Joseph, and anyone else who would listen.

The next day Dorothy wrote a note to Mme. Langlois, asking for an appointment to discuss the possibility of a tutor for Constance. She told Kingsley that evening that Constance wanted to have lessons and that she was arranging for a tutor.

"Whatever did you do that for, Dorothy? She is just a baby. She can't play the piano. It would be a waste of time!"

"Well, perhaps, Kingsley. We will just have to see. You know I started lessons when I was only five. It depends on whether she has talent and the interest to work."

"Huh!" was the grunted answer. "I suppose the next thing you will be starting the boy on piano lessons!"

"Not yet of course." Dorothy was composed. "But if he shows any interest later. You know, My Dear, music has been such a joy in my life, if they want it, I want them to have that pleasure too. And Margaret used to play when she was a child in Bremen. She told me her mother had a piano. If talent comes to the children from both sides of the family, it could be quite strong."

"Well," Kingsley could think of nothing to say. Dorothy seemed to know so much more about his parents than he did.

Dorothy arranged a meeting with Mme. Langlois and a young man who was a potential tutor. She invited Margaret to meet with them; she always had good instincts. And she insisted that Kingsley be involved. "This has to do with Constance's future, Kingsley; I need your insight regarding the suitability of this candidate. And Mme. Langlois is a woman of quality. She is doing us a favor by bringing this young man to be interviewed. Besides," she added with a secret smile, "she is a very beautiful and cultured woman. You will enjoy meeting her."

They were prompt. Mme. Langlois, elegant in lavender silk introduced her young protégé,"May I present M. Roger Archambault. He has been my piano student for eleven years. He is a very talented pianist, and he has acted on my behalf as a tutor for beginning students on several occasions. I have watched him work, and I can attest to you that he has a special gift for teaching. I am confident in presenting him to you, but no doubt you would like him to tell you about himself and his interests."

Dorothy said, "Mr. Randolph will ask a few questions if that is acceptable, Mme. Langlois?"

Kingsley said rather abruptly, "You are very young, aren't you?"

"Yes, sir, I am nineteen."

Kingsley waited, but when the young man said no more, he continued, "Why would you interrupt your own studies to tutor our daughter?"

The boy had an easy manner, respectful and courteous. "I do not have the talent to make a career of music. I love it and it will always be an important part of my life, but I am not a concert pianist."

"Why do you do this tutoring then?" Kingsley was more curious than aggressive now.

"Well, I like tutoring, teaching. I think it is part of my real future career. I am working toward a degree in psychology, and I believe I will end up teaching in some way, especially working with children who have problems learning. That is my dream, at least."

"Sounds very--------," Kingsley did not know quite how to end the interview.

Margaret fluttered her lace handkerchief and Dorothy nodded to her. "May I ask a rather personal question, Mr. Archambault? I am very curious. Are you a member of the family that is opening a sheet music store, sir?"

The young man grinned, "No, Ma'am. That is Mr. Edmund Archambault. We are distantly related by some connection, but not close. He is a real music lover, and I hope his business is successful. It is interesting that you know of his plans; it is a very new effort."

They talked lightly for a few minutes, then Dorothy called for Constance to come meet the potential tutor. Constance was shy, but said Yes, she wanted to learn, and No, she had never played at all. She seemed comfortable, and Dorothy asked Mr. Archambault to come twice a week until they could see how the lessons progressed.

Constance was a serious-minded child; she practiced diligently and began to show much progress. Many days she and Mr. Archambault sat and talked after the lesson. Dorothy usually sat quietly aside during the session, but joined the conversation over a cup of tea if the young tutor could linger. He told them how it was that he had become interested in psychology and teaching as a career. "I have a brother who is only six," he said. "He seems bright in many ways, but he has never learned to speak."

"Not at all?" Dorothy asked, astonished.

"No. Not any words, only odd sounds. And screeches," he added with a sad smile. "And he has peculiar mannerisms." He went on, "He won't let anyone touch him. If one goes near him, he flaps his hands and rocks back and forth, sometimes beating his head. And his screeches are so awful." The boy shuddered, thinking of the child.

Dorothy gasped, "How awful for you all, and for the poor boy! Has he been examined by a doctor? Is he allergic to something?"

"Yes, the family doctor. But of course, Emile won't let even the doctor get close. And our doctor is a good man, but he says he has no idea what is wrong. The worst is, Emile can't have friends. None of the other children will come near him, not even my other brothers and sisters. I want to learn more about this. I want to learn to help Emile." Young Roger Archambault turned away, his eyes brimming.

Dorothy touched his arm. "That is terribly sad, Sir. But you say the boy - Emile? - seems bright in many ways? Could you explain that?"

The young man brightened. "Well, for example, sometimes he gets one of those boxes of kitchen matches, and he makes things, patterns, all kinds of patterns with them. Sometimes it looks like numbers - a row of two by two, or three by three, or even fours. Other times it will be stars, or spirals, or something like a circle - all kinds of figures."

"Fascinating," Dorothy was listening intently, as was Constance who would not dream of interrupting.

"Yes! And music. If someone is playing the fiddle - all of our family are fiddlers!" He grinned at that. "Music seems to put him into some quiet place - almost beyond us - outside the world in a way. It's hard to explain, but he seems transported!" He shrugged restlessly. "I feel so hurt, so helpless. I want to know more."

Dorothy knew she had touched a very deep sensitivity. He had trusted her to understand; they had come close to being friends. "We will talk further another day," she said as the young man prepared to leave.

"What could be wrong with Emile, Mama? Why does he not let his mother touch him?" Constance could not believe such a thing.

"I do not understand it, Connstance. I have never heard of a condition like that. It is wonderful that Mr. Archambault wants to study and learn all he can about what causes his brother's strange behavior. Perhaps I will ask Dr. Michaels if he has heard of such a condition." Dorothy was thinking out loud, hardly aware that Constance was absorbing every word. That evening she wrote a long letter to Fizzy, relating in detail all that the young tutor had told about his brother. It had troubled her deeply.

Constance continued to progress because she had considerable talent and she loved music. But it became evident that she was more interested in how she learned and how music could be played than in a career as a pianist. One day, after her lesson, she said, "Mr. Archambault, "I think my little brother Charles has more talent than I. He is only four, but he seems to know rhythm. No one taught him, he just seems to know". She turned to Dorothy, "Charles is very talented, isn't he, Mama? I wish he could have lessons. Is he too young?"

"Generally speaking, four is too early to start lessons. But not always, of course. Mozart, for instance was composing at that age. But as I have told you, I have completed my studies at McGill, so I will not be available. I am moving to Toronto and will continue my interest in the psychological problems of troubled children at the University of Toronto."

"We are going to miss you very much, Mr. Archambault. We almost think of you as a member of the family. Constance has done well under your guidance."

"Thank you. It has been a real pleasure to work with Constance, and to get to know your family. And now I would like to make a suggestion. Before I leave, I would like Constance to present a recital. She is well advanced, and an appearance before a group would be a good experience for her."

"Perhaps," Dorothy hesitated. "We have agreed that she probably will not play professionally. She herself insists that is not her interest. She just loves the music and wants to play well. Do you really think a recital would be appropriate?"

"Appearing before a public group is a good experience for anyone, I think. It is an accomplishment in itself. And I believe it is especially worthwhile for a woman. I would like to see how well she can handle it."

The recital was a happy event. They limited it to family and a few close friends. Felicity and Grandpa Gordon came down from Toronto for the week. Mme. Langlois was invited of course. This would be the last time she would appear as Mr. Archambault's sponsor and she was always a welcome guest for Dorothy.

Constance performed well and was congratulated by all.

She talked about continuing lessons, and about an interest she was developing in teaching. She hoped to be able to study, perhaps at the University. The conversation turned to Mr. Archambault's plans and the reasons for his interest in psychology. As they left, Constance spoke to him briefly, thanking him for all he had done for her, she added, "I would be pleased to hear how your studies progress, Mr. Archambault. I admire so much your dedication to the problems facing your brother. It seems a very interesting field of study, and very important, too."

"I would be most honored to correspond with you, Miss Constance," the young man said and lingered just a moment at the door.

CHAPTER ELEVEN

Fractures

Montreal – 1910-1914

It was the issue of Charles' future that initiated the first serious disagreement between Dorothy and Kingsley. Charles had been studying piano seriously for several years by the time he was eight. Now he told his mother that he wanted to study the violin, "I believe the violin is the instrument that I really want to go ahead with, Mother. I want to be a violinist. I have to."

Dorothy had seen this coming, but she hesitated, "Have you spoken about this with your father? I think he hopes you will play an important role in the hockey firm, Charles."

"I can't do that, Mother. Father talks to me about the business. I know he hopes I will go into it. But I don't understand it. And, honestly, Mother, I just don't want to understand it. I want to be a violinist."

Dorothy sighed, thinking, 'This will not be easy. He

compares Charles with Little Kingsley anyway. They are both going to be hurt. Sometimes life is just not fair.' She said, "I will speak with Mr. Archambault about the possibility of a good violin. He has begun to expand his business into pianos and violins. But, Charles, you must tell your father that you do not intend to go into the business. That won't be easy, but he will have to know."

"Could you tell him, Mother?"

"I will tell him that I am looking for a good violin for you. But you should tell him about your decision, Charles."

Kingsley erupted angrily, "A violin? Why in the world would you get him a violin? The piano is bad enough. Now a violin? He doesn't need a violin. He needs to get some business sense into his head. I talk and talk to him, but he just doesn't learn anything. All this music just interferes with anything worthwhile. I won't have it."

That afternoon, Charles, nerves quivering like a piano wire, met his father in the hall. "Father I would like to talk with you. Could I have a few minutes?"

Kingsley flung his coat on a chair, "You want to talk with me, do you? Well I want to talk with you, young man. Get yourself into the study and wait for me."

He kept the boy waiting twenty minutes while he washed and changed. 'Let the little bastard cool his heels for a while. Let him find out what it feels like to push me around', he thought. 'A violin! The next thing, he will be telling me he is not going into the business!'

He stalked into the study, delighted to see that Charles was standing, pale and stiff. 'Right!' he thought as he sat down at the desk and faced the boy. "Now what is this nonsense about a violin, young man?"

"Sir, I want to be a violinist. I do not want to go into the business." He was trembling violently, but getting it said was a relief.

Shocked, Kingsley spluttered. Charles had taken his worst thought and thrown it into his face. "You-----You, what? What makes you think that you, an eight-year-old boy can tell your father such a thing? What makes you think you can decide what is good for the business? Or for yourself for that matter? You don't tell me what you will do, boy, I tell you!"

"I'm sorry, Father. I just cannot be a businessman. I have to play the violin." Charles' legs were shaking so hard now he could hardly stand.

"Your mother put you up to this! We will get it straight who is the head of this family!"

"Sir! No sir! Mother did not know I had decided until this morning. She only said that I must tell you."

"You decided? You decided? What makes you think you can decide anything? Go to your room and think about who works in this family, who pays the bills, who gives you a good home and nice clothes and food to eat. Then you may realize who decides things in this family!" He waved his hand dismissively, and Charles hurried out, frightened, stumbling against the doorjamb. He had never before felt the force of his father's anger. He had set off a terrible thing.

Kingsley stormed through the house shouting, "Where is Mrs. Randolph? Where is my wife?"

Joseph met him, "I believe they went shopping, Sir. Mrs. Dorothy and Mrs. Margaret, with Miss Constance. They took the cabriolet. Can I help you with anything, Sir?"

"Is Mr. Theodore here, then?"

"Yes, Sir. Shall I call him?"

"No. No. I'll see him later." Kingsley did not want Theodore to know that Charles had been able to make him lose control of a situation.

Kingsley went into the study, sat at his desk and shoved papers aside, spilling them onto the floor. He got up, paced from desk to fireplace, jerked around and strode to the window. His nerves were jumping; he wanted to smash something. Back and forth he pounded the carpet, his arms flailing spasmodically. His eye lighted on a glass ball with a snow scene, a Christmas thing Charles had given him when he was six. He picked it up, tossed it from hand to hand, put it down, picked it up again and hurled it violently at the brick fireplace.

He sat down, slumped and tired. Joseph was at his side holding out the box of Cuban cigars. He waited while Kingsley selected one and rolled it in his fingers. Joseph offered a light and silently withdrew. Kingsley sighed deeply and lay back against the chair, tasting the smoke and slowly exhaling.

Joseph hurried to Charles' room. He laid out fresh clothes for the boy and said, "Freshen yourself up, Master Charles. Agnes will bring you a mug of hot chocolate in a few minutes and you must drink it. Try to calm down and think of your music. Listen to the music in your mind. I will be back soon." He left as quietly as he had come.

Dorothy and Margaret arrived home late that afternoon. Joseph's bland face and worried eyes told the two women that the expected eruption had occurred. Dorothy said, "Constance, you go with Grandma Margaret. Thank you, Grandma. I will see you soon." She handed her packages to Joseph, "Mr.

Kingsley is in the study?"

"Yes, Madam."

"Please tell him I am home and will be down soon."

She dressed carefully, a modest grey silk with high collar and a row of black jet buttons from collar to waist. When she saw Kingsley's dejected face, she felt great pity for him. 'He does not understand what he has done to our son, and to our family.' "You look tired, dear."

Joseph was at the bar, "Can I get you something, Sir? Madam? A brandy? Scotch?" He poured drinks, faded back to the door, and at Dorothy's nod, left quietly.

Dorothy waited for Kingsley to open the issue that burned between them, but after several silent minutes she gave it a nudge, "Are you alright? Has something happened?"

"That boy! This violin business!" Then the anger and frustration boiled over, "Do you know what he had the effrontery to say to me? To me, his father? He told me he has decided - decided, can you imagine? Not to go into the business! He is eight years old, for God's sake! 'I will be a violinist' he says, the bloody impudent young pup! I wanted to smack him, beat some sense into him," Kingsley was standing over Dorothy now, breathing rapidly.

"But you did not," Dorothy said in a cold, hard voice. "And Kingsley, do not speak to me in that tone of voice. Do not use that language when you speak to me. Not ever again!" Dorothy's tone was so crisp and unflinching Kingsley stopped short.

"Oh, yes. Sorry. But that boy------"

Dorothy interrupted, "Kingsley, I mean that you must control your anger if we are to discuss this issue."

Kingsley gaped at her. His face reddened, he started to mutter something, then sat down and gulped the rest of his scotch. Finally he said in a calmer tone, "Did you know that Charles does not want to go into the business?"

"Yes, Kingsley. He told me. I said he must let you know so you can make proper plans."

"So you support him in this violinist nonsense?"

"I would be happy to see Charles go into the business if that were where his talents lie. But it is not. Actually, Kingsley dear, Constance might make a better 'businessman' than Charles. She is somewhat like Felicity in that respect, don't you think?"

"You are changing the subject, Dorothy. Can't you stick to one thing at a time? We have to make Charles understand that he must go into the business."

Dorothy realized that they could not go further now. They talked a few minutes more and Dorothy said, "Will you excuse me, Kingsley? I have some household affairs to deal with."

Dorothy found Charles curled up asleep on his bed. She could not wake him and he did not come down for dinner. The next morning Joseph shook his shoulder lightly; Charles answered groggily but lay back, immediately asleep again. By afternoon Dorothy was quite worried, 'Maybe I should call the doctor' she thought, 'but rumors get started so easily. We don't want family business made public.'

Charles finally roused two days later, Dorothy hovering anxiously, "You had quite a sleep, Charles. Are you feeling better?" He did not answer so Dorothy insisted, "Charles?"

"Yes, Mother," A hollow, bleak answer.

Kingsley came home early; he had finally become unnerved by Charles' long sleep. He found Dorothy sitting with the boy. "So, young man, you have finally decided to get back to life, have you?"

"Yes, Father,"

Dorothy flinched at the same hollow tone.

"So are we clear on this violin nonsense?" Kingsley tried a jocular note.

"Yes, Father."

"And you are ready to learn about the business?" Kingsley was a little less certain.

"Yes, Father."

Kingsley switched restlessly from one foot to the other, "What kind of answer is this? 'Yes, Father - 'Yes, Father'? Are you trying to be a smart aleck?"

"No, Father." Tears welled and rolled down his cheek.

Dorothy touched the boy's arm, leaned down and kissed the top of his head. "I will be back in a few minutes, Charles, dear." She motioned to Kingsley and he followed her out of the room.

In the days that followed, Charles wandered aimlessly about the house - the nursery, the garden, the kitchen. He peered out the front window or stood motionless near the heavy front door. His face had a blank look, his eyes unfocused. He spoke only in monosyllables - yes, Mother, all right, no, thank you, fine. Dorothy watched his trail, staying close, worried, but saying nothing. Kingsley tried to look unconcerned, but grew increasingly uneasy. Constance was

143

often at her brother's side, chattering animatedly, but expecting no answers.

At church Sunday Charles listened intently as the choir sang one of the hymns he loved, "All Praise to Thee, My God, this Night." The quiet music began to seep into his mind. He sat up straighter, but more relaxed as the song ended. He hardly listened to the pastor's words, but when the organist played the introductory chords to "Rock of Ages, Cleft for Me," the music flowed into him, filling him with a deep hunger. He glowed, wanting, needing, completely sure.

That night he slept deeply and had a vivid dream. He was standing on a balcony looking out over a wide, open yard. Roses, chrysanthemums, peonies, tulips, and lilies carpeted the ground, not respecting their season. Then the flowers became faces, turned toward him on a stage. He had a violin and bow in his hands. The flower-faces were smiling and cheering. He awoke, feeling music around him, smiled and went back to sleep.

Monday morning Charles appeared for breakfast, heaped his plate with scrambled eggs, bacon, and scones, and said cheerily, "Good morning."

They looked at him in astonishment, stammering greetings, not daring to break the spell. Conversation was sporadic, jumping from Theodore to Kingsley, from Constance to Dorothy, from Dorothy to Margaret. Each burst was accompanied by a sidewise glace at Charles. He calmly finished his breakfast, pushed his chair back, and said, "Thank you, Mother, Grandma." He added, "Please excuse me," and left the room. There was a collective sigh of bewildered relief as they looked at each other without comment. A few minutes later they heard the piano.

That afternoon Charles told his mother, "I would like to go to the music building at the university, Mother. Just to look around. I could walk there, it's not very far."

"I think that would be all right, Charles. But you should not go alone. Maybe Constance would like to walk with you."

When the two returned, they met their mother in her sitting room. "How was it?" she asked.

"There was a very interesting cellist," Constance said. "We listened to her for quite a while. It seems a big instrument for a girl, but I thought she played very well, didn't you, Charles?"

"She has strong hands, Mother. She wasn't afraid of the instrument. It was good. There were two violinists practicing at the time." He went off into a reverie.

"We listened to each of them for some time," Constance said. "They had very different styles, wouldn't you say, Charles?"

"What? Oh yes. Very different. You can do so much with the violin." Charles sighed and Constance and Dorothy exchanged glances of understanding. Charles had not given up on his dream, his intention to be a violinist.

Dorothy promised herself she would do all she could to make it happen. With Mr. Archambault's advice she helped Charles select a violin and arranged for a tutor. Kingsley did not protest.

The business thrived and Kingsley immersed himself in new projects. Their evening discussions often focused on ideas and plans. Theodore again brought up the possibility of developing an arm of the business that would tap into the growing interest in motorcars. "You remember Seth Taylor's steam buggy[2], Kingsley. It didn't go anywhere, but we are into a new century now. There are a number of American companies building the vehicles. Henry Ford is one company. They have developed several designs. But there are others coming along. There's Chevrolet, for example."

"Chevrolet? That name rings a bell. Wasn't there a Chevrolet who was a racing car driver?" Kingsley asked.

"That's right. But I understand he has gone into business under his own name and is designing a model of car with a racing car engine."

Margaret interrupted, "I think Monsieur Chevrolet was a Quebecer. I seem to remember he had a big family home down in the old quarter of Montreal."

"I believe you are right, Margaret," Theodore said, a little surprised that Margaret knew that much about a member of the French community. 'But'; he thought, 'that is just like her. Margaret is a social person, always knows about people.' He continued, "Louis Chevrolet was originally from France, but he did have a home on Notre Dame Street. Maybe he would be open to some cooperative venture here in Montreal. We can at least look into that, Kingsley. We need something fresh." Even at sixty Theodore had the visionary approach of an entrepreneur; he was always eager to explore new possibilities.

Kingsley jumped at the idea. "Maybe I should go to the United States to look into the factories, the setup and production, get a feel for what we would have to do to go that direction. I could meet with Monsieur Chevrolet and perhaps Mr. Ford. Test out whether either one would be interested in a Canadian operation. I should probably plan to spend a good amount of time to look around and get an understanding of how things are done. Maybe I should put my main focus on New York, stay there and travel to other sites."

Theodore looked startled, "I'm sure New York would be very interesting, Kingsley. But I believe that both Mr. Ford and Mr. Chevrolet are located in Detroit. And that is a long way from New York, at least a thousand miles."

"Well, I guess I'll just have to book rooms in a hotel. I'll check into it tomorrow."

"Isn't that going a bit fast? Don't you think you should get all the information you can about the motorcars that are being built - the mechanics, the production costs, the kinds of expertise needed - that kind of information so you would be prepared for discussions?"

"This would be just preliminary investigation, Father. It's more contacting the people involved, presenting our own credentials as a business, I think. All the details could come later."

Theodore was uncertain, but he thought, 'the boy will have to take over sooner or later. He will have his own style of doing business. Maybe I am getting old.' So he made no further objections.

Dorothy seldom entered into these business discussions, but now she said thoughtfully, "Isn't it amazing the changes that have taken place in our lifetimes."

"What are you talking about, Dorothy?" Kingsley asked.

"Well I was just thinking about how our lives have changed by so many new things. We used to have only oil lamps and candles, and now we have gas lights in every room. Almost everyone has them. And we have indoor water closets. That is a big change. And there are a lot of sidewalks downtown; remember the first plank sidewalks down near the Morgan company?"

"What has that got to do with motorcars, Dorothy?" Kingsley asked impatiently.

"We do so many things differently, Kingsley. I think motor buggies would make big changes. What about our horses? What would become of them?"

"Are you trying to throw a wet blanket on our plans? Why can't you be more positive?"

"I'm not trying to be negative, Kingsley. There could be big advantages. We could drive to Toronto, for example, not have to be limited by train schedules. I'm just thinking about all the changes a motorcar would make if it really worked out."

"And why wouldn't it work out? You do seem negative to me, Dorothy."

Theodore interrupted, "I can see what Dorothy is getting at, Kingsley. Motorcars would offer very good changes, but there would be problems we would have to work out. Such vehicles might have difficulty navigating our snow-filled streets in winter. There would have to be new services to go along with the cars. New inventions do change the ways we do things. But go ahead with your plans to visit companies in the United States, son. Do you think you should take Tom Allen along? He is involved in the production side of the business."

Kingsley snapped, "I can handle this. I don't need Tom Allen. It won't be his kind of issues I want to deal with." He stood and moved around the room restlessly, thinking about his plans. "I will probably have to stay for several weeks. It will take time to get to everyone and have good discussions."

Dorothy and Kingsley continued the discussion as they

were preparing to retire, "Since you will be away for several weeks, Kingsley, I think it would be a good opportunity for me to visit Father and Felicity. I haven't gone for a long time, and Constance has been wishing to visit Maria Elena. She might spend the summer with them."

"Maria Elena? Oh, yes, Felicity's adopted daughter. Isn't she very young? Just a baby?"

"She's six months older than Constance, dear," Dorothy said mildly. "They correspond constantly, are good friends."

Charles did not want to go to Toronto. "You know I love Aunt Felicity and Grandfather Charles, Mother. But I need to keep at my lessons. I can't afford to miss them."

"But both your father and I will be away, Charles. I don't see how I can leave you here alone."

"But I won't be alone, Mother. Grandmother and Grandfather will both be here. And I'm almost ten - you won't have to worry about me. And there is something I didn't tell you yet, Mother. Mr. Morrisseau just told me Monday, and it is so unbelievable, I just couldn't tell you yet."

"For heavens sake, what is that, Charles?"

"He says there is a new school in New York, founded just in 1905, that is for young artists, musicians even at young ages. He said he thought that if I work very hard for a couple of years, I might qualify! So you see, Mother, I just can't go to Toronto. Please!"

"Are you sure, son? What is the name of this school? Maybe it is just for local New York students."

"Mr. Morrisseau said the name is The Institute of Musical Arts[3], and it was the idea of a man who doesn't want young Americans to go off to Paris or Germany to study. But he is sure they would accept a Canadian, Mother."

"That is most amazing, Charles. It would certainly be wonderful if it is true. But about your staying home, I will discuss it with your Father. It's a big step, leaving you alone."

"Please, Mother, talk with Grandma Margaret. I will do everything she tells me. I just want to have my lessons, have a chance."

Dorothy, on the way to Toronto with Constance, thought they are growing up too fast; the family is breaking up.

CHAPTER TWELVE

War

Montreal – 1914-1918

Kingsley returned from the United States frustrated and irritated by the lack of interest in his ideas. "Monsieur Chevrolet at least met with me." He snorted a laugh, "He seemed to think that because I came from Quebec we should conduct business in French. And he thought I was proposing we wanted to invest in his U. S. operations. But at least he did meet with me. Mr. Ford was 'too busy.' I was awarded a tour of the factory with some supervisor. That fellow just went on about 'what a great businessman Mr. Ford is, how he comes down to the floor with a little notebook and checks everything. He counted the drops of oil they put on a crankcase or some such thing and told them to cut down by three drops! Can you imagine - three drops of oil! Why would he waste executive time on such penny-pinching?"

Kingsley did not notice the glance that flashed between

Theodore and Tom Allen. There were rumblings of war, and war would mean boots and heavy clothes, and tools for soldiers. Their operations could convert easily, and Henry Ford's attention to the details of production costs could give them an edge if it came to that.

Great Britain declared war against Germany August 4, 1914, and all of the Commonwealth countries rushed to support their new king, George V. Kingsley Industries was awarded a lucrative contract to produce boots and other items of clothing, as Theodore had anticipated. That operation was located in Halifax under the management of Dino and Pietro Chicachcio, the two sons of Theodore's old friend Ernesto.

Thousands of young men and women felt a desperate urgency not to miss fulfillment. Young men were anxious to join this 'war to end all wars' and young women were eager to support them. They married, somehow believing this bond would ensure a safe return.

Charles and Isobel Hamilton, a young flautist he had been courting for two years, were also faced with considerations about their future. They broached the subject with Dorothy one afternoon. Charles said, "We have decided we want to be married, Mother. We hope you will be pleased."

"Of course, Charles dear. And Isobel, I am delighted. We will be so pleased to have you join our family. But you sound worried Charles. What is it?" She looked at the pale young girl with some trepidation. Was she ill? Martha's cooking would put more color into her cheeks.

"The thing is, I should feel the responsibility of joining the war effort, the army. But I really don't want to do that. I just want to play the violin," he sighed guiltily.

"You see, Mrs. Randolph, Charles has a good chance of being admitted into the Institute this year. That would be so wonderful, even though he would have to move to New York."

They talked further and agreed that army or Institute, Isobel would make Redstone Manor her home while Charles was away.

Charles Kingsley Randolph II was born May 3, 1915. The birth was difficult; Isobel's labor lasted many pain-filled hours. Finally the doctor suggested a caesarian, but it was too late. The baby was saved, but Isobel survived only two weeks. Charles was devastated. He had failed this beautiful, fragile woman he loved. The only thing he was good at was the violin, and the violin was a useless thing. He took no interest in anything to do with the baby - except for the name. He was determined that the boy should be Charles Kingsley, Junior and shouted angrily when Kingsley said dismissively, "I suppose we'll have another violin player." But either name, Charles or Kingsley, would create confusion, so they began to call the baby King.

Charles isolated himself for days, going to the Music Faculty to hide out in a practice room, playing the music Isobel had loved. Even the arrival of a letter of acceptance into the Institute failed to cheer him. Dorothy and Margaret were delighted to have the baby to fuss over but they worried that Charles would do something rash in his despair. Dorothy knew this sensitive son all too well. When he came home Friday evening, shoulders stiff, she was frightened. "I think I've made up my mind, Mother. I think I should go into the army." He looked at his new son hopelessly. What was he doing with a son? He needed Isobel; she would have known what to do.

"You *think* you've made up your mind?" Kingsley's sarcastic snort shook him. "You *think* you'll go into the army? Well, that's a start at least. Maybe the army will make a man out of you!"

Dorothy flushed and started to speak. But she saw Charles' head go up and his back stiffen and she waited.

"No, Father, I *don't* think I will go into the army after all. I *think* I will play the violin." And now he was sure. Dorothy smiled contentedly.

The funeral for Isobel was small and private. The minister spoke of youth and loss, Charles played Brahms beautiful lullaby and Dorothy sang the English words softly: "Lullaby and goodnight, With roses bedight." Theodore sobbed brokenly and all knew that his tears were as much for his friends Ernesto and Riata as for this young granddaughter he did not know. Two of Isobel's fellow students came from Quebec City, Charles' friends, and the family - but the feeling was warm with regret at the loss of a talented and lovely young woman. And the sadness was somewhat tempered by muted congratulations to Charles on his acceptance into the Institute.

The day after the funeral Charles went into the baby's room and stood looking down at him for some tine. He admitted to himself that he had no feeling for the child. He did not feel like a father; he only desperately longed for Isobel to come back and make things right. He went back to his room, packed, and left for New York.

The war changed Constance's life also; she married Lawrence Tremblay in September 1917. She had met him at

Maria Elena's birthday party three years earlier. But Lawrence lived in Philadelphia. His parents owned a specialty bookstore and responsibilities kept him tied down, so theirs had been an on and off courtship. When Lawrence's number was called in the first U. S. draft, the couple joined the rush to the altar. Constance moved to Philadelphia to take over Lawrence's duties at the bookstore. Their first child, Jeanette, was born in June 1918.

News Item: Halifax, N. S. December 6, 1917. At 9:03:35 AM. The French munitions ship, the Mont Blanc collided with a Norwegian ship, the Imo. The collision sparked a fire on the munitions ship, which exploded. Many buildings have been destroyed. The casualties may reach several hundred.

A little before noon on December 6, the front door slammed open and Theodore rushed down the hall, shedding his greatcoat, tromping snowy footprints, and shouting hoarsely, "Margarethe! Margarethe! Mein Gott, Margarethe! Sprengstoff! Ernesto! Riata! Kaput!"

Margaret, hearing the horror and anguish in his voice, dropped her sewing and rushed to him. She took him firmly by the arm and urged him toward their sitting room, waving Joseph away. "Theodore, what is it? Calm yourself! Is Kingsley hurt? What has happened? Stop speaking German!" Then as the German words replayed in her mind, "What explosion? Where? At the factory? What about Ernesto and Riata? Calm down and tell me."

"Halifax! Explosion! Buildings kaput! Fuer! Hundreds tot!"

Margaret began to realize the horror, "Everything? Blown

away? Fire? Hundreds dead? It can't be that bad, Theodore. And you must stop speaking German, Theodore. Remember what happened to the Buchlers. Driven out. Do you want us all to be driven out of the country? We are at war, Theodore!"

"Ja! Ja! Liebchen."

"Do not Ja! Ja! Me, Theodore." She grabbed his chin and forced him to turn and look her in the face. "I tell you! Do! Not! Speak! German! You will get us all killed!" She slapped his face lightly, but with enough force that it stung.

The shock of this jerked his eyes into focus and he slumped down in the big chair. "Yes, Margaret" he said in a quieter voice. "But we have to go. Find out about the family. Do what we can to help. We should be there now. Tickets. The factory. Telegrams." He sounded confused, disoriented.

Margaret poured him a full measure of whiskey. "Here, drink this, Theodore. And then take an aspirin, I think. Just relax. I'm going to make a few calls." She rang for Joseph. "You have heard this terrible news, Joseph?"

"Yes, Madam. Some news at least. It is coming over the wireless, but in short items, a bit at a time."

"Mr. Randolph's partner and his family may have been in the direct path of the explosion and fire. It has hit Mr. Theodore very hard. He is to rest. Please do not let anyone disturb him, not even Mr. Kingsley. I must make some arrangements. You may pack a small bag for each of us, for a week I should think. But we must travel very light, and with serviceable clothes, nothing dressy."

"Very good, Madam."

Margaret went to her sitting room, a list of chores already forming in her mind. She called the factory, checked on Kingsley's schedule, requested Mrs. Thompson to get tickets for a double roomette to Halifax, or the nearest station open, and to find accommodations, if any were available. She called Dorothy in Toronto, learned that they had heard the news. She told Dorothy that Theodore, in his distraught state, had been speaking German. "I think you should come home in spite of Christmas plans. We need to defuse any hint of problems about the German," she added and Dorothy agreed.

They reached Truro three days later and rented a carriage for the final leg of the trip. Halifax was a shambles. The old shoe shop and all of the buildings along the street were gone, as if evaporated. Neither Ernesto's nor Riata's body was found, not even bones. Angelina, their daughter and her entire elementary school class were dead in the burned–out school building. People who had gone to a front window to see what was happening after the first small explosion, had been blinded, their faces splintered, their eyes pierced with hundreds of glass shards when the windows were blown in by the second, much more powerful, blast. Theodore and Margaret shuddered at the thought. It would surely have been the natural thing to do, to go to the window. They were almost relieved they had not found the bodies of their friends.

Finally they caught up with Dino and Pietro who had been at the clothing factory in northwest Halifax when the explosion occurred. They had heard the blast and pieces of the wreckage had blown past. Part of the roof was ripped off and windows were shattered. They closed down the operation and sent everyone home. Now they were burying their own grief by working eighteen to twenty hours a day helping wherever help was needed. There was nothing more that Theodore or Margaret could do. They attended a simple memorial service for their friends, quietly packed and returned home. Both were exhausted, as much by shock and grief as by anything they had been able to do.

Theodore seemed a broken man. He showed little interest in the business. Kingsley assumed charge. Good contracts with the army kept them busy; all divisions were pushed to their limits. But as events rushed past, it became increasingly clear that Kingsley was out of his depth. When Tom Allen offered a suggestion, Kingsley snapped at him.

Tom's increasing frustration almost boiled over. Kingsley is not half the man his father is, he thought. But his loyalty was to Theodore, and Theodore was still shaken by the deaths of his friends. The firm had lucrative army contracts; Theodore needed him. He bit his anger back, made his own decisions and kept production humming.

CHAPTER THIRTEEN

No! No!

Montreal – 1918

As the horror of war brought more and more injured men home, and brought, too, news of men who would never return to their families, Dorothy and Margaret spent hours at the hospital or in service centers, preparing bandages, organizing visits to distraught families, and assisting with care of the wounded. Without speaking of it, they shared the wonder and awe they received from this new life in their home. They turned to the baby to ease the hopeless misery they faced daily. This boy lives. He is the future.

In the summer of 1918 a worldwide flu epidemic spilled over into Canada and swept through the hospitals, taking its toll on workers as well as the injured soldiers. It hit suddenly, with the symptoms of a cold: fever, aches, and chills, and it progressed quickly. The medical community had no remedy.

Either the patient lived through it, or died within days, or even hours.

Dorothy came home about 4:00 pm June 6. Meeting Margaret in the front hall she, said, "I don't feel well, Margaret. I think I'll lie down for a half hour." She died at 6:00 the next morning.

Kingsley had slept in the spare room, 'so Dorothy can get a good rest.'

Margaret, checking on Dorothy about 5:30, found her ashen and still, breathing only faintly. She rang for Joseph, "Wake Mr. Kingsley. He must come immediately. And then rouse Mr. Theodore. Tell him I need him."

But Dorothy's struggle was over. Kingsley knelt by her bedside, holding her hand, still soft and warm, whispering, "No! No! No! No! No!"

Theodore touched him, patting his shoulder timidly, and the boy shrunk lower. Margaret said "Come, Kingsley, we must call the doctor and care for her, son."

Then Kingsley jumped up shouting now, "NO! NO!" He rocketed from the room, knocking his father off balance. And several minutes later they heard the front door slam. The business closed. Staff were met as they arrived, received the news, and were told they should come in the following morning. Only Tom Allen stayed to do what was necessary.

There was no word from Kingsley. Margaret and Theodore managed to get Dr. Michaels to care for Dorothy and provide the death certificate. All went about their morning duties with shaking hands and tear-filled eyes.

When Tom Allen arrived at the office at 6:30 two days later, he found Kingsley asleep in his office chair, very drunk and disheveled. He took Kingsley home and exchanged sighs of relief with Theodore and Margaret as they got their son into his bed. He knew they had feared for what their boy might do.

The funeral was a sober affair. This family had known too much bereavement in these past months. Still the church was crowded with mourners. Dorothy had touched so many lives. Family, and friends from Toronto drove down for the wake and the funeral. The music communities, both from Dorothy's own ties, and from those of Charles and Isobel poured into the church. The family business was represented, not just by executives, but by all the 'little people' who had loved Dorothy for dozens of small and gracious friendly nods or words. The groups Dorothy had worked with at the hospital, the church or just some unlikely small organization, all came silently to fill the huge church, spilling over to stand patiently outside to express their love and respect.

Through it all, Kingsley sat, quiet and shrunken, flanked by Theodore and Charles Gordon. He looked older somehow, heavy and tired, his face ashen and more lined, the vibrancy wiped out. It had fallen to Margaret to plan the service, and she had determined that it should be a simple, loving tribute to Dorothy.

But to everyone there was a more profound import. This was mid-June, 1918; at last this killing war was ending. In the hearts of all, this funeral was a tribute to Dorothy, to the hundreds of thousands who had suffered devastation and loss. They wept for Dorothy; they wept for themselves; and they wept because they could again look to the future.

The war had ended, but it left a ravaged family, and a decimated community.

The Armistice was signed November 11, 1918, and that meant contracts with the army would soon end. Kingsley turned distractedly from one crisis to the next. So Tom took over as Acting Manager, did what he could to fulfill commitments without official powers, and began to look around for other opportunities. He begged Theodore to return to work as Margaret nursed Kingsley and took charge of the baby and the household.

CHAPTER FOURTEEN

The Twig Is Bent

Montreal - 1920 - 1930

King realized when he was very young that his name, Charles Kingsley Randolph II, had a bitter note to it for the family. His full, rightful name was almost never spoken; he was called King. He knew, too, that his father's real name was Charles Kingsley Randolph I and he was always called Charles. So the Charles part of their names did not seem to be a problem; the bitterness must be about the Kingsley part.

The Kingsley part was very important. It had something to do with his Grandpa Kingsley Randolph. Father called him Pa - Pa Kingsley or Sir. And with the family business - that was Kingsley Industries. So maybe it was the Randolph part. He had heard Joseph and Martha talking about 'when Mr. Theodore and Madam Margaret Randolph were here.' He had thought maybe Margaret was the name of the nanny, but that couldn't be right; they wouldn't call the nanny 'Madam.' There just weren't any women except the ones who worked.

Maybe it was Industries; he didn't know what that was, but it was important. Anyway, Kingsley Randolph II meant he stood for the family and the business. It tied him to family and to the business. But whenever 'Kingsley' was spoken, Father and Pa Kingsley got a still, frozen look on their faces for just a minute. It left him confused about who or what he really was in the family. It was all very upsetting. His mind went round and round as he puzzled over why his name caused angry words and feelings. Maybe if he found out more about the business, it would make sense.

The business was the most important thing. The men who came to visit Grandpa all talked about the 'Industries'. When Grandpa talked about it, his voice got loud and it had a sound like 'don't argue with me' in it. And his words were angry. Grandpa talked to Father about it, too, saying things like "We have to get this boy started early so he will be ready for it. I want none of this violin nonsense from him", or "This boy will have a big job to keep things going." 'This boy' must mean him; he was the only boy there.

His father never said anything much about that, just "That's a long time off." Or, "He's just a boy." What was clear was that he was of no use unless he was in the business. Grandpa's tone said 'have to' with every word.

Anyway, Father was away a lot, and when he was home, he was always playing his violin in the big room with the piano in it. And there he 'was not to be disturbed!' He was never ready to answer questions; he was no help. King felt stupid, ignorant. He pursued every scrap of information that might help him understand. He sat behind the couch and listened when Grandpa talked with the men. And he listened to the people of the house as they went about their work.

The three of them, Father Charles, Grandpa Kingsley, and he lived alone in the big red sandstone house just below the mountain. Of course there were the people who worked. There was Nanny who slept in the small bedroom next to King's and took care of him. And Joseph ran the house now since Hubert had died, he was important. Martha, the cook was going, and Hilda would be cook. She was Joseph's wife, and they lived in the apartment over the garage. Then there were the girls who did the cleaning and dusting and started the fires, things like that. There were people, but they were not family, so they hardly counted. Except sometimes they talked as if he could not hear. That was good; he listened as much as he could.

It was a really big house, King thought; you could easily get lost in it, or hide in it if you wanted to. He had four rooms on the third floor in what Nanny called the North Wing. These were just for him - bedroom, sitting room, the small bedroom where Nanny slept, and the playroom. He only used the bedroom and bath, and the playroom when Nanny read to him, told him stories, or watched him play with his cars or blocks.

The rest of the third floor was closed up except for some rooms in the South Wing that were always clean and made up for guests. Only there never were any guests. The windows in the South Wing looked out over the city. In the daytime you could see the river, and in the night you could see the lights of the city. King liked that. From his windows you looked up the mountain at all the trees, but that was all there was to see. King roamed freely; he knew every closet, cubbyhole, nook, and cranny of the house. It was a great house for hide-and-seek, if only he had someone to play with.

The only women in the house were Nanny, Martha and Hilda the cooks, and the silly girls who ran around dusting and sweeping, giggling all the time. Once in a while some other names were mentioned, Dorothy and Margaret, and once Father said he got a letter from Constance. But he guessed they had always been dead. Of course Jacques, the chauffeur who lived over the garage had a woman friend who came in to help Martha sometimes. And King thought that Old Step the gardener had been married once. They wouldn't know anything about the family though.

Nanny was good to him, but she wasn't family either, and he could tell that she was more interested in some people she called 'my friends' than him. He had no one to find out things from. His father didn't talk to him much; he was always playing the violin anyway, or he was away. And Grandpa Kingsley was too stern; King was mostly afraid of him. Anyway he was out almost all day. No one was very nice, really, no one paid him any attention unless he did something wrong. No one ever laughed. He wouldn't have said he was lonely, didn't really know what that meant; he just felt alone.

He was always supposed to do whatever Father and Grandpa told him to do. Or mostly not do something they did not like. There was something about 'speak when spoken to', and 'watch your tongue', and 'mind your manners.' So he watched everyone with curiosity and considerable uneasiness trying to figure things out. He did not dislike the people, but the more he tried to understand, the more nervous he got. He felt something boil up inside him sometimes; then he went to his room and lay on his bed trying to make the feeling go away.

Martha and Joseph tried to spread a protective shield over him, but he did not understand this kindness. Sometimes it prevented him from finding out things so he avoided them and kept as close to Father as he dared. Often he hid behind some chairs in the salon while Father played the violin for hours. It was very strange about that; Father always played the violin when Grandpa was away. If Grandpa came home early and heard the violin, he got a mean look on his face and went into his study to drink whisky.

Neither Father nor Grandpa Kingsley explained anything. No one ever talked about his mother or anyone else in the family who was dead or not there - only about business, or the government, or the men who came and went.

King was not a part of anything. He was spoken to of course, or spoken about would be more true. "This is my son (or grandson) King. He's in second (or third) at Selwyn House. Doing very well - top in maths (or history)." It was like a formula, only the specifics changed. So King felt somehow shadowy, seen only in outline.

He was there like the piano was there in the salon, or like the portraits of Pa Kingsley and Great Grandpa Theodore that commanded the great hall. He was there like the servants were there. In a way that was good because most of the time the adults forgot about him. So he began to learn bits and pieces of the story from stray conversations, from the servants' gossip, from pictures with names written on the back, and later from papers he found in the attic.

King learned that he had aunts and uncles. He thought they must have come to him from his mother or his grandmother, but it was not clear. Someone was called Felicity, some letters to Grandma Dorothy from Toronto were signed Fizzy, and someone else was Maria Elena. There was a picture of a small boy and a big red dog with just the names Kingsley and Red of Glynmere and the date, June 1, 1894, on the back, but that didn't make any sense at all. The date was wrong for Grandpa. And it wasn't Father because Father's name was Charles. Besides it didn't look like the pictures of Father as a boy that were down in the library. He had tried to ask Martha about this boy Kingsley, but her face got stiff for a minute, and she turned away to the sink where she was scraping the carrots. "Some things are better not to ask about, child. Now get off with you. Don't you have studies to do?"

There was much that King couldn't figure out. There were no pictures of his mother. Her name, he was sure, was Isobel, but he could find nothing about her, no pictures of him with his mother, or of Mother and Father for that matter. He wanted to ask but he was afraid. Questions brought such terrible anger. He had tried once, had asked, "Father, where is Mother? Why doesn't she come to see me?"

Father's harsh, "She's dead. She died giving birth to you," had sent him retching violently in the toilet. He sat down against the wall behind the small bed, hugging his favorite book, *Jungle Boy*, and a soft pillow. But he was too exposed there. Anyone could come by and see him hugging that pillow like a baby. He crept down the back stairs to the closet under the grand staircase and lay silently.

Finally he slept. Nanny woke him hours later; she was cross, "I have been looking for you for hours. Why did you go off like this? I didn't dare say anything to your father. I could have gotten in real trouble. Don't ever go off like that again." The house was very dark and quiet. She just took off his pants and shoes and he crawled into bed.

He dreamed that he had come into his mother's room, and when she tried to hold him, he hit her with his pillow that turned into a rock. She had blood all over her face so he couldn't see what she looked like. His mother was dead, and he had killed her.

He woke with a fever and slept and dreamed fitfully for days. Nanny bathed his face and fed him soup and hot lemonade. When he finally got up, he did not remember what had happened or what he had dreamed. But he felt a heavy tiredness for weeks.

In 1925, the year King was four, family unexpectedly did appear. Aunt Felicity came from Toronto in May for some important thing that was for Father. He was going to get something that sounded like an 'ornery degree'. Everyone had to get dressed up and go to the university for that. It was very long and boring, but everyone clapped for Father.

Aunt Felicity was going to stay until after Christmas. Father seemed to like her, "Mother Dorothy would love to see you now, Aunt Fizzy. You get younger every year. Whenever she played the piano, she'd say, 'If only Fizzy were here. We'd play some hot music to get all of you youngsters dancing.' We'll get you to play for us while you are here, Felicity."

"Oh, Charles Kingsley, no wonder Isobel fell for you. You do have a way with words." She kicked a little dance step, twisting her feet and knees, and flicking her hands criss-crossing her knees.

King gaped at her, and Father laughed, "The Charleston. Trust you to learn the latest steps, Fizzy."

Grandpa cleared his throat heavily, "We hope you had a

pleasant trip down, Miss Felicity. And we hope you have a pleasant stay with us."

"Kingsley Randolph, you old goat. You can call me Fizzy, you know. You've known me for well over fifty years. We're long past the Miss Felicity - Mr. Randolph stage. Dorothy would want us to let the past die. I just made up my mind that this might be my last chance to get acquainted with my young nephew. So we are going to be family for this time, regardless of old worn-out problems."

King turned avidly from one to the other, his eyes alert. This was the first time that 'family' was spoken so openly. Unexpectedly, this strange 'aunt' turned to King, "And this must be Charles Kingsley II."

King started and shot a timid glance at Grandpa, as he realized she was speaking to him. Charles Kingsley II. No one called him that. He stuck out his hand, "How do you do, Ma'am...Miss...Aunt....". He was confused. He didn't know how to act with a woman, certainly not this woman who danced and called Grandpa an Old Goat. She didn't seem to realize that she was an old lady. And she was old. She must be; her skin looked thin. You could see black lines through the tissue-paper skin, like rivers on a map. And her heavy hair was white under the big black hat with its lavender rose. He couldn't take his eyes off her, and he couldn't pull his hand away - she held it with a strong grip.

"Aunt Fizzy is just fine, Charles Kingsley Randolph II. You have the Randolph look all right, just like your Grandpa Kingsley there, but you got your red hair from us Gordons. We're going to have seven or eight months to get acquainted. I'll call you King if you'll call me Aunt Fizzy." This was another startling revelation; he looked like Grandpa Kingsley. He

170

looked up quickly but Grandpa glared at Auntie and then at him, hunched his head into his shoulders and turned his back on the three of them.

Normal routine was greatly shaken up by Aunt Felicity. A bed was moved down into the small parlor so she wouldn't have to climb the stairs. That cut off one of King's favorite retreats under the great, winding staircase, but she was so willing to talk, and he was so eager to listen it seemed more of a bonus than a loss. She invited him into her makeshift bedroom every day after her nap. A sweet fragrance filled the room and clung to her dress, her gloves, her handkerchief. King was dizzy with something he had never known. She insisted that King accompany her on frequent short walks on the western mountain. They talked about the trees, the small animals, the pond where ducks rode, and about King's studies and things he liked.

Conversations at dinner became lively and King listened eagerly. "Maria Elena and George will be here October first, in time for Thanksgiving," Aunt Fizzy said one day. "She's due in six weeks, but George has been transferred down to CP here, so better to come early."

He wanted to ask about that; "coming October first" and "due in six weeks" was very confusing, but he didn't quite dare that. Instead he tried, "Who are they, Auntie?" He had arrived at Auntie as a name for her, not quite daring Aunt Fizzy, and feeling that Aunt Felicity was too unapproachable.

Pa Kingsley scowled at him, and Father said, "Don't be impudent!"

But Aunt Felicity smiled, "Maria Elena is my daughter, and her husband is George Orwell. They are your aunt and uncle."

So there was something else he'd better not ask. Aunt Felicity was a 'Miss.' Grandpa had called her "Miss Gordon," so how did she have a daughter? He thought only a Mrs. could have a daughter. He was trying to get all of these new pieces of the family picture in his head, but it was very difficult. He would ask Auntie more; she didn't seem to mind questions.

"Auntie," King asked on one of their slow, easy walks, "who is Constance? I found a picture of Constance and you, I think, in the attic. Is she related to me?"

"Indeed she is, little King. She is your father's sister, your Aunt Constance. That picture was taken in 1897, the year after your father was born, Charles Kingsley. A long time ago. I was fifty then, and Maria Elena was eight, a pre-teenager. Dear little Constance was still a child, only seven. She lived with me in Toronto for quite a few years when she was little.

"Your Grandma Dorothy and Constance came up for a visit when she was just five or six. And then....and then it seemed best for her to stay with me while...when...for a while. She was a little sweetheart - but a real tartar. She knew her own mind from the git-go. Don't you know your Aunt Constance and Uncle Philippe?"

"Aunt Constance and Uncle Philippe? No, I don't know them. Are they alive? Where do they live? Are they very old too?"

"Well, I suppose it would seem so to someone your age, but not to me. No, not to me. Constance is six years older than your father, child. They have a son, my other nephew Lawrence is about your age - only one year older in fact. They live in Philadelphia in the US of A."

"Is their name Kingsley Randolph, too? Is Philadelphia a long way off? There is so much I don't know," King sighed.

"No, it's Tremblay. Philippe Tremblay is a good writer, and he and Constance have a wonderful bookstore in Philadelphia - Woodstock Books. They are very highly regarded in the literary world. You really don't know much about your family, do you, child? Isobel would have made such a difference in your life if she had lived. You would have loved your mother. She knew Constance and Philuppe because her father, Florent Graham, was a painter."

"Please tell me about my mother, Auntie. Did...did...did... I really kill her?" King trembled violently as he dared this frightening question.

"Of course not, child. She died because the doctor wasn't careful, and she got an infection. Whatever put that notion into your head, foolish child? But I'm tired now. Let's get back to the house so these old bones can rest."

"Auntie...oh, nothing."

"What is it, boy, don't be afraid to ask questions."

"I just wondered...but I guess I shouldn't say it."

"Oh for goodness sakes, child, speak up. Don't dither."

"Well, you look sort of old, but you don't seem old. I just wondered...-."

"Aren't you the one! I just had my eightieth birthday in January. And eighty is pretty old, all right. But inside I don't feel old. I was seventeen years older than your Aunt Dorothy, your Papa's sister, but we were always good friends. Strange isn't it, some people die so young, and some of us just live on forever - no sense to it at all. Now, get me into my room and be off with you."

King had a lot to think about; he climbed up to the attic and sat on the old rocking horse in the corner. King liked the attic. There were so many family things there. He felt close to the family when he sat up there reading, or when he examined the old things. He felt closer still now; everything was so much more friendly with Aunt Felicity here, and now Aunt Maria Elena and Uncle George were coming soon; maybe he could ask about other things. He wanted to ask why Grandpa was so cross all of the time, and why Father didn't talk to him.

Aunt Felicity seemed to like to talk. A few days later King said, "What happened to Grandma Dorothy, Auntie? Why did she die? Was she very old?"

"No, child. She was not even fifty when she died. There was a terrible flu epidemic in 1918, and...." She broke off, "Do you know what an epidemic is, King? No? Well it is when someone gets very sick, and then another person catches the sickness, and then another, and another. Hundreds of thousands of people died from the flu in that epidemic, and your Grandma Dorothy was one of them. That was very hard on your grandpa. He loved her very much, and she loved him too. There had been just too many really sad things happen for your Grandpa Kingsley to bear. It took a lot out of him when your grandmother died. She was a beautiful person, child. You would have loved her, too."

"Did she look like you, Auntie? I think you are beautiful."

"Child, child! You will break my heart with that sweet talk." She pulled a soft white handkerchief out of her pocket and wiped her eyes. "Your grandmother was beautiful in the way you mean - to look at. We both had red hair and creamy complexions. But your Grandma Dorothy was beautiful in a more important way. She was a beautiful person, a good, kind person. She loved your Grandpa with all her heart, and she was strong, which was a good thing for her, and for your father. But that is enough said about that. I am old, and tired. I need to go home and rest now, King."

King could see that she was very tired as they walked slowly back home. She fumbled and dropped the soft handkerchief at the door of her room. King picked it up; he would give it to her in her room.

Because Auntie was so willing to answer questions, King became bolder. "Father," he said Thanksgiving Day in early October when everyone around the big table was quiet for a minute, waiting for coffee and the crème brulée, "there's a good old rocking horse up in the attic. Was that your horse when you were little? Did I ever ride it? I don't remember riding it. Did I?" There was a deathly stillness around the table. Everyone's eyes shifted quickly to Pa Kingsley, who snarled, "Get out of my sight! Get out! Out! And stay out!" Gasping for breath and clutching his chest, he thrust his chair back, and left the table.

"Now see what you have done, King! You've upset Pa! The day is spoiled! You have to learn to hold your tongue!" King froze. Father was angry too, and everyone was staring at him. Auntie was gasping, clutching her chest. Maria Elena was up, leaning over Auntie.

Grandpa Kingsley hated him. Everyone hated him. He always made everyone angry. He mumbled an excuse and fled to the attic to lie numbly on the pile of rolled up carpets. He sighed heavily. His questions were all bad. But why? Memories squashed his mind. Like the time he had asked, "Grandpa, why

175

is the business called Kingsley Industries when our name is Randolph? I saw something about Randolph Cobblers once. Is that the same?"

Grandpa had growled, "My God, child! Do you have to get into everything? What are you trying to do to this family, stir up trouble every way you can? Some things are none of your business. Go read or something, but keep your nose out of other peoples' affairs."

And then there was the day so long ago when he had asked if he could have a dog. "I'd like a big dog, just like that Red of Glynmere in the picture." That, too, had brought the unexplained snarling fury. One by one the memories tramped through his mind.

Finally he stirred and shifted restlessly. He wanted to get up but there was nothing he wanted to do. His mind was numb, he had a stomachache, and his arms and legs felt heavy, dead. He looked over at Grandma Dorothy's old trunk under the dormer. He had never thought of opening it. There was a padlock, only a small one but he recognized the lock as a signal of privacy and he had never thought of breaking it. Now it didn't matter. He could never please Father Charles or Grandpa, so he could open the trunk. He felt unreal, in a strange new place where he no longer cared about rules or boundaries.

The trunk held children's clothes and baby things. There was a small gold and ivory music box that played a soft, sweet melody when he lifted the lid. In the bottom of the trunk, in a separate box, there were yellowed papers and a small key. King didn't think; he just touched and turned things. He handled the clothes without unfolding them. The musty smell of the old clothes seeped into his mind, like fog over his thoughts. He tucked the key in his pants pocket, took the papers out of the box and hid them under the pile of carpets. Carefully he put the box back in the trunk and laid everything on top. He fixed the padlock as well as he could and threw an old shawl over the top, not really caring if it hid everything.

King suddenly did not feel like a child. He was beginning a secret life, hiding his true self from the family. He would find out everyone's secrets and then they would be sorry they always got mad at him. This was the way things were for him; they needed him but did not want him. He would show them. The seed of loneliness and humiliation had taken root and was turning into passion. This passion was a cold thing; knowing things would make him strong. He would make his name, King, important. He would prove his right to the name.

He sat for hours with his back against the old trunk, watching the sunlight move across the attic floor, seeing its warmth but not feeling it. He had no energy to go about the rest of an ordinary day. Just before he fell asleep against the carpets, a fleeting thought tugged at his mind. Something about Auntie, but he was too tired for it to be clear.

When King finally returned downstairs, he met Joseph passing through the great front hall. Joseph's glance mixed protocol and sympathy. "Good evening, Master King. The family are in the drawing room. Will you be joining them?"

King hesitated at the foot of the stairs, his mind still focused on his thoughts. "May I brush your jacket, sir?" Joseph had noted King's rumpled state and, fully aware of the dinner table disturbance, determined that the boy should make a proper appearance now. King dutifully stood to be brushed and twitched into shape. He did not recognize the kindness in the attentive hands, nor did he feel his customary small-boy impatience. He just didn't care. Joseph sighed and shook his head slightly as the boy turned to join the family.

CHAPTER FIFTEEN

Fast Friends

Montreal – 1930 - 1942

King had always been a quiet, observant child, making meaning out of words and the way voices sounded. Tonight he watched even more carefully, and listened more intently. He no longer thought of himself as a boy, as the least one in the family. He did not think, either, about becoming a man, an adult. He would become strong. He would be stronger than Father Charles, even stronger than Pa Kingsley. His new mind refused to think of him as Grandpa.

He now focused on learning everything about the family, even about the business. He would use everything he learned, to be someone important in the family. He was tired of being a small, unimportant boy. The meanings he wanted now were how to use what he heard and saw.

To become this new King he would find the weaknesses in others. Their weakness would let him be stronger. He did not understand this change in himself. It was hardly a conscious change, but it was very real. He sat straighter, was quieter even than usual. Without the burden of hope and fear, his mind began to slice away confusion and ignorance, to focus more sharply, to seek only ways and means to one purpose: he would become the person they all looked at, spoke to, sought out.

He focused fiercely on Pa Kingsley; he would learn the secrets that made the Kingsley name both painful and powerful.

He did not move toward Aunt Felicity's hand reaching out to draw him to her; she was no longer important. He did not notice her heavy breathing, paid no attention when Maria Elena stood abruptly and led her mother out of the room.

Felicity's death was an event outside of King's new purpose. He allowed himself to be dressed formally for the funeral, sat patiently through the songs and tributes, not thinking about what he was hearing. Only at the graveside, as the coffin was lowered into its black hole, did he feel an emptiness. He watched Pa Kingsley throw a handful of dirt on the coffin and hated him. He glared at the old man, blaming him for this loss too, suddenly finding him to blame for everything - for Father's anger, for his mother being gone, for his loneliness. It was Pa Kingsley who made everyone unhappy. He would make Pa Kingsley sorry for causing everyone to die.

King walked through the days that followed wrapped in his mind. He saw and registered events, but could not connect to them. He saw himself in a bubble, floating along with activities around him, but sealed off. He spent long hours in the attic, doing nothing, thinking only of his faults, of how bad he was, of how always, always he caused problems.

When he was hungry he went to the kitchen where

Martha or Joseph urged him to eat something - perhaps a bowl of hot soup, a piece of cold chicken, or warm biscuits fresh from the oven, perhaps a glass of cold milk and a piece of sharp cheddar cheese.

He wandered through the house, absently touching things: a door knob, the acorn newel post on the grand staircase, the gold twisted serpent handle of Father's walking stick, a soft key on the piano in the salon. He brushed the leather spines on the set of Dickens in the library, gave a listless twirl to the heavy chair at Pa Kingsley's desk, slumped in the window of the front parlour, and stared at the winter birds pecking through the dirty snow at the edge of the driveway.

Joseph, moving quietly about the house in his daily work routine, caught glimpses of the little figure on its lonely trek. He shook his head and, returning to the kitchen, reported sadly, "He just wanders, or sits and stares at nothing, Martha. There's no spark to him anymore."

"It's like he has lost himself," Martha fretted. "You can't get through to him. He eats anything I give him, but it's like he's eating cardboard. He just chews and swallows."

Rubbing the silver coffee urn absentmindedly Joseph said, "I don't understand why Mr. Charles doesn't see what is happening to the boy. They don't even speak to him - more than 'good morning,' or 'wear your boots, not those shoes,' or 'hold the door for your Aunt Maria Elena.' It's the way they speak to the maids or the gardener. It's not good."

Christmas came and went. King thanked everyone politely for his gifts - a warm jacket from Father, new skates from Maria Elena and her husband George, and a night-glow wristwatch from Grandpa Kingsley. He took his presents to his room anger boiling up from his stomach as he looked at the watch. He wanted to throw it in the wastebasket because it was from Grandpa. But he did want the watch. For weeks he had been looking at these watches in the stores. He would be able to tell the time in the dark. So he hardened the hatred into a ball and determined that he would not wear this watch around the house where Grandpa would see him enjoying it. He would wear it when Grandpa was away.

He tucked the watch underneath his sweaters and shirts in the bottom drawer, and slowly pulled out the small white box hidden there weeks ago. He had bought a dainty linen handkerchief with a beautiful scrolled "F" embroidered on it. He had been delighted at the thought of giving Aunt Fizzy something so pretty. Now misery melted in with hatred so he could not tell how he felt. He threw the handkerchief in the wastebasket, and then sat with one arm flung over the basket, the other hugging the new skates. Finally he picked the handkerchief back out and buried it with the watch in his bottom drawer.

Early in the New Year, Maria Elena and George were preparing to move into their new home on Trafalgar, and there were serious discussions in the library. King sat in the window seat listening.

"Someone has to go up to Toronto to close up Felicity's house," Pa said. "I was surprised that Felicity wrote me in as Maria Elena's agent to act with her lawyer as executor, but I suppose she was thinking of Maria Elena's condition and your new responsibilities at CP, George." Grandpa did not look at George when he spoke, as though he was addressing the air around them. That meant that George was not important.

Exactly the way he talks at me, King thought. He saw again clearly his own place in the world about him. And he saw that he could talk to Pa the same way. He would try out the cold voice and blank stare on Pa one day. Everything had become part of the struggle with Pa.

In late May Tom Allen asked, "How old is your boy, Kingsley? I think he's about the same age as my son Michael."

"Charles? He is almost thirty, much older than your boy, Tom."

"I meant Charles' boy King. Isn't he about seven? I think he and Michael were born about the same time?"

"Oh, that boy. He's seven, I guess, or will be next month. Why?"

"I thought so. Do you have him enrolled at Selwyn House? Michael is starting there in September; I had Mrs. Sorenson do the registration last week. I thought we might get the two of them together so they would know each other before they start. Might be nice for them to have a pal on their first day, don't you think?"

"Hadn't thought much about it," Kingsley muttered. In fact he hadn't thought about it at all. But he should get the boy in school. He'd get the secretary to take care of it.

"I'm taking Michael to the apple farm in the Townships on Saturday - pick some apples and have lunch. Would King like to go along?"

Kingsley's grunted 'Huh!' was a good enough answer for Tom. It was settled. What in the world did that boy do all day long alone in that big house! It was about time he got to know someone his own age.

The boys were shy at first, but King was hungry for a friend and Michael was cheerful and talkative. By the time they had picked a sack of apples, they knew which books they liked and that their favourite thing was a train set.

When King took his sack of apples to Hilda in the kitchen, he stood hesitantly in the doorway. "Uh!" was all he could get out.

"What is it, Master King?"

"These apples."

"Do you want me to make an apple pie for dinner?"

"Would you? Could you? I love apple pie! Uh.... Are there enough? Could I have one or two for myself? But if there aren't enough?"

"That's a big sack, Master. King. You can have five or six if you want. I can make a nice big pie."

"Lord love him," she said to Joseph later. "I'd have gone out and picked more apples myself if there weren't enough. You should have seen his face - happy! He was happy, Joseph!"

At Selwyn House the boys were tested, questioned about reading and general knowledge and numbers. They found themselves in a classroom with more than twenty other boys and looked around. "There are so many, and they are all so different." King had never seen other children except from the window of the family car.

At recess a few days later they stood near the fence. "Do you know that kid with the long name, Michael? Florenzo Genovenzi? He must be Italian. He doesn't look big enough to be in school - only comes about to my chin! How old do you think he is?"

184

"Yeah! I don't know, but I think he is really smart. He's in some special class I heard. And they say that whenever Mr. Howard asks him a question, he just rattles off the answer, right every time. Why?"

"I was watching him. He sort of stays off there in the corner all the time. But that big kid they call Gordo - do you know him?"

"Gordon Johanson. I know who he is. Dad knows his father, Dr. Johanson at the University. He's pretty famous. And his wife is a poet, they say. What about him?"

"Well it kind of looks like Gordon is crowding Florenzo. And Gordon is so big. I just thought------." They walked over, ambled around, and Gordon edged away. They kept an eye out in the next few days, and moved in whenever Gordon seemed to crowd the smaller boy.

Florenzo finally confronted King and Michael one day. "What is it with you guys? Don't you think I should be friends with Gordon?"

"We just thought…." Michael started.

"He's so big." King added.

"And I'm so little!" Florenzo laughed sarcastically. "You think I can't take care of myself? Well let me tell you, jerks! My father taught me a thing or two. He learned a lot of tricks on the streets of Florence when he was a boy! You don't have to worry about me. And I'll thank you to let me take care of myself!"

"Sorry! Sorry!" King and Michael backed off."

"You're from Florence?" King asked. "Isn't that in Italy? Is that where your name comes from?"

"Yeah! So?"

"Your dad owns that trucking firm - what is it called? Ike's International Transport? My dad is Tom Allen; I think he knows your father. Dad works for King's father, Kingsley Industries." So they cooled the tension and began to talk about school and things they liked to do.

"Ma---," Gordon hesitated, wanting to talk to his mother, but afraid he was right and then it would be worse.

"What is it, son?"

"I'm too big!" Gordon's face twisted, ready to cry.

Hilda Johanson put her arms around the boy, giving him a big hug. "You're not too big for me, love. But whatever is wrong? Why do you say that?"

"I think the kids are scared of me," he blurted. "There's this little kid, and I like him, and he's so smart. He knows so much, and I just want to talk with him. But every time I get near him, the other kids crowd me out. They think I want to hurt him, Ma!"

"You get it from my family, son. Your Grandpa, and even farther back. You know, I was sure your father would never want to marry a big woman like me. I fell for him the first time I met him, but I was sure.... well it took some time, but you know how much we love each other. It takes time, son. Maybe some day you could invite them over for a swim. Talk to your father, maybe he knows the families."

King watched Gordon the next day. "You know, I'm going to ask Gordon if he wants to have a coke with us after school. Get acquainted. What do you think?"

"I think that's what I like about you, King Randolph! Take the bull by its horns, as they say. You always figure out a way to

186

do something, and you just go ahead and do it!" The four boys began to meet during lunch break and after school. They arranged to go to a movie together. They laughed to see Florenzo hop out of his stretch limousine, and joked about Gordon in his family's 'little' Mercedes. Suddenly King felt connected, a part of something. He was happy.

When King met Mrs. Johanson, he ached inside, really understanding what he had missed all his life. She was such a 'mothering' person. She just reached out and gathered them all in, and king felt what it might be like to be loved.

They started privately calling themselves the 'fearless foursome,' and for King it was a heady feeling. He had friends and they liked him! He had something to think about besides the family and the business. He had places to go – maybe to Gordon's for a swim, maybe to Floro's to examine the huge transport trucks, or with Mr. Allen on some drive in the country. He always asked his Grandpa, and took Kingsley's grunted "Huh!" as permission enough. Joseph and Martha saw the difference in the boy and were relieved. "He's going to be all right," Joseph said.

Eleventh grade was to be their final year at Selwyn House. They had another year before they could get into any regular university program. Ontario had four years in highschool, but Quebec was different. They could go to an Ontario high school for that extra year, but McGill did offer a pre-acceptance year. There were class tests and Provincial exams, but all four were good students. They would make it. So the Fearless Four were on their separate ways but they knew they would always be friends.

The big question was who would they invite to the graduation dance! King had no doubts. "I'm going to take my cousin Lehlia Orwell," he announced. "I've met her a few times, and she's nice. She's not a real cousin - only through my Great Aunt Felicity. I already asked her, and she said yes. Her dad is at CP Rail."

"Ah ha!! Methinks something is afoot there!" Michael laughed. "How about you, Floro? Who are you going to ask?"

For the first time ever they saw that Florenzo was flustered. "I...I..." He turned to Gordon. "Do you think your sister Anita would...?"

They looked at him in astonishment. Anita was a big girl, big like Gordon was big. "She likes you, Floro. I know she does. She blushes every time I say you're coming over. Ask her. I think she would."

"She's nice," they agreed, mentally rolling their eyes at the image. She could pick him up and dance around with him, but Floro could handle it. He is big in spirit as Gordo is in body, King thought.

And that was not the end of the surprises. Gordon shifted uneasily. Heck, might as well just say it, he thought. "I want to ask your sister, Marianne, Floro. That would make us quite a picture! She's about half my size. So everyone will get confused about who is whose partner!" The ice was broken; if Gordo could laugh at himself, so could Floro.

The biggest decisions agreed on, they went on to the details - tuxes, which restaurant for their dinner, corsages - all the details of their first formal affair.

By the time they graduated they knew they were friends for life even though they were going separate ways. Michael would go to medical school; he had always known he wanted to be a doctor. Floro was equally sure of himself. He would study mathematics and physics. What that would lead him to he wasn't sure. He would explore. Gordon was heading for Agriculture School. He would be a biologist, a plant scientist, make things grow.

King was less sure. He wanted to go into the family business, but was not sure how to go about it. He talked it over with Mr. Allen. "I think I should get a university degree, Sir. It seems important these days to have something beyond high school."

"That's right, son. But why are you hesitating?"

"Well, what I really understand is the best is a Master's Degree in Business Administration. But that would take at least six years. And I would like to know more about the family business so it all would make sense to me. I think I would have to know something about production before I could be a good administrator."

"That's sound thinking, son. What do you want me to do?"

"I thought maybe I could work in the shops at the same time I go to university. I'd like to work in the shops somewhere. It wouldn't have to be an important job - just get better acquainted with how things are done, what problems and issues come up. I guess I was hoping you would put in a good word for me, sir?"

"That I will do, my boy. I think your Grandpa will be pleased." Even though he would never admit it, Tom thought with amusement.

King finished his breakfast and, rising from the table, asked to be excused. "Just a moment, boy."

"Yes, Sir?" Surprised, King sat back down.

"Hmm. Your Father and I have a graduation present for you." He held out a paper. "We needed another car anyway. Can't have you calling on Simon and the car all the time. Got you a little Mercedes."

"A...a...car? For me?" King was too stunned to think. "You? And Father?"

"Boy to drive you. Bertie. Someone Simon knew of."

"Oh Grandpa! That's wonderful! I don't know how to thank you. Just wonderful!"

"Go on. Boy's in the kitchen. Write your Father. Thank him."

"Oh, yes sir!" A car! He couldn't believe it. Wait until the others saw this!

CHAPTER SIXTEEN

Charles Kingsley Randolph III

Montreal - 1943

King dropped the flowers on a chair, shed his coat, and went quickly to Lehlia. "Sorry I wasn't here, darling. Couldn't get out, flights all cancelled - storm was really bad. Are you all right? You look tired?" He leaned to kiss her, whispering, "Charles Kingsley Ran....." He stammered to a stop, glancing at the child and back to Lehlia. "Is he well? His face looks so.. ... so pinched."

"The doctor said he is fine, healthy - seven and a half pounds?" Lehlia's voice rose plaintively.

"He's so tiny. His face is so...thin. And his eyes! Almost like...I don't know...strange!"

He reached out as if to smooth the black hair back from the broad forehead, but drew back with an uncertain shake of his head, changed direction, and straightened the twisted cord of the call button lying by Lehlia's pillow, then brushed a stray red-gold curl back from her cheek.

"He doesn't look like... He's got Pa Kingsley's pointed ears right enough. But he doesn't look ... he looks like a...like a...little drowned rat." The gruff inflection bit the words off.

The boy, black hair plastered from a widow's peak low on his forehead, seemed little more than a wisp in the curve of Lehlia's arm. He moved in the blanket, tiny hands fluttering.

"I'm...sorry, King. Babies ... always tiny, aren't they? His face... fill out...?" Her voice wavered.

King pulled a chair over to the bedside, dropped heavily into it, and sat holding her hand and stroking her cheek. He was so tired. Those words! Miserably he tried to erase them, but his mind shouted at him - his own words, and then the lines from The Rubaiyat[4], "The moving finger writes, and having writ, moves on." Over and over. "Nor all your tears wash away a word of it." He kissed her fingers, pressed her hand to his tired eyes, and restlessly smoothed the ribbons of her peignoir. "I thought I'd never get here," he said tiredly.

"But you are here," Lehlia smiled up at him, her face warm.

King relaxed; it would be all right. He shook himself and wrapped the ribbons around his fingers. "Good thing we had the nurse. I was frantic when I couldn't get a flight out. Why don't you sleep a bit? I'll go in, check in, see what's needed, come back this evening."

Lehlia wiped her tears from the baby's face.

They wrapped him in soft warm things and took him to a new place. He could hear the woman but could not feel her near him. He was warm, but he felt alone. This place was big and empty. He whimpered, beginning to cry. He felt the woman again, soft and warm. Something came in his mouth. Sweet filled his mouth and he sucked greedily. Sweet and warm filled him and he slept.

In the time that followed he saw light and dark and began to know the rhythm. A brisk, busy woman bathed him. She rubbed him with something nice, his arms and legs and down between his legs and all over his back so he began to know his parts. Her hands were big. The brisk woman put warm things on him and took him to the soft woman..

"You want to go see your mama, don't you, little one," she murmured. "Here you are then, here's your mama. Here he is, Madam, a sturdy little one, I must say."

So she was called Mama/Madam. Again he sucked and the sweet warm filled him. Mama held him awkwardly for a minute. His eyes looked at Mama's eyes. Mama was not like the brisk woman. Her face was not square and wrinkled. Mama's face was round and smooth. He liked Mama's face. But she held him away from her.

"Isn't he the handsome one, Madam, all dressed up for the ceremony? It's a beautiful dress, Madam, the hand embroidery and the lace."

"Yes, a family heirloom. You take him please, Nurse." She turned uncertainly to King, "Well here he is then. We'd better go on to the church. Everyone will be there. I hope Beth and Morris come. I want them to sit near us. They don't know everyone." Morris was King's friend from the office, the Vice-

President for Finance, and Lehlia had become friends with Beth.

"'Everyone!' Won't be many,"

"You know our friends will be there—Mr. Allen and our group. A christening is not supposed to be a big public affair anyway. It's a sacred moment in our son's life. We only want our closest friends to be there, to witness the commitment." Besides, she thought, Anita told me that Floro spread the news throughout the whole Italian community; we may have a good many we don't even know.

Simon dropped them at the entrance to St. George's on de la Gauchetière Street. "Simon, you go back and get Mr. Charles and the others, and then park in the lot west of the station."

"Yes, sir. We'll be right back."

"I hope Flora is here. I want them to sit up front with us, King."

"Everyone can sit up front, Lehlia. Won't be many here."

Charles Kingsley Randolph III was born at the baptism. Someone said that name patting water on his face. That name frightened him. It was big. He didn't belong to that name. He was The Boy - Little Rat, and the big name hid in a dark hole in his mind.

The family party after the ceremony was held at Redstone Manor on Fort Street. The guests were in a jolly mood. It had been more than a year since the Fast Friends and their wives had gotten together. They were eager to congratulate King and Lehlia on this addition to the crowd. And they were in the mood to give King a bit of ribbing for being the last to add to their numbers. They now counted three 'nephews' and two 'nieces', as they called them, or 'godsons' and 'goddaughters' assigned unanimously to all.

King's uneasiness melted as the friendly banter flowed. "Just look at those eyes! He's taking everyone's measure— probably knows all our secrets!" And "That forehead—a big brain. I'm putting him down for Harvard!" Then the more modest comments from Anita and Marianne: "He's adorable" and "His eyes are following movement—that's unusual." Lehlia glowed.

Morris and Beth lingered after the other friends left. They had been overawed by the noisy familiarity of the others. Beth hung over the bassinet, looking at the child. She couldn't see the great things in this child that the others had raved about. He really looked quite peculiar to her. But she had to say something. "So cute. Isn't he cute, Morris? He's so tiny. Such a tiny face, sort of shaped like a little...... well.... mouse. So cute." Her voice was thin and high and she giggled when she said 'cute'.

"Yeah." King replied, suddenly depressed again. "Yeah, a mouse. Pa Kingsley wished those pointed ears on him, a family trademark."

This was the voice that had called him a little rat. This was The Man who belonged with Mama. The Boy looked carefully at him. He was bigger even than the brisk woman, and his face was sharp. His mouth turned down. Small eyes. The Boy felt alone when he looked at The Man.

"Look at his eyes," *another man's voice.* "Looks like he's

listening, or thinking."

"He can't be; he's barely two weeks old." That was Mama talking. "I don't know. He's just different, Flora. He makes me feel... well... strange."

"Not surprising. To have a baby around after all these years. It will take some getting used to." *The Flora woman.* "You're lucky to have him at your age, you know. "

"Yeah, lucky." The bitter sadness in King's voice cut off the conversation.

Lehlia trailed her fingers across her face, brushing away guilty, unshed tears. "Take him upstairs, Nurse. I'm so tired."

Flora and Morris left soon, stammering good-byes, "So lucky...bright eyes...didn't make a sound...really very cute."

"That's all they can say about him--cute!!" King's voice was harsh, raw. Why, he thought. 'Cute'! Why couldn't he just be a normal baby? Why did this happen to me?

CHAPTER SEVENTEEN

He wants To Belong

Montreal - 1945

The days were spent in cold time and cold, empty space. The brisk woman, who was called Nurse, bathed him, dressed and undressed him, and fed him. She said things to him, "Here, now. Time for a nice bath;" "Arm in;" "Phew, what a mess;" "Let's turn you a bit. More comfortable that way?" She moved him from sleeping bed to riding bed, to warm red blanket on the floor, to a seat that swung softly and let him sit up.

When Nurse took him down to the kitchen, though, she talked a lot with The People. The People were two men and two women. Cook/Hilda belonged to the kitchen, he knew. She was always there and was always doing things at the stove and the long shelf. She made the kitchen smell good - sometimes sweet and sometimes tingly in his nose. She always smiled at him. Her face was round, and it was red when the stove was hot. She wore a white dress on top of her other dress. Sometimes she took it off when she sat down to have a cup of tea. She said, "I'll just take me apron off for a bit and have a cup of tea, eh?"

He learned the words and stored them in his mind with the pictures of things and the smells and tastes of things: apron, cabinet, sugar, saucer, spoon, milk, teapot, spice, saltnpepper, toast, graham cracker.

The other one wasn't old like everyone else. Cook called her Meggs sometimes, but most of the time Little Miss or You There. You There went all over the house, he saw her everywhere he went. She carried a fluffy thing and flicked it around on chairs and pictures. But sometimes she did things with the beds, and other times with a pail of water. She did strange things, too. Sometimes she closed her eye at him and poked him in the middle. Then Nurse scolded her, "Leave the Boy alone Little Miss. You'll set him off and then who has to manage? Not Little Miss Meggs, for sure." You There/Little Miss laughed and ran off.

Cook and Nurse sometimes talked about the man and woman. He listened carefully.

"They're very strange for parents."

"Well, they are pretty old to be new parents - middle aged, don't you know." That was Cook/Hilda's voice. She talked slow, and her voice sounded like something he had heard - music. It went up and down like the music Mama played in the small parlour, low and soft. He felt warm inside when she talked.

"I try to get Madam to hold him, but she makes some excuse - she's tired, or she has a headache. And Mr. King is worse. He just freezes up if I even bring the boy near him."

"Mrs. Randolph was sick a lot, eh?" Cook tried to explain. "And he was a peaked little newborn, that is true enough, see?"

"I've heard Mr. King say Little Rat. What if he understands? Look at those big eyes; always looks like he's watching and listening."

Why was Nurse whispering?

"Madam feels like she disappointed Mr. King. She wanted a perfect baby so Mr. King would be proud. A man needs to see himself in his son, to see what he wants to be. It's normal."

Cook liked Mama, and Papa too, he could tell. Her voice was louder now. And it just went down this time and stopped hard. She didn't want Nurse to go on any more. She didn't want Nurse to say bad things about Mama.

"Well he's healthy, and he's strong. They could do a lot worse. He's filling out more, too - doesn't look so pinched and old. He did look a bit like a little drowned rat at first, I must say. That thin little face and tiny chin, and with that black hair way down on his forehead, and his pointed ears. Not everyone can have a Gerber baby. Might as well accept it." Nurse's brisk voice settled the discussion.

Little Rat was not his name; his name was Boy, or Child, or The Boy. But Little Rat was the dark shadow that lurked underneath.

That image was there. So they were disquieted, disturbed, but somehow not surprised that he never crawled in the normal way. He scurried around on all fours, hands and feet propelling him from room to room, like a dog, or...a... cat...a... They shied away guiltily from the hurtful word.

In time Nurse went away and Nanny came. He was seldom taken to Mama now. Nanny watched over him in the big rooms upstairs, fussing in a low, soft voice. When she took him down to the warm, happy kitchen, Cook and Nanny talked and laughed for long periods. The Boy sat in his chair carefully picking up the Cheerios[5] on his tray one-by-one. He put his finger into each little hole, concentrating intently.

"He's strong enough, and he can do things with his hands," Nanny told Cook. "He never drops anything. You should see him stack up the blocks, five or six high and he never fumbles them. Just look at him with those Cheerios, so careful and precise. That's the way he is with everything."

"It's a caution." Cook handed him a piece of the hard bread he liked to chew on.

"A caution is right. That's a true word. He's a strange one. And always on the go now that he walks - not walks, runs! He's so quick I have to watch him every minute he's awake. Take my eyes off him and he's gone - no telling where. Down in the parlour or the drawing room, sometimes in the conservatory."

"Funny," Cook said. "You'd think when he goes like that, he'd come down here to the kitchen. He knows the kitchen; you'd think he would want to be around people."

"Oh, I think he wants to be around people all right," Nanny's voice was sharp. "If you want my opinion, he's after his mama and his father. He goes where they go, the conservatory where his mama does the flowers, Mr. King's library. He was scooting around in the parlour the other day when Mrs. R. had her bridge group here - peeking behind the ladies and grunting away like he does."

"That was really odd, queer; he went around behind every one of the ladies and then stood behind his mother grunting and rocking. Almost like he was trying to tell her something. But the grunting got everyone nervous, and Madam was so upset she just threw down her hand and everything stopped till I got the little rascal out of there. You can be sure Madam gave me the what-for later."

"Strange about that grunting. He's old enough to be at least saying a few words."

"At least the grunting is better than his screeching. You didn't hear him the time I put the baby harness on him. You never heard such a caterwauling - him kicking and screaming, Madam crying, Mr. King shouting. I thought the boy was going to have a fit. It took Simon and me both to hold him and get a tranquilizer down him. I didn't try that again. No more baby harness!"

"They should get him tested." Cook sighed, "Joseph tells me to mind my place, but I think they should do something."

The Boy was hungry and tired and began to rock and grunt. "Uh! Uh! Uh!"

"Well, it's back to Siberia for the two of us," Nanny barked out an angry laugh. "The view is good, but the third floor is a long way from anything you might call ordinary family life. That's what they want, so that's where we have to be. Not good for The Boy though, I'd say."

Back upstairs Nanny sat him in his table chair with quick harsh words, "Sit there. Stupid kid. Can't even let me have a few minutes with Cook." She busied herself at the small kitchen area, "It's going to be squash and applesauce for you today."

She made it sound bad, but The Boy didn't know why. He liked squash; it tasted good and filled his empty spots. He rolled it around in his mouth, tasting strong at the back of his tongue, yellow sweet in the middle, and sharp on the edges. Squash was interesting.

Nanny continued to grumble as she spooned the squash in, "Crazy family. Don't want you is what I think. Leastwise they can't seem to stand having you around them. Especially Mr. King. That Little Rat business - enough to chill your heart. OK now, let's finish this squash up, every bite. You want to see Peter Rabbit smile at you, don't you?" Nanny kept chattering, talking to keep herself company. She certainly did not believe that the child took in a word she said. He was old enough to understand, but she was sure there was something not quite right with him.

Nanny put The Boy down for a nap and wound up the music box over his crib. The soft sounds tinkled up and down in his head and the red and yellow and blue birds flew around and around over him. The Boy lay quietly watching them, feeling warm and full of squash. He slept.

Nanny cleaned the little kitchen humming to herself. She gave the counter a final swish with the damp cloth, peeked at the child, and took herself down to the kitchen for her afternoon tea.

When the boy woke up it was quiet. He sat up and looked around. Nanny was gone. He stood up against the side of his bed and rocked quietly. Then he pulled himself up and over the side and roamed around the room. He smelled the squash in his bottom, enjoying it again. He wandered out and down the stairs to the next floor. He liked the big mirror in the sunny room with yellow and green walls; he stood for a while looking at himself, and touched the face of the boy in the mirror.

But no one was there, so he climbed down the stairs and went to Father's library. There were men at the big table, blue suits, talking seriously. He stood in the doorway. The tiny old man with a folded-in mouth sat on one side of Father. The Boy could see only his face and shoulders above the table. His eyes were closed. Sleeping. The other-side man was big and he moved a lot, reaching across the table at the others. The Boy could see two backs. More men. These were all Father's men.

Father said "dollars" and then "hockey arena," and "sports centre." The men nodded and wrote on papers they had.

The pushing man with the loud voice said, "It's too much; we can't make it, King."

Father banged his fist on the table, "We will make it, John. It's the ideal location - streetcars, access, parking... everything. We need the new arena for Montreal to stay competitive. We don't just have Toronto any more - we've got all of the teams in the states. To say nothing of the Russians." He looked around the table and, glancing up saw The Boy in the doorway. His face froze and he muttered, "Jesus Christ, how did you get down here?" He walked toward the child, then stopped, sniffing and scowling. "My God you stink!" Snatching up the house phone he called the nursery, Nanny's room, and finally located her in the kitchen. His angry voice brought her hurrying to the library.

"Take this child and get him cleaned up. He shouldn't be down here. Take care of him. Take him for a walk or something, but keep him out of these rooms."

That evening as King mixed their pre-dinner drinks, he complained angrily to Lehlia, "For Christ sake, the Board was here! There he was in his sleeping shirt...and dirty! Just staring with those big eyes. It was embarrassing. I don't know what they thought. Why is he like that? What is wrong with him anyway?" King stammered in frustrated, angry phrases.

Lehlia decided to talk with Nanny, see if they could come up with some strategy to persuade the child to talk. She asked Nanny to come to her sitting room when the boy was sleeping.

"What do you think, Mrs. Michaels? Shouldn't he be talking by now? Saying a few words at least?"

"Children develop at different rates, Madam. You really can't say there's a rule or anything." Nanny was not going to commit herself. It could reflect on her. But of course he should be talking, she thought.

"But he should be saying words, shouldn't he? Mama...car...bye-bye...cookie? Things like that? Most babies say things like that by two or three, don't they? Even sentences, don't you think? He's almost three. Has he ever spoken to you? Or to Hilda or anyone?"

"I have never heard him speak, Madam. And Hilda says he has never spoken to her."

"He has to be able to communicate. I get so worried." Lehlia twisted a soft handkerchief in nervous fingers.

Oh he communicates, Nanny wanted to say; his screeches and grunts make it pretty clear what he likes and doesn't like. "Well, he lets you know if he wants something."

"Have you tried to teach him to say words?"

"Teach? No, Madam. I can't say I have. I don't know how to teach. I point to a picture - a boy, a girl, a cat or dog and I say the word, and I point to the picture again and say the word again and wait. But he never repeats anything ."

"That sounds good to me. I just don't understand it. He does seem bright in other ways. Maybe we could try to sort of...force him? Keep something away from him until he says the word? Like 'milk' for example. He likes milk?"

"Might work, Madam."

"We'll try that tomorrow morning before breakfast, when he's hungry." Lehlia thought, maybe it will work, I have to try.

CHAPTER EIGHTEEN

Potential

Montreal – 1945-1947

"Where were you, Lehlia? Where did you go?" King turned impatiently from the drinks cart. "I wanted to talk to you. We've got a real problem. It's this western development business. Some of our best men are quitting - moving to Toronto. Even Sam Holton. He told me today. I can't believe it." King took another sip of his brandy. "Oh, sorry. What do you want?"

Lehlia waved a 'not important' gesture and leaned her head against the wing of the chair, covering her eyes with her hand.

"Well, do you want a brandy? Or wine? What do you want?"

"Wine, I guess, King," her voice was low and shaky.

King poured the wine and brought it to her, but she didn't look up or reach for the glass. "What's wrong, Lehlia? What's the matter? Don't you feel well?"

She shook her head, reached out for the wine glass and took a long drink. "We...we...Nanny and I...we were trying something."

"Trying something? What? With the Boy?"

Lehlia nodded mutely. "We...we thought we'd get him to just say one word, King. Just milk! We decided not to let him eat anything until he said 'milk.' Just milk, King. I'm sure he could say it. I know he can." She wouldn't meet King's angry glare. "I told Nanny we had to teach him to talk. She reads to him, but..." She turned away rubbing her left arm nervously.

"You don't have to teach a kid to talk. No one taught me to talk. Every kid talks, for Pete's sake. We've got to find out what is wrong. We've got to stop shilly-shallying. When is his next appointment with Westover? You've got to get him to do some tests, find out what can be done. He's four years old, for god's sake. All kids talk by the time they're four."

"Tuesday. Dr. Westover did say something last month about a hearing test and some coordination tests."

King shifted restlessly, "I don't want to just hear this 'he's healthy and strong' business. We've heard that for three years. I want to know what is wrong. They've got to be able to tell us something."

When Lehlia returned from the visit with Dr. Westover, she sent The Boy upstairs with Nanny and met King who was pacing around the study, squeezing an exercise ball, unable to relax. "Well, what did Westover say, Lehlia? What about those tests?" King kneaded the ball automatically, then tossed it to his left hand and squeezed again.

"I don't know, King. He said he couldn't find anything

wrong," Lehlia's voice wavered unhappily. "He said he is growing normally, and his hand-eye coordination is good. He said that was important. His hearing seems to be all right, though he didn't always respond - as if he was dreaming. And there's nothing wrong with his mouth or vocal chords."

"We don't need the doctor to tell us that!" King snorted. "We hear his screams and grunts loud and clear. He can make enough noise. But what about talking? A four-year-old should be able to talk, for God's sake! Didn't he suggest anything?"

"He did say he would make an appointment at the Neuro for some kind of special test if we really want it." Lehlia wasn't sure how King would take that suggestion.

"What kind of test? What does that mean, a 'special test'?" King froze in his restless pacing, "Does he think there is something wrong with his…?"

"I didn't really understand it too well." Lehlia felt battered by King's demanding tone. She shut down what she had planned to say. It was better not to offer too much when King was in this impatient, critical mood. "I think we should both go and talk with Dr. Westover."

"Does it mean a tumour or something?"

"I don't know, King. Maybe you should call him. You would understand it better."

King paced again, tossing the exercise ball nervously from hand to hand. "Why, Lehlia, why? Why should this happen to me! No, both of us will go." He turned to his desk and opened his agenda, "Monday morning at ten or Thursday afternoon at three are possible. Make the appointment." He picked up some papers from his desk. Lehlia turned toward the door, hesitated and turned back. She wanted to suggest a speech pathologist, to say that Dr. Westover was just a general family doctor, to talk about special schools. But King was already focused on work. Lehlia and the boy had been dealt with and dismissed from his thoughts.

On Thursday afternoon Lehlia and King sat stiffly on the blond oak visitors' chairs in Dr. Westover's office. King had been in the office before and took no time to examine the decor. He took quality for granted, expected it of anyone he dealt with. So he scarcely noticed the curly maple panelling (though Lehlia had talked about how beautiful it was) or the pair of water colours that surely were Turners, or the small Lladro figure of a woman with child that sat on the bookshelf behind the desk. Suddenly that figurine irritated him, reminded him of their own problem. He spoke brusquely, "What is this business about a special test, Westover? What are you saying?" King demanded.

"Actually, I've been thinking a lot about the boy since I talked with you, Mrs. Randolph. Probably the test I was thinking about should not be necessary," Dr. Westover said. He had begun to realize that he should protect himself. He should be very careful of what he said, what he recommended. It was time to get some backup support. "The thing is, Mr. Randolph, Mrs. Randolph, the boy seems bright enough, alert enough"

"Bright enough. Alert enough." King interrupted. "What we want to know is why he can't talk!"

"Not talking is only part of the syndrome, Mr. Randolph. He doesn't respond to people. Or, that is, he reacts by watching, by seeming to throw up a wall, or a shield."

"Syndrome. What does that mean, syndrome?"

"Yes, the syndrome, the pattern, the not talking, the

209

watching, shielding. It all makes me think that perhaps some work with a child psychologist, or someone trained to work with special children would be useful."

"Well, what do you recommend, Westover?" King spoke impatiently. "There must be something that can be done. There has to be someone who can give us some idea of what can be done." King was accustomed to getting answers; he wanted a solution.

"It might be worthwhile to get a child psychologist to work with him for a while. They do quite remarkable things to bring children out of a shell, so to speak. I could give you names of some very good people."

"I think we should try, King. Nanny is good to the boy, but she's not trained, not even a teacher. We have to get professional help, someone who knows more." Lehlia spoke hesitantly, but she was desperate to do something positive, to make this child into a son King could be proud of.

"You would want to meet with several psychologists to select one you both feel comfortable with."

"Give us the names, Westover. We want to get The Boy started. He's already four. He needs discipline. The nanny is too easy on him."

"Well, yes, OK." Dr. Westover recognized King's readiness to find some excuse, to place blame somewhere. He would not accept the responsibility of working with the child himself. They would have to get the boy into a programme.

"I've put three names and phone numbers on this card. All three are very well regarded."

Lehlia read the names slowly, "Dr. Joseph Aarons...Dr. Mona Carlucca...Dr. Francine Roy..."

"It's pronounced more like 'Rwa,' Mrs. Randolph. Dr.

Roy is French."

"Well, do they speak English, Westover? We want the boy to be able to talk. That's what this is all about."

"Would they know how to help the boy - find out why it is that he can't speak? Why he reacts so wildly to anyone? That's what I want, someone to find out why. To help us so we can help him learn." Lehlia wanted more for him than just talk; she wanted a normal, ordinary child.

"As I say, all three are good. Dr. Carlucca takes only individual children. That might be good. I spoke with her; she uses a variety of techniques. Dr. Aarons usually asks both parents to be involved. Many psychologists do, of course. Talk with all of them before you choose, face-to-face."

"No need for all of us to spend the time. Mrs. Randolph can meet them, she'll be the one who takes the boy in. There's nothing wrong with us, Sir."

Dr. Westover stood to walk them out of the office, continuing as if reading from a card, "Take the boy in. Choose someone you are comfortable with, someone you feel you can work with." He shook King's hand, and nodded at Lehlia. "Let me know how it works out. And good luck."

CHAPTER NINETEEN

A Special Child?

Montreal – 1947

Dr. Nona Carlucca was always pleasant, always courteous, but Lehlia still felt very much in awe of her. She was a tall, spare woman with salt and pepper hair cut in a short bob. Her eyes, slate grey, were not unkind, but focused, watchful.

She wore what Lehlia had concluded was her uniform: a straight skirt, taupe, ending at mid-calf and loose enough to move around in easily. Her tailored shirt, buttoned to the collar, had a faint rose stripe and dusty rose collar and cuffs. She wore a narrow satin tie with rhodolite pull; the taupe jacket hung over the back of her office chair. A colour-coded façade, the thought flashed through Lehlia's mind.

The whole office complex had made Lehlia somewhat uneasy from her first visit. It is severe, she thought. The furniture is solid and quite beautiful for a doctor's office, rosewood and creamy leather. The Persian carpet is a good one, filling the large office and just worn enough to reveal that it must have been in someone's family for a long time. The two framed reproductions are good, Picasso's blue period Man with a Guitar, and the Modigliani, Head of a Woman in Orange.

Lehlia liked both of the prints, and she wondered again why it was, after all these months, she still felt overpowered by the office. Suddenly she thought, there is nothing in the office that says this is a place for children to get well. There are no toys, nothing cuddly and soft, no pictures of children - not even family pictures, she realized. There is nothing child-sized either, except in the viewing room. Everything is warm looking, softly pleasant to the eye, but definitely for adults, not children.

Months later Lehlia and the psychologist watched the child and the young para-professional from the viewing room. The Doctor spoke quietly, "You see, Mrs. Randolph, he turns his back on Clara. If she moves in front of him, he swings his back around. He does the same with me - has done every session - from the first one last June. As now, he just sits and rocks, and brushes something against his face - anything, whatever he happens to pick up, a block, the doll's blanket, the little bottle."

"Does he talk at all - say anything? That is what we are so worried about. It's been almost a year - every week. Surely something should get better. He's nearly five years old. Can't you do anything for him, Dr. Carlucca? Won't he ever be able to talk?" Lehlia's voice shook.

"I'm sorry, Mrs. Randolph. I don't think we should accept it as a failure. He is a very special child, but I don't want to mislead you either."

"What do you mean by 'special child,' Dr. Carlucca? Why do you say 'not a failure?' I just want him to be normal, a normal little boy who talks. 'Special' sounds so…so…hopeless."

"We have tried many different techniques: mirroring, physical manipulation, withholding things he likes, music and rhythm. I am convinced that he is aware of what we say, and of all that goes on around him. He just doesn't react in typical patterns."

Dr. Carlucca was using textbook phrases to skirt around her message. She recognized Lehlia's weak self-confidence, and believed the problems lay as much with the family as with the boy. She was going to suggest a school for special children, but she wanted Lehlia to see the need for it herself. "Watch what he does when no one is with him." She touched a button that activated a silent pager and Clara glanced up at the two-way mirror, nodded, spoke briefly to the boy, and left him alone in the room.

The boy sat for a minute, and, ducking his head, looked around in all directions without changing his position. He's checking to make sure he is alone, Lehlia thought. Then he got up and started moving around, touching things. He climbed on Clara's chair and, standing up and holding on to the back, rocked it and moved it around the room, smiling to himself. Soon he turned around on the chair, hung over the seat and scooted the chair with his hands. Tiring of this, he went to the big blocks in the corner and, piling them carefully, built what was clearly a house.

"Now watch," Dr. Carlucca said, and told her assistant to return to the room. Clara did, making considerable noise with the doorknob. The child quickly laid the small doll's blanket over the house he had built as if to hide it, and Clara found him in the position she had left him, brushing the small red wooden bottle against his face.

"You see, Mrs. Randolph. He won't, or can't, relate to people - can't, or won't, communicate. I could say I would continue to work with him, but I truthfully do not see the potential for much progress in working with him in this single client situation."

"But that's what you do, isn't it? Isn't that what you said was best? Work with each child alone? Why have we gone on like this all year then?"

"You will remember, Mrs. Randolph, I suggested when you first brought the boy in that it might be useful to have you and Mr. Randolph work as a family unit with young Charles. You did say that you were both only children, and that you were not very close to your own parents. It often helps to have all of the members of the family work through the problems together."

Lehlia could not meet Dr. Carlucca's eyes; she knew that King would not accept such a programme. "Mr. Randolph is so busy with the company and with his community activities. He's around the boy all the time at home anyway, so an hour or so here couldn't make that much difference, could it?"

"Does he talk with the boy? Play with him?" The Doctor controlled her impatience and probed.

"Play? No, King never plays. He has so many demands on his time," Lehlia recognized implied criticism and defended King self-consciously.

"Well, we do believe he needs social stimulation in a training situation. We suggest as an alternative, the type of school described in this brochure. They work with children of limited abilities. I am sorry that we have not been able to reach him, in spite of all we have tried." She touched Lehlia's arm, directing her back into the office.

Lehlia vacillated between fear and anger. Dr. Carlucca acted sympathetic, but it is a cold, impersonal kind of sympathy, she thought. How can she dismiss the child as "hopeless" so easily? We are being thrown out. What is a "special child?" What does she mean "limited abilities?" Lehlia was trembling, unhappiness pinching her eyes. She wanted to cry out in frustration.

Clara had turned the child over to Nanny in the reception room, and they left hurriedly. Lehlia stumbled into the waiting car as Simon opened the door. Turning her back on Nanny and the boy, she huddled in the corner and burst into hysterical sobs.

At home Lehlia hurried into the house. Simon and Nanny exchanged unhappy glances, and The Boy rocked and grunted wild unhappy sounds, "Uh--uh--uh--uh!" That doctor made him feel bad. She watched all the time. He felt her eyes trying to make him do things. She made Mama feel bad too.

That evening Lehlia waited for King in the small parlour, drinks cart and newspapers at hand. She was determined to be calm and rational, to discuss the necessity to take more positive action for the boy, to talk about the different choices that had been worrying around in her head all afternoon. She started calmly enough, but her fears and her insecurity took over. She spilled it all out to King, "I can't...I don't. She said...said he's hopeless! It's my fault. How dare she? No potential. Why, King, why?" She sobbed again.

King's face grew hard. "Don't cry Lehlia. It's not your fault. It's got to be something from way back in the family - Pa

Kingsley's heritage. He was always unstable."

Lehlia turned away, "Heritage," she repeated in quiet desperation, then turned back, determined to make King help her. "Surely it's not all heritage, King. He seems so bright in so many ways. She made me so angry. How can she possibly say he is aware of everything but has no potential? 'No potential', what does that mean? How can that be? We have to find someone who can give him the right kind of help. Do you think he is hopeless, King? What was there about Pa Kingsley that has come to this?"

King crushed the paper he had picked up, "Pa, yes, Pa Kingsley," he muttered. "You didn't know him. You wouldn't understand." His mind flashed an image of Pa Kingsley - the first Kingsley Randolph born to the immigrants Theodore and Margaret Randolph now long since dead. And Pa's sneering glare that had always told King he was a dead loss - that he would never measure up. He slumped in his chair.

No potential. Hopeless. He huddled inside the armoire, whimpering silently inside himself. Mama and Papa couldn't help him. It was heritage. He wanted to tell Mama and Papa that the doctor stood over him and squashed him down. But they knew what he was. The words ran through his head again. Hopeless. No potential. Unstable. He hated that doctor. She made Mama cry.

He had to find some potential. He would learn to read all of Papa's papers and he would listen to everyone. He would get some potential so Mama would not cry.

217

CHAPTER TWENTY

He Learns To Read

Montreal – 1947

That doctor told Mama he had no potential. He hated that doctor. She made Mama cry. He felt himself in a great emptiness.

He was four. He didn't know what four meant exactly, but it had something to do with him, how big he was and what he should do. He knew all his body parts, but he didn't know what he was inside.

The People were around him and they talked and laughed and touched each other. They told each other what they were. "You are so good-hearted, Hilda." "We can always depend on you, Simon." "Joseph, you are so wise." They even told Meggs, "You are a caution, girl." Sometimes Nanny called him "Little Pig" but he knew what a pig looked like, so he knew he wasn't a pig. He wanted to be part of the people so he would know what he was inside. Maybe then he would have some potential.

They dressed him and gave him food and moved him from one place to another. They talked at him, said 'eat this' or 'nap time now'. And they talked about him, called him The Boy or The Child or whispered Little....... But they didn't tell him who or what he was. He wanted to know who he was. He wanted to belong with Mama again. He thought he remembered belonging with her once.

He remembered two quite well - there was a cake with pretty blue flowers on it. There were pink and blue twisted things sticking up. Father touched them with a little stick of wood that burst into a bright light when he hit it on the side of a box. He learned the names they said: candles, matches, fire.

Mother said, "One--two, one--two candles." There was a brown teddy bear, and Mother touched its eyes and said "One - two," and then she touched his eyes and said "One - two." He banged his spoon on his dish one--two, but no one said, "One--two." Mother took the spoon away and said, "Don't do that, you'll break your dish."

Now they said four and he ate his cake upstairs.

Nanny said, "Come here, child. I'll read to you." When she told him the pictures she talked very slow and pointed at the little black marks on the page. Nanny showed him a picture of brown, feathery owls with big yellow eyes sitting near the old barn. She pointed at the owls and said in a sing-song voice,

"Three big barn owls sat
Behind the old barn door.
One flew in beside them
And then there were four."

She pointed at the black marks as she said the picture.
"Four, four. That's what you are, child, four." Then she
pointed at the marks at the beginning and said, "Three, three.
That's what you were last year. You were three, now you are
four."

This was very exciting; the black marks said three
and four. He liked it when Nanny showed him
pictures in his books and told him about them.

Nanny went on, telling him about the lamb.

"Ma--ry--had--a--lit--tle--lamb
Its--fleece--was--white--as--snow.

Nanny always stopped and pointed to the picture and said,
"See the little lamb? See how white it is - like snow before it
gets all dirty." Then she started over in her sing-song voice,
"Ma--ry--had--a--."

He began to see that the black marks told the
story to Nanny so she could tell it to him. That was
what Nanny called 'reading'. Some marks said "Mary"
or "lamb." All of the little black marks were in
bunches that Nanny called "words," so he began to
look for the words as Nanny's finger pointed.

Nanny liked the book about the Grinch. She made her

voice go all wavy and scary.

> "Every Who
> Down in Who-ville
>   Liked Christmas a lot
> But the Grinch did not!

She went on:

> "And the Grinch
> grabbed the tree,
> and he started to shove....

He remembered a tree like the one in the picture, with all the lights, and the pretty coloured things hanging on it. He began to wriggle and scooted down into the cushions on the couch. He was as bad as the Grinch. He had grabbed the silvery strings - they were so shiny. He pulled and the whole tree fell on him. Mother cried. Father yelled, "You rotten little--."

Nanny grabbed him and dragged him upstairs. "Now you've done it" she scolded. " Gone and spoiled the whole tree and the pretty decorations. It's into bed for you." The tree was gone the next day.

He hated the Grinch. He pushed the book away and kicked at it. So Nanny started a different book about Jack and the Beanstalk and the bad giant. There must be books that would tell him how to do good things, where to find potential. There were so many books in Father's library. If Father read them, they must tell good things.

The next day he slipped quietly into the library. The

biggest book in Father's library stood on a narrow table of its own. He pulled the little stepper over and climbed up to look at that book. It was always open and the pages were very thin. His fingers twitched to turn the pages, but he was afraid so he looked at the ones that were open.

There were lots of black mark words, but not many pictures. He saw a bird. It was kind of fat but not very big, and it had a long thin nose where a mouth should be, and long skinny legs with big toes. The bird had its name, SAND... and something more. He knew SAND from sandman. He ran his finger under the name words like Nanny did, and his mind said, SAND - SAND. Maybe SANDMAN was there too.

He looked for the man with a bag of sand like the picture in his book. He wasn't there but there was sand, sand, sand over and over again, lots of black marks saying sand... all down the page. There was sandman! But there was no picture. His fingers fluttered over the words. There were some queer shoes that had the name sand... something. He pored over the two pages, studying all of the sand words. He wanted to look at the other pages, but he was afraid he might hurt the book and Father would be angry.

He sighed. He was very tired, and Nanny would find him here if he didn't leave. He would come back tomorrow. He began to spend time in the library whenever Nanny was busy. He always went straight to the big book, eager to see what was there today. He studied each new page, examining any pictures carefully to make sense out of the black words. He listened and watched more and more intently as Nanny read and pointed.

So he soon knew many words, and he began to know the sounds of the black marks that made the words - hard sounds and soft sounds, clicking sounds and humming sounds. He was enchanted; he could put the sounds together to make the words Nanny said. He made Nanny's voice come into his mind saying the sounds as he studied the words in the big book. He thought he could make those sounds, maybe, but he was afraid. They would know he had been in Father's library. They would take the library away from him like everything else. He must keep Nanny's voice in his head.

The pictures in the big book were small, but they were very interesting. Some looked like they would do things - turn and turn, or lift things. He cut out pieces of his collared paper to look like parts in the pictures and tried to fit them together. He made a big wheel and a small wheel with stick-out bumps but they did not fit well enough to work like in the picture that said "cogwheels" and they wouldn't do anything.

When Nanny came in she scolded loudly, "Just look at the mess you've made. And who's going to clean it up? Not Mr. Rat the mess-maker. We'll just put the paper and scissors away for a week. Then maybe you'll learn." She stooped to take the scissors, but he began screaming in his piercing voice, so she threw everything back down, "All right, make a mess then. And live in it. A little pig is what you are."

The Boy held the two wheels, absorbed again trying to turn them together, to make them fit each other.

Lehlia's experience with Dr. Carlucca had disturbed her greatly. She investigated the school Dr. Carlucca suggested,

The Infant School for Special Children. It was in one of the renovated townhouses on St. Michael Street, just below Ste. Catherine. The sign had French words, l'Ecole pour les enfants inadaptés. "Enfants inadaptés" doesn't sound as promising as "special children," Lehlia thought.

The door was gaily painted, blue and yellow, and bright sun-catchers in the shapes of birds and fishes hung in the window. It looked cheerful and welcoming at least.

A young woman whose long brown hair flowed loose around her face met Lehlia at a desk near the front door. Lehlia introduced herself. "And this is my son. We have an appointment with Mrs. Sorenson."

"Ah, oui, un moment s'il vous plait." The woman, a girl really, Lehlia thought, hitched up her long granny dress and ran lightly up the stairs, calling, "Sarah, Madame Randolph est ici." A minute later she hurried back down. "Mme. Sorenson vient. Venez voir la salle de classe." Without waiting for a reply she opened a pair of wide double doors into what would formerly have been the main parlour.

Bewildered, Lehlia followed. She did not know what the girl had said. No one had ever spoken to her in French before. She knew that King had to speak French in the business world, but she had been shielded by money, cocooned by the deference paid to her as a desired customer. She was not pleased with the girl's casual dress and manner, nor by her presumption (that's what it is, Lehlia thought, presumption) that she should speak French. Already she was forming an unfavourable opinion of the place.

She recognized that the room must be a classroom. There were two low tables, several child-sized chairs, what looked like a ragged pile of dolls in one corner, a fire engine with red hats and rubber slickers piled on it in another, and an assortment of other toys, mostly wood or soft cloth. Four children each accompanied by an adult were in the room. Lehlia's guide addressed the room, "Bonjour tout le monde." She turned to Lehlia, "Mon nom est Marie, et--."

Lehlia interrupted hesitantly, "I don't speak French, I'm sorry."

"Oh, je m'excuse, madame. I am sorry. I say my name is Marie. Et cet petit la, that little one there is Franklin." She pronounced it as if it were two names, Frank Lynn.

Lehlia held her son by the shoulder, confused by the rapid flow of words, and by her efforts to absorb the meaning of what the children were doing. Franklin was fitfully attempting to fit different shapes of blocks into their matching holes. He looks at least ten or twelve, Lehlia thought. The Boy did better than that when he was two. His face, she shuddered mentally, he doesn't have any expression at all. And that little girl; at least she's clean and neat, but she is just sitting there. They don't seem to be doing much to teach them anything.

A small, thin-faced boy sidled up to Lehlia and took The Boy's hand. "Don't let Leon take his hand, Madame. Sometimes he bites." Lehlia jerked away frightened. His eyes had the look of a wild animal. He really might bite, she thought.

The Boy was interested. Frank Lynn was lonely. The woman didn't care whether he got the blocks right. He went over and stood watching. He took Frank Lynn's hand. He patted it and gave him the red block that had three sides. He took Frank Lynn's finger and made it go around the three sides. Then he took the finger and made it go around the three sides of the hole it should fit. He passed the finger around the block again. A little light came on in Frank Lynn's eyes. He put the block in its hole, twisting and turning until it fit. He sat rocking and smiling to himself. The Boy held his hand.

Lehlia looked at her watch. It was half past eleven. They had waited thirty minutes for Mrs. Sorenson and Lehlia didn't like much that she had seen so far. "We must go," she said to Marie. "Perhaps we will come at a more convenient time."

Her report to King was brief, "That is not a suitable place. The children there are not bright, and the women did not seem to be teaching, just sitting with the children, keeping them occupied. Nanny does more than that. If Dr. Carlucca actually visited that school, she must not expect much. I'm going to speak to the principal at The Study. She's the oldest Henderson girl. You know the family. Her mother was a MacIlvey, the chancellor's aunt. She would know the kind of school we should look for."

"Well, fine. But you need to find something soon. We have to find a place for him."

"I don't want 'a place for him,' King. I want someone who can help him. I want him to be able to lead a normal life."

Lehlia persisted in spite of the fact that King continued to distance himself from all of her efforts. She called The Study and made an appointment. This time she would not take The Boy.

Miss Henderson was very sympathetic. "The child sounds very interesting, Mrs. Randolph. It's quite unusual for a child almost four not to speak at all. Especially given the kinds of things he creates, and the physical dexterity you describe.

226

Unfortunately we don't have the facilities at The Study to deal with such special difficulties. You have had him tested, of course?"

"Tested! It seems to me we have had every kind of test known to man." Lehlia felt warmed to the sincere interest of this young woman. "Nothing the doctors have said really tells us anything. They just say, 'He seems normal physically, and healthy,' but no one has any idea why he doesn't talk, or what to do about it. Why he is so...so easily disturbed." Her face trembled; the sympathy released her buried misery, and she controlled the tears with difficulty.

"You know, Mrs. Randolph, I have learned that there is a Montessori[6] school opening in Montreal soon. Montessori has a very good reputation. It encourages freedom of expression, but offers a well-designed program of instruction as well. They have a worldwide system, and they train the staff members in their techniques. And, they do take young children. This might be ideal for your boy."

Lehlia took the name and phone number of the man who was opening the new school, heartened by this prospect. She called Mr. Timmins the following day and made an appointment to meet him at the Windsor Hotel.

The room at the Windsor was elegant. The hotel had the gracious feel of old money and style. Wood panelling, thick green carpets with a brown and dark green geometric border, heavy dark oak tables and chairs. Lehlia could see the bedroom off to the right. Mr. Timmins met her at the open door, ushered her into the sitting room, and offered tea and tiny sandwiches. Lehlia was impressed.

Timmins listened sympathetically to Lehlia's recitation of

the child's history. He was a tall, well-dressed man, about fifty Lehlia thought, and he had a serious, gentle manner. "We have rented an elementary school building on Waverly that closed because of declining enrolments. We are renovating the building, painting, installing new equipment, and so on. We will open in about a month. We are accepting only thirty students to start, and will have a staff of eight. Including myself, of course." He smiled pleasantly. "This gives us a ratio of one to five, one teacher to five students, that is."

This sounds very good, Lehlia thought. So when Mr. Timmins requested a thousand-dollar registration fee to cover the first three months, she quickly wrote the check.

"Thank you, Mrs. Randolph. We are happy to have you in our Montessori family. We will be in touch soon with final arrangements."

Lehlia returned home, happy that they finally had a promising situation for the boy. When two weeks had passed with no further word, she called the number. The secretary said, "Mr. Timmins is out right now, but he will call you this afternoon."

Another week passed without word. Lehlia tried the number again, but got only the busy signal. Finally she called Miss Henderson at The Study. "I haven't heard anything more, Mrs. Randolph. But the Montessori system is quite particular about who is permitted to use their name. I'm sure it is all right. You might want to call the Simpsons. We have Marcia in second grade, and I understand they were interested in the new school for their three-year-old."

Gloria Simpson said, "Yes, we registered Samantha six weeks ago. We were so lucky to get a place, Montessori has such a good program. They screen the applicants very carefully.

We haven't heard anything more though. Yes, we paid the fee--
eight hundred dollars."

"Your fee was eight hundred? We paid a thousand. I
wonder why ours was more. We haven't heard anything more
either, and Mr. Timmins has not returned my calls."

King stormed, "It's a scam. It's got to be a scam." He
called Lawrence Simpson, and between them they learned that
the man who called himself Timmins had vanished. He had
duped at least fifty couples, and had disappeared with over fifty
thousand dollars.

Lehlia became depressed. She could not think of anything
else to try. She felt old, tired, useless. King shrugged off all
interest in the boy, busied himself with work and community
affairs. The child was left to Nanny and the staff.

The help talked freely among themselves, puzzling over
the boy and his problems. They, after all, were the ones who
had to deal with him day after day. Lehlia and King now
seldom brought him into their daily life. They saw him when
there was an emergency, or when the boy thrust himself into
their lives suddenly with some wild, strange behavior.

They did not know how to cope with this strange,
uncontrollable child. They fretted for someone, something
other than themselves to blame – the nanny, the food. But
Lehlia could not rid herself of the nagging worry, the constant
thought that there must be some help somewhere. But not an
institution; she could not face that thought. They took reports
on the boy's behaviour and his needs from Nanny. Hilda
occasionally spoke to Lehlia, or Simon to King, but Lehlia
could only mumble, "Yes, good. Take care of it."

King might add, "He needs supervision, Nanny, a firm hand."

When some question was brought to Lehlia and King, they avoided the issue, unable to respond in any coherent, united way. Their eyes shifted from each other, neither knowing what more to say, unable to talk even to each other about their unhappiness.

Nanny was becoming increasingly worried. She told Hilda, "What if something goes missing? They'll blame me! My red beads were gone from my chest the other day. They are back now. But you never know what that boy is up to. What if something is gone from the silver, or something! You know who always gets the blame! He's too much!"

On Saturday Nanny took the boy with her as she did her shopping. In Simpsons he saw a big box with bright colored pictures of wheels and blocks like the pictures in Father's big book. He pulled Nanny to the box and pointed. He grunted, "Uh! Uh! Uh! Uh!"

Nanny said, "Yes, Lego[7]. Come on. We've got to hurry."

The Boy stood stiffly in front of the counter and began to scream and flap his hands. He tried to grab the big box but Nanny pushed it back and hauled him away. "Stop your caterwauling," Nanny said irritably. She jerked him around and marched him home. "I couldn't finish my shopping, Hilda," she complained. "He wouldn't stop screaming. He was trying to grab things off the counter. He kept trying to get the Lego set. He's a terrible handful. I had to drag him almost all the way home, squealing like a stuck pig."

Hilda was thoughtful. "He does like bright colored things. You've said yourself that he's always fooling around with little pieces of paper - making patterns, you said."

"That's right - the beads, the colored glass, and those shiny green beetles I always have to clean out of his pockets. Where he gets them, the Lord only knows. He's a queer one, all right."

"Poor little child. There's not much fun in his life. Maybe he would like the Lego. You tell Madam that you think a Lego would be good for him. She'll give you the money, so get him a big set."

When the big Lego set was delivered the next week, Simon carried it up to the boy's room on the third floor. He removed the brown wrapping paper and started to cut off the plastic wrap. But the boy flung himself at the box and covered it with his arms and body, crying "Uh! Uh! Uh!" softly and running his hands over the bright pictures. When Simon said, "I just want to open it for you," and tried to take the box, the soft cries turned to screams, and the hands flapped wildly.

Simon stood back uncertainly and watched the boy smoothing, smoothing the pictures and crooning his soft, "Uh! Uh! Uh!" Again he touched the box and said, "Let me open it for you. You'll like the blocks." And again the soft cries turned to screams. Simon turned to Nanny, "Can you take it from him?"

"Not on your life. He gets this way and you can't do a thing with him. Let him be. Maybe he just wants the box."

Simon told Hilda and Joseph, "He seems to have something in that mind of his, but Lord only knows what it is. He certainly wanted that box of Lego. Nanny thinks it's just the box he wants. But he doesn't want just any box, it's the Lego box - maybe the bright colors."

"He probably doesn't realize what is in the box. Maybe he'll get it open himself. Those little fingers of his are very clever. If he doesn't get it open in a day or two, you can open it when he's outdoors, or asleep. "Meggs," she turned to the young house girl, "go call Nanny down for a cup of tea. Seems like when he's alone he'll do things he won't do even around Nanny. It's like he thinks if no one sees him do something, he won't get in trouble. Not that anyone treats him bad," she sighed.

The Lego set was a success, but it was a source of puzzlement and frustration, too. Nanny watched the boy sit fingering the pieces, turning them over and over, brushing their smoothness against his lips. As long as she watched, he did nothing more. But whenever she was out of the room, some remarkable construction appeared - a tower, a car, a crane. The construction was covered with a shirt or towel or pajama pants, and anyone who started to uncover it was quickly warned off by the boy's screams.

Constructions soon rimmed the bedroom, each covered with some piece of cloth. Cook found her kitchen towels; Meggs found pillowcases, Simon found his soft chamois skins. They marvelled over the works when The Boy was asleep.

Finally Nanny, Hilda, and Simon delegated themselves to speak to King and Lehlia. "You need to see what the boy does with the Lego, Sir, Madam. It's very...unusual," Nanny said. "If you please, Madam, you should go to his room when the boy is out. He gets so upset sometimes."

"Nonsense!" King snorted. "Sneak around in my own house, behind my son's back. Nonsense. We'll go now."

"Maybe..." Lehlia hesitated.

"No. Let's see these things."

The Boy looked up startled when the delegation appeared. His eyes jumped wildly around the room and he covered the piece he was working on with his body. King strode over to the wall and pulled covers off of standing constructions. "Well..." he started, but The Boy's piercing screams interrupted him. The child flew about the room knocking down everything he had built, sending Lego blocks flying. And he screamed, and jerked, and flew wildly, kicking the blocks, the box, bits of cloth and papers.

Lehlia shrank back to the doorway, her hands at her throat as King roared, "Stop that! Stop that noise this instant!" The child's face was a frozen mask, and his screams became hysterical sobs. "For God's sake. Give him something to quiet him down, Nanny. And get rid of this stuff. Simon, take it out of here, all of it!" He strode out of the room and Lehlia trailed after him. Nanny, with Simon and Hilda's help, gave the child a cup of warm milk with a mild tranquilizer. Eventually the wild screaming sobs turned to hiccups, and the small body relaxed as the boy dropped quickly into a troubled sleep.

Feeling deeply guilty for their part in the affair, the three employees picked up the Lego pieces, the papers, the towels and shirts, and the brightly colored box, and silently took the lot of it to the trash. They would not interfere again.

It was weeks before The Boy returned to the library. He sat in the corner of his room, brushing his hand back and forth across the carpet. Nanny dressed and undressed him like a baby; he moved only when someone moved him. He drank juice or milk when it was held up to him. He opened his mouth for food, but didn't chew. Finally Nanny told Hilda, "I can't

take it. It's a sin and a shame. I can't do anything with him."
She told Lehlia, "I have to go to New York. My sister is ill."

A new nanny came. Over the weeks a series of nannies
came and went. The Boy grew more secretive, disappearing for
hours at a time. The nanny ran frantically around the big house
looking for him, calling, "Boy, Little One. Come. It's time for
lunch...or for your bath." Suddenly he might appear behind his
nanny, startling her by tugging at her skirt. His silent grey eyes
watching the nanny's every move made her uneasy, nervous.

"What in the world do you do with him?" she asked Hilda.
"Where does he go? He's just all of a sudden <u>there</u>! He'll be
dressed, or undressed, in the bed, in the tub with the water up
to his armpits, or at his table, and I never see him do it. He's
just there, staring at me with those big grey eyes. Gives me the
creeps. I think he gets into my things, too. I can't find my pin
with the blue stones, and my blue satin scarf was gone the other
day. It's back in the drawer today, but I'm sure it was gone for
two days. I don't know. What if something was missing from
the house - they might think I took it."

These nannies did not read to him, so the child began to
pore over his books in secret. There were many corners in the
big house where he could hide and study the books. With his
finger following the lines of words, he listened to Nanny's voice
in his head saying the stories.

He went from his own books to the big book in the library
where he found all the marks whose sounds he had learned
from Nanny's voice. He puzzled, wondering why
sometimes a mark made different sounds. Like the
one he called "rolling mouth," because it was round

234

like a rolling ball. But it was open like a mouth. It had a hard sound in candy and cat and candlestick and Christmas, but a soft sound in city and Cinderella and chair and circus. Ah, but there in circus, that was strange - one was soft and one was hard. So he began to hear the black marks in his own head. He whispered the sounds to himself when he was safe in the attic.

There were many other books in Father's library. He sounded out long words like "go-ver-ne-ment" and "ec-on-om-i-cs," and short words like "t-he" and "la-w," trying out both hard and soft sounds. He listened to Father and the suit men talk and looked for the words he had heard. The sounds and rhythms of language began to flow from the black words so they seemed to be alive, marching across the pages. On the bottom shelves he discovered a row of books that kept him engrossed for weeks. They told much better stories than the ones Nanny had read. There was Moby Dick and Treasure Island, and a heavy book by Edgar Allen Poe. It had beautiful, scary pictures in it.

By now he was reading everything he found in Father's library. He read all of Father's papers, and could understand when Father and the suit men talked about "The Business." The Business was many things he learned. Hockey skates and figure skates seemed to be the main part, but there were skis, and motor scooters, bicycles, huge trucks, and some pulling, lifting machines like he had seen in the big word book. And there were sport clothes of all kinds. The shiny book called Annual Report for 1939 had pictures of Father and many of the men who came to the house. There were pictures of lines that went up and down, and bars and circles that said things about different parts of The Business. And there were lists of numbers with many zeros and dollar signs.

As he read and studied and listened, something grew in him, something filling him up so he felt that he was about to burst. He was afraid to look at it because it was a terrible thing, and it was a Charles Kingsley Randolph III thing, pushing itself up out of the black hole. He became very nervous and screamed when anyone surprised him.

CHAPTER TWENTY-ONE

Black-Eyed Peas

Montreal – 1948

By the time he was six, new words filled his life, "He's getting older...", "guard him...", "institution...", "cousin....,", "take over...", and "permanent care...".

One day the grey suit man with the heavy briefcase came and Mother and Father met him in the library. The Boy crept onto the window ledge behind the heavy leather couch and lay quietly to listen.

Father sat in his business chair and did the talking. "Hanford, we've got to see what can be arranged. We can't expect anything from The Boy," he sighed heavily. "Mrs. Randolph has investigated everything that anyone has suggested, the psychologists, the programmes, the schools. There just isn't anything helpful at all. We just can't expect things to get better for him.

"We have been thinking about Cousin Lawrence's boy, Theodore for the business. At least he's family. He must be fifteen or so by now, a good age to begin thinking about his future. And we hear he is very bright," he sighed again and he and Lehlia exchanged unhappy glances. "I have to get someone in line for the future of the business. The Boy..."

"The thing is," Lehlia whispered, "we haven't been in contact. We don't know either of the children - Theodore or Jeanette."

Mr. Hanford glanced at the sparse information on the sheet they had given him, "What about Lawrence himself? He is your cousin. Would he take over the business?"

"He'd never consider it. He was so angry about Pa Kingsley's will, leaving his mother Constance out completely. It was just like Pa; he could be mean spirited. Oh, Lawrence is capable enough, he must be. He has built his bookstore up from nothing; it is quite famous. But anyway he's wrapped up in that and they are very much involved in the Philadelphia art and literary community. And he travels a lot for shows and sales. I'm sure he's not a bit interested in manufacturing or in sport equipment or developing new vehicles. We need someone with a clever mind for... for inventing, for mechanical things, for tinkering in a way, not just for building a business.

"No, Lawrence wouldn't be the one, but maybe Theodore. He is a cousin, family, and at his age he might be ready to consider a move. We just don't know him well enough to begin to plan seriously. What we want you to do, Hanford, is to find out about this cousin - what he's like, what his abilities are, what his interests are. Maybe he would be able to take over. That's what we want, isn't it Lehlia?"

"And the other cousin Jeanette too, Mr. Hanford?" Lehlia

interrupted.

"Yes, both cousins, we should get to know them both. Then maybe we could make plans for the business...and something permanent for The Boy, right Lehlia? You'll do that for us, Hanford?"

The Boy lay for a long time in the window, the words worrying around in his mind. "Cousin...future...The Boy....business....clever mind....take over... permanent.....Cousin...Cousin!" Over and over the words tumbled.

He began to hide often, and to listen more carefully at doors and from behind the couch, the chairs, inside cupboards. They were planning something. They were going to take Charles Kingsley Randolph III away from him and make him be The Boy forever. The thing growing in his chest filled him with terror. He would do something first.

He stole the bags of beans from Cook's pantry and arranged the beans in intricate, intersecting patterns. Circles, arrows, triangles - red, white, brown, pink. The white ones with black eyes he always put in the center - four rows together, back to back, with their black eyes looking out in all directions, careful, watching. The eyes would watch everything the others did, protect him.

Meggs saw them first because Nanny had the afternoon off. She told Hilda, "They're beautiful, Hilda. You should see them. He's used the colours to make patterns. It's like he is an artist. You have to come up and see them."

Hilda looked at Joseph and shrugged her shoulders, "We

don't want another day like the Lego day." But she had been sure that the boy had unusual abilities - especially after the Lego. She had thought about that day often, had wished they had handled it better. "Where is the boy now, Meggs?"

"Well, he's not in his room, and I looked everywhere downstairs. I don't know where he is. He's a slippery little devil - he'll show up just before Nanny gets back. But please, Hilda, you have to see these pictures he has made."

Meggs was so urgent Hilda could see that she was really impressed. She looked at Joseph again, "You speak to Madam, Joseph. Get her to go up there now while the boy is out. You must, Joseph. Madam would want to see them."

Reluctantly Joseph agreed; sometimes it was hard to know what would be best to do. Mr. King would not be happy if there was another difficult scene, but Madam would be eager to see these newest creations - If they were as unusual as Meggs said. He went up to the boy's room and stood amazed, staring at the designs. Meggs is right, he thought, they are beautiful. He turned and hurried down to the salon where Madam was playing a Schubert sonata, a dreamy smile on her face.

He waited until the piece ended, then cleared his throat and stepped to the side of the piano. "Excuse me, Madam, but we would like you to see something new the boy has made." He put his request clearly so Madam would know it was not bad news. "In his room, Madam, he has made some quite unusual designs."

"Designs, Joseph? What kind of designs? Where is the boy? I don't want to get him upset again."

"No, Madam. He is not in his room at the moment. Meggs saw them first, and then I went up. Indeed they are important, Madam. May I suggest that we go up right now, before Nanny comes back? And may I suggest that you take the Polaroid - we should get pictures to show Mr. King, in case they get disturbed later?"

Nervously Lehlia followed Joseph to the study where they picked up the camera and film, and then to the small elevator. Joseph opened the doors and pressed three for the child's floor. At the playroom door she stopped with a gasp. "Oh! Oh! Joseph! Did he truly make these pictures himself?"

"He must have, Madam. Meggs found them and there is no one else."

Lehlia began snapping pictures from all angles, but soon tears blinded her. "This child, this child. So beautiful. Why? Why this, and still he can't talk?"

Joseph quietly took the camera from her shaking hands and finished a series of photos. "You must show the pictures to Mr. King, Madam."

King too, was shaken by the pictures spread out on the coffee table that evening. When Lehlia laid her head on his shoulder with a heavy sigh, he held her close. They seemed to be on a continual roller coaster of emotions about the boy never able to understand and not able to find a productive course of action. "What does it mean, Lehlia? What is it about?" When she only shook her head, King asked, "Did you call Dr. Foster?"

"Yes, King. He's coming tomorrow at eleven." Lehlia was exhausted, tears ready to flow at any provocation. The whole house felt heavy to her, uneasily quiet, expecting something. It was as if the house itself knew that something should happen, but was not able to bring it forth. It's because everyone is holding their breath, she thought, tiptoeing around.

By unspoken agreement everyone stayed out of the playroom until Dr. Foster arrived the next morning. Lehlia met him in the small parlour and showed him the photos. This psychologist, the most recent in a long series, was a small thin man, nearly bald except for a rim of wiry grey hair above his ears and across the back, His brown suit was a heavy wool tweed that made him appear hot and uncomfortable. He squinted and blinked nervously through thick wire-rimmed glasses.

But Lehlia liked him in spite of his strange appearance and fidgety manners. He's so serious, Lehlia thought. He doesn't say much, but he is interested. And he doesn't upset the boy either, just sits and watches and puts things nearby. She had told King. "It's as if he respects the boy - respects his space."

King had snorted, "Respects his space! What we want is for someone to teach him to talk, how to act around people. We all respect his space, for God's sake. What does that mean anyhow?"

"Well, Dr. Carlucca didn't get anywhere pushing him around, King," Lehlia said heatedly. "Maybe this is what he needs."

Dr. Foster had been studying the photos carefully. "You say the boy made these, Mrs. Randolph?"

"He must have, Dr. Foster. There's no one else goes into his playroom except Nanny, and it was her afternoon off." Maybe he won't believe me, she thought. He wasn't too convinced about the Lego constructions. Just my word that they even existed. At least we have the photographs this time.

They went up to the playroom, opened the door and stood staring, silent. Dr. Foster caught only a glimpse of the designs before the child dashed from the corner of the room and flung himself protectively on top of his creations, arms outstretched, crying loudly, "Uh! Uh! Uh!"

They retreated to the small parlour where Dr. Foster studied the photos again with great interest. He was reminded of reports of the extraordinary drawing capabilities of some autistic children. He had been reviewing all of his notes and old texts on autism since first meeting with the child in January. He was especially attentive to the works of Kanner and Asperger in the 1940s. Some of the characteristics they had identified were evident, especially the fluttering hands, rocking motions, and wild grunts that were the child's only vocalizations.

"Some special children do have extraordinary gifts in certain areas. I have been studying…. " Dr. Foster cut himself off. He should go carefully with this family. Many people are afraid of problems like autism, even the words. Moreover, Dr. Foster was not convinced that autism was the answer. The grunts, he had learned, were almost a language; their tone and intensity expressed a variety of emotions: anger, fear, happiness, contentment. Such a variety of emotional reactions, both to people and to some objects, if the story of the Lego constructions was accurate, were not typical of autism. Moreover, the effort to hide, to protect the things the child constructed were not typical autistic behavior as he understood it.

He had not discussed this possible explanation of the child's difficulties with the Randolphs. He saw that the family relationships were extremely vulnerable; he wanted more information, both about the child himself and about autism. Now with these photographs, and the fact that he had himself observed the child's protective behavior, he had something to take to specialists.

Perhaps he would write to Lorna Selfe whose account of the child artist Nadia he suddenly recalled, or to Dr. Oliver Sacks who had done so much work with neuro-pathologist patients, among them many autistic savants. In his own small way, Dr. Foster was becoming quite excited.

"May I take these with me?" he asked. "I would like to consult with some people who have studied children's artistic abilities. This may be quite important."

"I don't know. I don't think so, Dr. Foster. I don't want to lose these." Lehlia longed to believe him - to believe that these designs were important - that they meant something. She wanted to have the photos near her as some tangible evidence of ability in the child. She wanted to carry them around with her, hold them close, as if by holding these photos she was holding her son. She did not see the irony in that.

"I would be happy to have colour reproductions made and get these originals back to you very soon," Dr. Foster urged. "Or you could have the prints made."

"I'm not sure, Dr. Foster." She trusted this strange little man, but she still hesitated. "I'll have to speak to Mr. Randolph. We have to think about everything, about what can be done. Mr. Randolph will have to decide what is best for the child's future."

Dr. Foster left, repeating, "Please let me have copies of the photos, Mrs. Randolph. I do think this might give us something to work with."

The Boy had crept downstairs to hear what Mama and the doctor would say. He heard only the last few words, 'decide what is best for the child's future." Blood pounded in his ears. He ran to the attic and banged his head on the pile of carpets, moaning softly. He was getting more frightened and more frantic every day. He must do something to make a safe place for himself.

He drew great jagged slashes of color on the walls, the windows, and the marble floor in the great entry hall. He peed in each of the four corners of his bedroom and of his playroom. He pulled the sheets off his bed, carefully cut them into narrow strips, and tacked the strips across the doors of his bedroom and playroom, of all of his rooms. He did all of these things when Nanny dozed off or sat talking with Cook, or at night when they thought he was sleeping. He never swallowed the pills they gave him, and he had a big bag full of them hidden in a hole inside his mattress.

CHAPTER TWENTY-TWO

Jeanette Is Cousin

Montreal – 1949

One day early in October Nanny took him for a walk down the hill to Papeterie Hancock on Sherbrooke Street to get some Christmas paper. It was a wonderful day. There had been an early wet snow that clung to the branches of the trees and pulled them down. It felt like they were walking through a snowy cave and the boy was giddy with the beauty and the mystery of it. He stuck out his tongue and felt the feathery flakes vanish like icy bubbles as they touched. He kept pulling away from Nanny, jumping to touch the branches and let the snowy shower fall over him.

This nanny was very old - maybe a hundred, and she walked funny. Her right foot toed out and turned under at the ankle, so she rocked from side to side walking on her inside ankle. The Boy had tried it, and it really hurt, so he didn't see why she kept on walking that way.

He slipped away from Nanny's hand again and walked on his ankles, keeping just ahead of her. She hurried to grab him, slipped and fell hard against the curb. She just lay there, and people stopped to try to help her.

The Boy danced around her, fluttered his arms, screeching. A woman in a brown fur coat said, "I think he pushed her." A man in jeans and a plaid jacket grabbed The Boy's arm so he bit the hand, and the man batted his head and shook him hard.

When they finally got Nanny up, two policemen took them home. Everyone stood around in the big hall, Mother and Father, the two policemen, Joseph and Simon, and Nanny. He huddled down on the floor, shivering.

The tall curly headed policeman said, "He bit a man and punched a lady in the stomach. Someone said they thought he pushed this lady into the curb. She said No, but it was pretty hard to settle him down."

That was when Nanny said, "That's it. I've had it with this child. I quit."

Mother begged, "Oh, please no, Nanny! So close to the holidays! We'll never be able to get someone on such short notice."

"Can't help it, ma'am. He's too much for me. Can't say he pushed me; he slipped away and I tried to grab for him. That's honest enough. But he's too much. Ought to be in a home somewhere, he's more than one person can manage. Not as if there's much future for him, poor little.... Needs full time care, and that's my honest opinion. I'll just get my things and be off." And glad enough to be shut of the little rat, she muttered under her breath as she headed for her room upstairs, limping and rubbing her hip. She gathered her things and left hastily.

The policemen followed her out, with a final comment, "The child needs help, more direction. Take care of him."

"What are we going to do now, King?" The four stood around in a stunned huddle, gazing blankly at each other and the boy.

The door chimes rang.

"What now?" King

"Nanny's come back!" Lehlia

Simon met Joseph's eyes and turned to the door. A young woman stood there with a card in her hand. "I believe this is the home of Mr. Charles Randolph, is it not? I am his cousin Jeanette Marie Tremblay from Philadelphia. May I speak with him?"

Simon resisted the impulse to turn and look at the group surrounding the child. "Please come in, Miss. I will see if he is available."

His eyes swept across the new woman - grey suede jacket, shiny silver blouse, black wool pants, a long black narrow coat with slits up each side, and grey suede boots buckled at the ankles. And then - flaming red hair clipped back with curly wisps pulling loose around her face, creamy skin, blue watching eyes. She was 'cousin'. She would take him away. He would watch her.

Jeanette Marie looked closely at the boy. He was shivering violently in spasms. He seemed tense, frozen, listening. There was a crisis. "I seem to have come at an awkward time. I am sorry, I can come back later." She stepped back to leave.

248

King forced himself to attention. There was no sense in trying to pretend. They had all heard her say she was family; they would welcome her and explain later. "Simon, ask the young lady to wait in the small parlor. We will welcome her properly in a few minutes." He turned, "Lehlia?"

"Yes, of course. Ask Hilda for hot chocolate, Joseph." As King and Simon picked the child up and left, Lehlia touched Jeanette's arm and motioned to the right. "This is a wonderful surprise Jeanette Marie, although we are, as you say, in a bit of an awkward situation. But you are most welcome. Please come with me."

Jeanette Marie followed Lehlia into the small room with its windows opening onto the city below. "This is just so beautiful," she cried. "We have snow in Philadelphia all right, but it gets dirty so fast. There's so much coal dust and smoke in the air. You can see clear down to the river from here, and the air is sparkling - so clean and fresh. This is a lovely home, Lehlia."

"It is nice, isn't it. Theodore and Margaret had it built in 1889, just before Kingsley's wedding. At that time it was pretty much at the edge of the city - very few houses around, and none of the tall buildings you can see below us now. It was a showplace then - the red sandstone. There are bigger homes, but I do like ours - the red is a warm colour." Talking about the house had calmed Lehlia, even put a spark of pleasure into her voice.

The two women looked inquiringly at each other. Lehlia asked, "You are from Philadelphia? You must be Aunt Constance's daughter? This is a coincidence. We were speaking just yesterday about getting in touch with the family. Your father's name is Lawrence? And you have a brother? Theodore.

Is that right?"

"Yes, just one brother, Theodore - after Great-Great Grandpa Theodore. But Constance is our grandmother. , not our mother, and she was married to Philippe Tremblay. You probably heard the story that Grandpa Kingsley was so angry that she married a French man and moved to the states? And that he cut her out of his will? How angry Grandpa was at Kingsley? What a family!

Grandma and Grandpa had just one son, out father, Lawrence Tremblay. Our mother's name is Veronica. So it's Veronica and Lawrence who are our parents. You will meet her later.

Theo is quite a bit younger than I - twelve years, in fact. Papa was in the war, you see, and he was badly injured. He was in the hospital for several years before he really recovered and came home. So I was an 'unexpected blessing' as Mother always says." She laughed, a bright happy sound.

Lehlia smiled; she liked this cheerful young woman who seemed not at all non-plussed by the awkward beginning. "Have you just arrived in Montreal?"

"This morning. But Mrs. Randolph...Lehlia?"

"Yes of course, Lehlia."

"Lehlia! And Jeanette, I really prefer that - no one calls me Jeanette Marie. The Jeanette is from my father's family and Marie from your mother's name, Maria Elena. Do you know that connection? Our families have not been good correspondents." She laughed ruefully. "My grandmother was Constance Randolph, your husband's Aunt Constance."

"Yes, Father Charles' sister."

Jeanette nodded, "You know that Grandma Constance lived with Aunt Felicity and Maria Elena in Toronto for several years. That was where she and Grandpa met, at a birthday party. Our Grandmothers were very close."

"My 'twin sister,' that's what Grandma always called Constance. Except that she had black hair, not the Gordon red you have inherited. I was born in this house, Jeanette. Right upstairs in the room you will be in. Did you know that?"

"No, I didn't. But Maria Elena was your grandma, wasn't she, and Aunt Fizzy was your great-grandmother?" Jeanette was trying to get the picture of family ties clear in her mind. "How did it happen that your mother was here when you were born?"

Lehlia happily talked on about the family. "That was the fall of 1922, the time that Great-Grandma Felicity died and I was born two weeks later. Grandma had come down to Montreal from Toronto - to heal old wounds, Mother told me when I was old enough to wonder. Grandma Felicity - I was never allowed to speak of her as Fizzy, you know, still can't either. She and King's Grandma Dorothy were sisters, but Pa Kingsley wouldn't have Grandma Felicity in the house after my mother was born - the family scandal. Grandma Felicity never said who Mama's father was." Lehlia hesitated, looked embarrassed, and added. "She told Mama in 1917 when the Halifax explosion killed Ernesto and Riata Ciccacio. Mama thought it probably had been an 'open secret,' but at least she did tell Mama the truth. I always felt awkward around Pa, though."

"I don't think you should have. King told me that he overheard Great Grandpa Theodore say there was some shame about Pa Kingsley himself in that story - that he had been drunk and had tried to force himself on Felicity. So there are always more to family stories than get told openly!" Jeanette was angry that Lehlia had been left with that half-truth version

251

of the story. "I guess we just have to let that water flow on under the bridge, but I certainly don't think there is any shame attached to you, Lehlia! But go on. I know so little about all of you here in Montreal."

"Grandma Felicity (I have always just left off the 'Greats and the Great-greats - so much simpler) hadn't seen any of them since Dorothy died in the flu epidemic of 1918. Now she was eighty years old and it was time to clear up old misunderstandings, she told Maria Elena. Besides her heart was bad, and she didn't want to die outside of the family. She wanted to know this youngest one of the clan, her nephew King, and maybe make friends with Pa Kingsley again after so many years.

"My father George had been transferred to Montreal - to take over his new position at CP Rail, and Grandma Felicity insisted that they should join her at Randolph House. Grandma said that George and Mother should meet Pa and connect with the family. So Mother and Father were here, Grandma was old, Mother was close to her time with me, and there was some terrible upset. It was between King, who was five that year, and Pa Kingsley. It was at Thanksgiving dinner. Pa was very cruel to the boy, and Charles just let it happen. Mother said it was an awful day.

"In the trouble Grandma Felicity's heart gave out and she died, then I came along early, so we were still here when I was born. We moved to our own home on Trafalgar soon after and never were close to Pa, never were a close family. Mother always said Pa was rigid, moralistic. A tyrant, living in the past."

As King joined them, Jeanette explained how she happened to be in Montreal. "My fiancé Richard Hamilton and

I were attending a conference in Toronto this past week. Since it is so close, I wanted to get acquainted with the family. We are at the Queen Elizabeth Hotel. Richard is meeting with some colleagues at McGill this morning."

"How long do you plan to be in Montreal?" Lehia asked. "You must not stay at a hotel. You must stay here with us. We have plenty of room, and would like that very much. We have no family here."

"Except Father Charles, of course." King interrupted. "But he is in Berlin this week, and his tour will keep him away for six more weeks. He is away more than he is here - always has been. We would be very pleased to get to know your part of the family better. This is wonderful."

Jeanette left a message at the hotel asking Richard to call her. She mentioned that Richard's colleague was a child psychologist and caught the quick glance Lehlia and King exchanged. Then conversation faltered; the commotion that Jeanette had come upon was uppermost in everyone's mind.

Lehlia sighed, glanced again at King and said, "Our son has problems. He is a difficult child, hard for a Nanny to handle sometimes. Today....today..." She stopped, hesitant, her hand touching her cheek.

King interrupted, "How is Aunt Constance? She and Lawrence have a fine bookstore, I understand."

"Yes, it's very well known. I worked there until I went back for my degree."

Lehlia realized that King wanted no part of a discussion about the child's problems; they needed time to distance themselves from the morning's events. She said, "Perhaps you would like to freshen up, Jeanette, get settled in. We can talk this evening."

Hours later Richard came, bringing their luggage from the hotel. Jeanette told him about the situation she had stumbled into. "I think Lehlia wanted to talk about it, about the boy," Jeanette said. "But King shied away from any mention. I got the impression that the child is very troubled, four or five, I think." They were interested and curious since it was their field, but agreed they should let the parents bring up any discussion.

Dinner, at the dark oak table, the heavy chairs with their red leather seats, was somewhat formal. Joseph served and it was clear that this was customary. King and Richard sized each other up. They were about the same height, but King seemed taller because he was slim and had narrow shoulders, his face a lean triangle. Richard was of a sturdier build; his frame was heavier, and his posture more casual so looked shorter. King wore a dark blue suit; the two-button jacket had wider lapels than the business suit he had worn earlier. Richard's tweed jacket and tan shirt were his custom. He had decided that a tie would be appropriate, a brown and tan knit he had brought along. Both noted the differences, but decided they were agreeable.

Conversation was easy, about family, work, the upcoming Canadian Thanksgiving, (Jeanette knew from her mother that it would be in early October instead of November) and events the young couple might find interesting. They began to feel at ease with each other. That informality continued over coffee, until at last there was a long pause. Finally Lehlia said hesitantly, "I'm sorry you caught us in an upsetting moment, Jeanette. Our son…"

Again King interrupted, "Do we have to talk about that,

Lehlia? Can't you just drop it for now?"

"We are interested in the child," Jeanette said. "It is a failing of ours. We can't keep our paws off children. We do so love to work with them." She glanced at Richard and they laughed at themselves. "But why don't you and I talk tomorrow, Lehlia, after we have had a good rest. Richard and I have had a full week. Would you mind if we say goodnight for now?"

The tension was relieved and they all retired.

In Lehlia's bedroom, the issue of care for the child had to be faced. King said, "Simon's niece says she can be here for a week but you have to get something done, Lehlia. We can't go on like this."

Lehlia's pent-up emotions spilled over into sobs. King alternately tried to calm her, to quiet her fears, and then stormed angrily from window to door. "That child. We have to do something, Lehlia. This can't go on upsetting the whole household this way. I've got to be at work tomorrow. I have a business to run. We're in the midst of a recession and our hockey sales are down. This French-English tension is growing. It's a real hassle. I haven't got time for this nonsense with the boy every time I turn around. Get someone who can cope, for God sake."

Lehlia's sobs grew more frantic. "I'm s-s-sorry, King."

King's frustration quickly turned to regret; they were all caught up in this. He leaned over and kissed her cheek, "It's not your fault, my dear. I should not storm at you that way. We are both tired and upset. We'll figure something out tomorrow. Why don't you talk with Richard or Jeanette? They said they work with children. Maybe they will have some ideas." He urged her to get up, held her and soothed her until they were able to prepare for bed.

Jeanette and Richard were down early for breakfast. It was a bounteous spread before them on the low buffet - scrambled eggs and crisp Canadian bacon, fresh hot scones and jam, fruit and coffee or tea. Joseph immediately began serving them. They ate, expecting their hosts any minute. When neither King nor Lehlia still had arrived as they finished, Jeanette sat back, "That was good! I haven't had a breakfast like this for years - two pounds at least! It will have to be back to the bicycle for me!"

Richard grinned and patted his stomach, "Me, too! I have to walk some of it off this morning."

"I hope nothing has happened. I'm not sure we should stay on, Richard."

"Let's give it one more day and see how it goes. I thought I would excuse myself today, and contact my Quebec relatives. And meet King for lunch? I would like to treat him, and learn more about their hockey business. What do you think if I just go ahead with those plans? If you would make my excuses when you see them? We can't expect them to be too attentive to us today. They have a lot to deal with."

Jeanette agreed; they had also talked about the child before retiring. Jeanette described what she had seen and added, "I am sure I overheard the nanny say 'Little Rat' as she stomped out." That was significant they agreed, how much so depended on whether it was an isolated incident. They decided it would be wiser not to double up on either King or Lehlia. And they thought it would be good to have some discussions in the boy's own room.

"It would be good for him to get accustomed to having people around him, in and out," Richard said. "That is, of course if either parent wants to talk." But they both knew they would bring the talk around to the child. They had already decided they would get involved; the child needed help, and so did the parents.

When Lehlia had not appeared an hour later, Jeanette decided to check on her, to see if she could help in any way. She knocked on the door to Lehlia's sitting room and at an answer, stepped quietly in. Lehlia huddled in her wing chair; King stood silently at the window. She said "good morning" and touched Lehlia gently on the shoulder.

"Oh, good morning, Jeanette," King turned toward the two women. "Did you sleep well?" Though Lehlia was still in her soft velour robe, King was immaculately dressed, Jeanette noticed: grey silk suit, white shirt, French cuffs pinned with silver and grey links, a pale grey silk tie with faint threads of red and black, black shoes and socks. A gold tie clasp was decorated with crossed green and blue sticks - hockey sticks she recognized as identification with the business.

"I--I'm fine, King, thank you. But can I do anything? Lehlia, can I get you something? Tea, or coffee?"

"We're sorry, Jeanette," King was still speaking. "Have you had breakfast? It's ready in the small dining room. Just ring the bell and Joseph will serve you." This was disconcerting to Jeanette, this host-like formality completely out of tune with what their postures suggested.

"Thank you, King. Joseph served us. It was delightful. Have you eaten, Lehlia?"

"Yes, Lehlia, you must have something. You must eat. I

have to go. We have a meeting of the Centennial Committee at ten. We're coming up to the 350th anniversary for Montreal, Jeanette. I've got to go, Lehlia," King went on distractedly. "I'll have Simon bring the car right back - in case you need it."

"Richard is meeting some of his Hamilton relatives this morning. He asked me to tell you that he would like to meet you for lunch later. He thought if you are free he might tour the facilities, get to understand the hockey business better."

"Fine, fine, good idea! We'll talk about what we can arrange for the boy this evening. You must eat, dear." The words spoken, King seemed to feel that everything was settled, organized, back in place for the day. He kissed Lehlia on the top of her head, patted her arm, straightened the collar of her robe, and briskly left the room.

Lehlia's tears flowed again. "I don't know what to do! I can't...." She looked frail and helpless huddled deep between the wings of her chair. Her long dark hair was loose and tangled around her face. The forest green robe and the shadows deep in the chair accentuated her clear pale skin, blotched with red from weeping. She was a forlorn sight.

Jeanette felt a stirring impatience. What is wrong with this family? Why was there this angry frustration from King, and why the weeping vulnerability from Lehlia? This is the same tension I felt last night. All of this distress to stem from one small boy - it seems exaggerated, over-charged. But she should go down and get some breakfast. "Come on, Lehlia. You need something to eat. We can talk or not, however you feel."

"Oh, I can't go down. I'm not dressed, and I haven't had my shower."

"That's no problem. Let's just go as we are. Did you ever

have a 'come as you are party?' That's what we'll do, come as we are to breakfast." She took Lehlia's hands and urged her out of her chair. "Come on. Give a quick brush through your hair, and swipe a washcloth across your face. You look lovely. Against that dark green robe you're like a beautiful pink forest flower." The small compliment washed over Lehlia, and for a moment she stood straighter and her eyes brightened. Then the wave ebbed, and she shrunk into her unhappiness again.

"But the boy. King gets so upset when he hides off like this. Where could he be? Maybe he's hurt or sick. Maybe I should look for him, but I don't know where...." Lehlia looked as though she might weep again.

Trying to lighten the atmosphere, Jeanette said, "Meggs is looking for Charles, and Simon will be back soon. She tells me he always just reappears after a while. Is that so? Rub a magic lantern and there he is?"

Lehlia followed Jeanette into the small dining room where sbe again stood looking out at the city. "This is a beautiful city, Lehlia. I think it must be that it is built on hills. You get the view of the city and the river. Philadelphia has many very beautiful spots, many historic points of interest, but you don't get the perspective of the whole so easily."

"We call them mountains," Lehlia smiled. "Mount Royal and 'Outremont,' that means other mountain, she added.

"San Francisco is another city that is built on mountains," Jeanette wanted the conversation to be about other interests until Lehlia was ready to talk about the child. And she needs to eat Jeanette thought as she continued, "It's a port city too, but right on the ocean. Montreal is very far inland to be a major port - because the river is so navigable, I suppose. This is an interesting city to visit, Lehlia, and of course we are both so pleased for the opportunity to visit family here."

She is cheerful enough when we talk about most things, Jeanette thought. She doesn't have much self-confidence about the child, although it seems she really has investigated a good many possibilities.

Lehlia had eaten as Jeanette talked, fruit, hot sausages and boiled eggs in their little Delft cups, a split cherry tomato and sprig of parsley on the side. Now she toyed with a crust as Joseph poured tea and replaced the cozy not even blinking to see Madam in her robe - unheard of in this house. Miss Jeanette seemed not to think it a bit strange. The two women chattered away about the house, the city, that other city Philadelphia.

"It's very strange," he muttered to Hilda on one of his trips to the kitchen. "Not a word about the boy, or where he is, or if we've found him. Not a word."

"Well we haven't found him, have we," Hilda said sharply. "He'll turn up. He always does. Thank the Good Lord Miss Jeanette has got Madam's mind off the boy for a while at least."

Jeanette and Lehlia lingered over their tea, but their chatter soon died out. Both wanted the same discussion, but it was not easy to get started. Finally Jeanette thought, just say it. If Lehlia doesn't want to talk, we will drop it. "Could I see your son's rooms? Does he have any pictures or designs now?"

"See his room? Well, I guess so, if he isn't there."

"We wouldn't have to speak to him, disturb him in any way. It might be good for him to have people in and out, don't you think?"

"Oh, do you think so? We have worried about upsetting him. We don't go in."

"If he gets upset, we can always leave. I'd like to see what he does have, toys, anything he has made, that kind of thing."

The room was empty so they sat down and looked around. "Tell me about your son," Jeanette said. And the story flowed.

Lehlia told her about the boy not talking...at all, never. And about his screaming fits, especially when someone touched him or something he had made.

Jeanette listened without interruption, handing out tissues when Lehlia broke into angry, frustrated sobs explaining about Dr. Carlucca and all the other efforts she had made to find someone or something to help. And touching her arm encouragingly when Lehlia defiantly asserted her belief in the boy's unusual abilities.

When Lehlia described the Lego incident and the 'black-eyed peas' designs, Jeanette finally did interrupt, "Maybe Richard and I could try to get close to the child, to see if we can reach him some way. Richard is very good with children."

Lehlia brightened, "He is so easily disturbed. I don't know."

"Richard has good instincts. He will not intrude."

Jeanette suggested she would like tea, and Lehlia rang for it. The two women lingered and as conversation continued, tjey grew more comfortable with each other. Jeanette was amazed at how freely Lehlia spoke when not around King. She would try to move the conversation further, but move slowly. "So you were born during the holidays? You must have a birthday coming up?"

"Yes, October 31. Mother said Pa Kingsley called me their 'hobgoblin baby'. He meant it for a joke, I guess, but I used to think I was going to turn into a witch when I grew up."

Lehlia laughed uneasily and glanced at Jeanette.

"Family jokes!" Jeanette smiled in vexation and shook her head. "Not so funny sometimes, are they!" Her mind flashed to the story Grandma Constance had told of the pain Pa Kingsley had suffered at the death of his first son. And how Pa had turned that bitterness against Constance herself and her brother Charles. Pain begets pain, she thought.

She decided to ask the most troubling question. "I thought I heard the nanny call the child 'Little Rat'. What was that about? Did she mistreat him?"

Jeanette heard a soft gasp; she glanced up in time to catch the quick movement behind the hall door. It was Charles ducking quickly out of sight. She ached with sympathy for the child, felt a desire to know more, and would not give the boy away. She hoped he would come to them of his own accord.

"Oh..." Lehlia turned away and hid her face with her hand. "That was...I was so angry at Nanny. I didn't know. The staff...they must have heard. It was King." She stumbled through the effort to explain, to apologize. "He had such a tiny face...and his ears....King just said it.....looks like a little rat. He didn't mean...I know he loves the boy." She felt a momentary shock; that was the first time she had used the word 'love' in connection with her child.

Silently Jeanette touched Lehlia's hand, and watched as sympathy brought the tears again. "Tell me," she said. "What is the problem for Charles?"

"We don't know! We just don't know!" Lehlia sounded angry, but Jeanette thought it was really desperate unhappiness.

"You don't have to talk about it, Lehlia. But he seems so

aware, so attentive to everything. Have you had any help from a psychologist?"

"A psychologist! Dr. Carlucca, Dr. Falconer, Dr. Andrews… they were all alike. They all just said, 'Put him in an institution!' Oh, they didn't say it in so many words, but that's what they meant. Dr. Andrews said we should put the boy in his full-time programme. I watched twice. They punished him when he wouldn't talk. So he screamed and screamed, and screamed! I was so upset. I just brought him home and told King he wasn't going back there! Never!"

"No child should be punished for things he can't help."

"Dr. Foster is the only one who seems to see something good in him," Lehlia continued. "I can't believe it. The boy is so clever in so many ways."

"Charles, Lehlia, Charles."

"Well, Charles then!" Lehlia snapped. But her voice was stronger now, passionate. "You should see some of the things he does, Jeanette. The things he built with the Lego set. And he rides his bike - or did before we took it away - he went out on the avenue, so dangerous - and he swims. And he draws - colors - the most unusual pictures. And the beans! Let me show you the pictures." She rushed to her desk and pulled an envelope out of a drawer. "Even King was amazed! He doesn't know I kept these, but they are almost beautiful!"

Jeanette examined the photos, struck by the intricate patterns. "They are beautiful, really beautiful - and very creative. Did you show these to the psychologist?"

"Yes, Dr. Foster, the fourth one, the one we are working with now. He said 'strange!' Well we knew they were strange. But he meant strange in a beautiful way, I think. At least he said it like he was interested. He said he has some ideas to look into about these things Charles makes."

She's not weak or childish when she talks about the things Charles does, Jeanette thought. She has the right instincts. "Are there special schools here in Montreal? We have such a wonderful staff at our Academy. Have you inquired about programs for special children?"

"Enfants inadaptés they call them. They just baby-sit. I went to see. And then the Montessori school - that was a scam. Everyone was so disappointed when it fell through". Seeing Jeanette's disbelieving look, she continued. "Oh yes, it was a scam. The man took our thousand dollars, and similar amounts from several other families here and then just left. Everyone was furious, but no one could find a trace of him. That seemed the last straw. I've tried everything anyone suggested. But it seems so hopeless."

This conversation is irritating Lehlia, Jeanette thought, but she forged ahead. "I'm sure you have had tests?"

"Oh, yes, tests. On and on. Hearing tests, vocal chord examinations, eye-hand coordination tests, test with blocks, with pictures, with music. Every kind of test invented. Dr. Westover, our family doctor, finally scheduled him for a psychiatric test, but King and I both just put our foot down!. Psychiatric test! That was just too much!"

"Did anything at all show up in any test? Did they tell you anything? Could anyone suggest any patterns, anything at all?"

"The only thing they said was that he seemed terribly disturbed when people around him talked - especially us. But they said that was 'to be expected.' He would react more to King and me. They just keep saying, 'Nothing appears to be wrong physically.' But something is wrong; it has to be. He just looks at us with those big eyes and hunches down, or starts

264

screaming. It's like he's afraid of something!"

"Yes, that's what I noticed. Certain things seem to trigger the fear for him. My friend Richard, Dr. Richard Thomas, says some children begin life frightened. They seem to have been affected in some way by the birth process."

Lehlia listened eagerly, afraid to accept any hope that it was not her fault. That, too, was what Richard had taught, that parents had to be freed from their guilt. Suddenly Jeanette wanted to talk with Richard again, to work with him, try to help the child. "Did you have a difficult pregnancy?"

"Yes, quite bad. I was sick a lot, and I was in labour for fifteen hours. They had to turn him; he was a breech delivery. I was very weak. King was so frightened. The nurse said he cried when they told him I was all right."

"I believe, and Richard does too, that babies, even new born babies, know more than we realize. Somehow he may have felt your worry and King's fear."

"King worried all the time I was carrying. His mother had died when he was born, you see. And somehow Old Pa Kingsley made him think he had killed her. And then Pa was so harsh on King, it had something to do with the first boy in the family."

"That must have been Little Kingsley, the boy who died of pneumonia."

" I don't know. King doesn't talk about it, but Pa was hard on him. He blamed King for everything."

Joseph, clearing away the remnants of breakfast, let his mind go back to those "days of trouble" as Madam Dorothy had called them. He had started as the young yard boy under Old Step, only twelve years older than the boy King. He had picked up bits of information about what was going on in the big house from Old Step, and from guarded conversations in the kitchen. Hubert, Theodore's man, had liked me, Joseph remembered, he brought me into the house and trained me. I was lucky.

Young King changed after those days. He had always been quiet and reserved, but friendly and interested in everything. Something dreadful happened between the old Mister Kingsley and the boy. King was never the same. Joseph sighed; I don't think Mister King remembers that I was in the service here when he was young. He just quit being a boy after that time. Hubert never talked about the old trouble. Even when King was cold or unkind to the servants, Hubert just said, "Poor young fellow. He had it hard."

Joseph could not shake his own troubled thoughts. As he went about the day, his mind turned again and again to his early days as yard boy, to old Miss Felicity (this young Jeanette somehow brought the old lady to life - there was something about this one). And to the young Master King and harsh, autocratic old Mister Kingsley. Those days were good to me, Joseph thought, but not to the boy.

CHAPTER TWENTY-THREE

Connections

Montreal - 1949

Jeanette sat quietly at the small writing desk near the window, alternately thinking and jotting something down in the notebook before her. It was mid-afternoon and the house was quiet. She had decided that she would write a letter to little Charles. She had a hunch that the boy could read, and she knew that he was curious, that he investigated everything. She would tell the boy who she and Richard were, and that they hoped to talk with him. She would make some promises, and some suggestions. She would just leave the notebook lying around in her room and hope that young Charles would nibble. She shuddered momentarily at the realization of the image her mind had allowed - using that word 'nibble' shows just how infectious an idea is, she berated herself. She began to write.

Dear cousin Charles,

My name is Jeanette Tremblay and I am your cousin from Philadelphia in the USA. Actually, I am your 'second cousin.' That is because your father King and my father are the 'first cousins.'

My friend Richard Hamilton and I are visiting your mother and father for a few days. We are both psychologists and we are teachers, too. We work with children in Philadelphia.

But while we are visiting in Montreal we are trying to get acquainted with the family here. We would like to get acquainted with you too. So here is my first suggestion – I could read to you some afternoon. If you have a favorite book, just leave it out on the little table in your playroom, and I will come and read it to you.

Now here is my second suggestion – if you have a question you would like to ask me, write it on a page in this notebook and I will try to answer it.

And here is my promise to you – I will never tell anyone else anything you write or tell me unless you want me to.

So that is my letter to you for today. I will write more tomorrow.

Your cousin,
Jeanette Tremblay

She looked back over her letter and thought there is so much more I would like to say, but that's a start. I am sure he will read it, and I can just hope he will connect.

Richard arrived at King's office complex on Union Street south of Morgan's at 11:30 and was ushered into the office with the gold nameplate on the door. Not an imposing building, he thought. All of the buildings look old, some very old and re-conditioned from a former existence.

"Montreal has an Old World feel to it, like some parts of Philadelphia," he said. "And I'm a bit surprised that there are no very tall buildings. Is that a city by-law or something?"

"I'm not sure, Richard. But all of the buildings down here in the old quarter were built long ago. Whether it was regulation, or just the difficulties construction faced in the old days is hard to say. But I like them - not what you would call modern, but beautiful, I think."

"The detail on such buildings is more interesting. Philadelphia doesn't go quite so far back, but it has some of this historic glamour about it too. Craftmanship - maybe they had more time for it in those days."

"To change the subject, I have made reservations for lunch at a small restaurant near here. I am not sure - how much do you really want to know about my business here, Richard?"

"I am interested in business in general, I guess. We are involved in the two things in Philadelphia - Jeanette has always helped her parents in their bookstore, and we run the Academy. I know your business started out in Halifax as a cobbler's shop, didn't it? It was your great-grandfather, wasn't it? He must have been far-sighted?"

"Yes a real entrepreneur, though I don't think they used that term in those days. Let's go to lunch and we can talk there. I can talk for hours about Grandpa Theodore and hockey!"

They did linger for hours over lunch while King told

Richard about the immigrants, Ernesto the boot-maker, and Theodore and Margaret, both of whom were always on the lookout for new opportunities. Then about the terrible explosion of the munitions ship in the Halifax harbor that killed Ernesto, his wife and several of his children. "That was long after the partners had more or less gone their own ways, but it hit Theodore and Margaret very hard," King said. "Theodore never had the heart to go on after that - turned everything over to Kingsley, my grandfather. He wanted my father, Charles Kingsley to take over, but Father only wanted to play the violin. He just left and the violin has been his life. Comes back once in a while, but never for long."

Richard had heard some parts of that story from Jeanette, but didn't ask for details. They talked on for a time and Richard asked, "Would it be possible for me to look in on some of your production sites? Should be quite interesting."

King was pleased, "I'll set it up for tomorrow."

"There's an exhibition of ladies' dresses from the 18th and 19th centuries at the McCord Museum," Lehlia remarked at breakfast. "Would you be interested in that Jeanette?"

"Yes, very much. And maybe we could do some shopping while we are downtown. I'd like to get a few gifts, and just look around a bit."

They spent a couple of hours browsing. "Such gorgeous gowns!" Jeanette said. "But aren't you glad we don't have to wear those heavy ornate styles today? By the way, did you know that Great Grandma Margaret had a smart eye for fashion, Lehlia?"

"She did? I always think of her in black bombazine from neck to ankle! Stiff and unbending."

"Grandma told us that Margaret grew up in the garment industry in Bremen. After they came to Canada, her mother often sent her pictures or sketches of the latest Paris styles. Margaret copied them and she adapted them to suit her Halifax friends. She was in great demand there as a dressmaker among her close friends."

"That is certainly different from my image of her. I don't think Mother liked her. She always believed that Margaret would never forget the gossip about her father."

"Probably, but Constance admired Margaret, at least respected her. She was musical - played the piano for her church in Halifax. They held music soirées, showcasing Dorothy, but with invited artists too. Charles' musical talent came from her side of the family too. When eight-year-old Charles told Kingsley that he wanted music as his career, she helped Dorothy select a good violin for him. Constance always believed she was more lenient with her grandchildren than with her son. That's pretty common."

"Well, Mother didn't think highly of her," Lehlia said stubbornly. The two women browsed and chatted, their conversations always returning to family, its history or their present concerns. "Do you want to walk over to Morgan's? It is only a couple of blocks."

"Yes, Let's."

In Morgan's Jeanette shopped for gifts and treats, and indulged herself with a golden fox fur jacket. "I've always dreamed of having something like this. It's beautiful isn't it." Jeanette stroked the soft fur and turned, preening in front of the mirror.

They gravitated to the toy department where they discovered a small farm set. The barn door and the hayloft door opened; there was a farmer dressed in blue overalls, and animals - two cows, a horse, some pigs, a wagon. "Charles would love this, Lehlia! There are so many interesting pieces."

Lehlia nodded, her face bright with anticipation. She bought the set and told the salesgirl to send it down to the pick-up door. "My driver, Simon will collect it."

"What do you want to do now? We could go across to Birk's, or go have a cup of tea at the Tudor Room in Ogilvy's?"

"Why don't we just go on home, have tea there, and see how our purchase fares? I have some writing to do anyway." She wanted to write Charles another letter today.

Lehlia was more than pleased. They walked out the big double doors on Ste. Catherine Street, and Jeanette laughed to herself as Simon swished in to pick them up. He certainly knows her routine, she thought. They debated how to present the set to Charles. "If Simon just empties the set out on the playroom floor," Lehlia said, "maybe he would set them up some way. Maybe he will have some idea of how it should look. What do you think?"

"I'd bet that he would. At Least it's worth a try. We could even take before and after pictures to show your psychologist Dr. Foster if he does something interesting!" They were both excited about the idea but agreed to wait until King and Richard got home so they could all observe.

Richard accompanied King on his trips to various production sites. They had become at ease with each other and King talked more freely about his role in the business and his hopes for the future. "Montreal is a city that has a lot going for it," he said. "It has an important role in the history of the country, is the heart of Canada's financial activity. And it has many strong industries - furs, insurance, manufacturing, construction.

"I'm very young, but I've thought a lot about it. Montreal is a producer city, and these years - the late1940s - are good years for us. That's not all there is to it of course, but Montreal produces things that get sold; that stimulates jobs and other businesses in other cities. I came into the family business when I was just eighteen. And I confess I got into it as much because I was family and knew I could go to the top pretty fast. But I'm glad I'm in it. I think we have a future." He sat back, a little embarrassed. "I told you I could talk for hours about the business."

"Don't worry, you should hear me go on about the Academy. Philadelphia is rather like that, too. It is an important national historic city, and has strong industries that make it important financially." As they talked on, Richard bought new boot skates and some hockey outfits for family at home. They had the beginnings of a friendship.

Simon dumped the set as instructed, but they could not control their excitement. They kept popping in and out of the playroom to see what the boy might have done. Nothing was changed by that evening. King was impatient. "Why don't you just set it up like a farmyard and see what he does then? How would he have any idea of what to do with those bits and pieces?"

"There are stories and pictures of animals and farms in some of the books Nanny used to read to him, King. He could have some idea, don't you think?"

"He's sure to know about animals," Jeanette said thoughtfully. "And this might be important for another reason,

King. The Lego and the beans are objects - things. These farm pieces are more human. It could say something about his feelings. What do you think, Richard?"

"Well we shouldn't read too much into this. But it is worth a few more days at least." They tethered their disappointment and turned to other activities and plans. Jeanette took the opportunity to write another letter to Charles

Dear Charles,

This is my second letter to you. I hope that you read the first one. This time I am going to tell you a little about the family – who we are and how we are related.

Some of our family lived many years ago, but you will meet Grandma Constance. She is my Grandma, too. So you and I are cousins. Richard and I are good friends, and we plan to be married.

Those are just a few of the people in our family, but they are the names you might hear.

Richard and I have to go back to Philadelphia soon. We work at a school called The Academy. I hope you will visit us in Philadelphia soon.

With affection,
Your cousin Jeanette Tremblay

She closed the notebook and laid it on the table near the window in the playroom, looked at the farm set that had not been touched, sighed and went to get dressed for dinner.

Richard had just returned from his tour with King and they showed each other their purchases.

"Did you get the plane tickets?" Jeanette asked.

"Yes. Monday - 10:35. We should be at the airport by 10:00."

"It's been good, hasn't it! I'm so glad we decided to stay over. I like them both, and I really would like to follow Charles's progress. I think he might be quite bright."

"You might be right. But remember, you are getting the story based on Lehlia's hopes. I didn't get anything really from King. He never mentioned Charles, and I didn't press it. From what Constance has told you, King had a very rough childhood himself. Helping Charles will not be a simple matter - King and Lehlia both have their own hang-ups."

"I know. And I don't want to interfere. That would just cause more problems. But, Richard, you saw the things he does. It breaks my heart to think of him. He needs help somehow! I'm going to invite them for Christmas. Grandma Constance would love to have them. Then at least they could see The Academy, get some idea of our program."

"I'd say, just talk about Christmas and family. I wouldn't mention The Academy."

"I'm sure you are right. I'll try, but if Lehlia considers coming, it will be The Academy she is thinking of."

Richard smiled, agreeing, and they went down for dinner. All the while, Jeanette continued planning. Charles could spend time with the other students at the Academy. We could see how he takes that, and maybe Dr. Foster could find something similar here in Montreal. It would be a fine line between helping and interfering. But she would do whatever she could that might help the boy.

They told King and Lehlia that they planned to leave on Monday, and proposed the Christmas visit. Jeanette noted the quick glance Lehlia and King exchanged. "We'll think about it. Wouldn't be easy," King said. They discussed the invitation that evening. "I can't stay away from the business that long," King said.

"You could take almost a week, and I could stay a little longer with Charles. I really would like to see what they do at that Academy. If I learn how they manage, I could talk with Dr. Foster about it. Maybe he would be interested in visiting the school himself. Please, King. I have to try. They seem so kind and so understanding."

"They are. Richard has a sharp mind for business, and he gets along with people. He impressed everyone he met at work - the staff in the office and the men on the floor too. I like him. I could manage the time. But the boy. How could we manage him? That's a long trip - two days at least."

"You could figure some way. And now that we have Mrs. Neal, it might not be too difficult. She is good with Charles. Very different. Doesn't treat him like a baby - more like an ordinary child who understands, but just can't speak. I think we are lucky to have her." Lehlia smiled happily to herself. At least he didn't say no; he'll figure out something. He's good at getting things done.

Meggs had kept a constant check on the set. She seemed almost more eager than the family to see the boy do things that showed he was clever. The next morning she rushed into the kitchen, "Hilda, he did it! He did it!"

"Did what, child?"

"He moved something! The barn is standing up, and there

is a chicken in the doorway of the loft! He did it! I know he did! No one has been in there but me!" Meggs was so excited she could hardly speak straight. The adults trouped in a few at a time, and all agreed that the changes had been made. They hoped. When Lehlia told King, tears welled again. She had to believe that there was reason to hope.

Lehlia did the Christmas shopping with enthusiasm, and wound up with boxes of gift-wrapped presents to take to this celebration. King decided on the train. They would leave Montreal December 19, and would have two roomettes - one for them and one for Charles and Mrs. Neal who had agreed to go. "I will require that we have some clear guidelines for Charles," she said. "I must have full charge of his behavior on the trip, Madam. Charles has begun to learn that I will expect certain things, and a trip must not give him the idea that it changes anything. I will see to it that he gets to explore the train and has things to do. But I must have charge."

Lehlia was only too happy to agree. "You are already getting him calmed down, Mrs. Neal. We are so pleased to have you with us."

Letters and phone calls flowed back and forth between the two families as plans were finalized.

CHAPTER TWENTY-FOUR

Potential II

Philadelphia – 1950

The train slowed and rumbled into the Broad Street station late Thursday. "This is where Jeanette said they will meet us." King was standing, scanning the crowd of people pushing along the platform. "There's Richard," he shouted. "And it looks like he has a Redcap and a trolley." He moved to the end of the car to be ready. Lehlia waved at Jeanette happily and stood to gather their things.

Mrs. Neal said, "Look Charles, there are your cousins. See the man with the red cap on his head; he will help us with our bags and boxes." She always spoke to Charles as if sure he understood, and Charles appeared to listen intently. She had told Lehlia and King that they should follow her example. They should never talk about him in his presence, she had insisted.

Lehlia had tentatively begun to follow her advice and now she said, "Look, Charles, there is Jeanette with the beautiful golden fox fur jacket she bought in Montreal. Doesn't she look happy?"

   ·   With everything efficiently organized by King and Richard, they piled into the two cars. Mrs. Neal manoeuvred Charles into the car with Richard and King. "Charles, you will want to ride in this car with the other men." Lehlia gave a startled gasp and started to object. But thinking better of it, she slid into the front seat of Jeanette's car, feeling a giddy sense of freedom.

In his car Richard kept up a running tourist guide talk, addressing himself to King, Charles, or Mrs. Neal. King had not yet spoken directly to Charles, but by turning his head occasionally to face the back seat riders, he was including the boy in the conversation. "Black Gold, isn't that what they call coal?" King asked.

"Yes. It's our lifeblood along the Appalachians, but it's a dirty business, dirty and dangerous. Lung problems, injuries and deaths, young men who never get a chance for education." He sighed. "I shouldn't get started on this. I would hate to have a son of mine in the business!" He switched back to the city's history and points of interest.

Jeanette pointed out a few of Philadelphia's landmarks as they drove. But their conversation focused on themselves, the family, and Charles. "Your Mrs. Neal seems to have things pretty well in hand. She has a nice way with Charles. How did you find her?"

"We were so lucky. Miss Henderson, the Principal at The Study brought us together. She had suggested what everyone thought was going to be a Montessori school. When that turned out to be a scam, she kept an eye out for us. Mrs. Neal was a teacher, but after she was retired she wanted something to 'learn from' she said. She is interested in what she called autism, said she had read a bit about it, and would use the opportunity of working with Charles to read and study more. It was almost as if we were doing her a favor. Can you imagine! Not that she doesn't know her worth; she set a fair price, and she laid down some rules for us, too. We're her students, too!" Lehlia laughed a bit uncertainly.

Jeanette laughed too. "She certainly doesn't consider herself a nanny then, does she?"

"No. She told Charles she is his tutor, or teacher, and companion. And he is to think of her as Mrs. Neal! She talks to him as though she assumes he understands everything."

"That's probably good, don't you think?"

"I guess so. She says we must do the same - always talk _to_ Charles if he is there, not _about_ him." Lehlia wanted Jeanette's confirmation that this was good.

They continued their lively discussion as they reached Jeanette's home, "Well, here we are, and there's Grandma Constance at the window, waving at us!"

Richard pulled in behind them and they all got out, standing in their small group. "You go on in. I'm going to get the luggage organized", Richard said. "Send Theo out to help me, Jeanette."

They trouped in and Constance grabbed Lehlia and hugged her. "Lehlia, love, let me look at you. You are almost my own granddaughter; Maria Elena was like a sister to me. It is so good to see you again. Far too long. And this must be Charles Kingsley; how are you, young man? Did you enjoy your first train trip?"

Charles looked uncertainly from this old woman to Mother, then to Mrs. Neal. "This is your Grandma Constance, Charles. She is the sister of your Grandpa Charles." Mrs. Neal turned to Constance, "He may think of you just as 'Grandma Constance' may he? Without the 'greats'?"

"Of course. And this is your Grandpa Philippe." She turned and grabbed King giving him a big hug, to his embarrassment. "King! King! King! You were about two years old the last time I saw you! As they say, you have grown!" She laughed joyously. "I just can't tell you how pleased we are to get the family together."

She introduced her son Lawrence and daughter-in-law Veronica. Then Richard and Theo came in with luggage and boxes. Theo went directly to Charles, put an arm lightly around is shoulders and whispered, "You are my very own cousin!" Charles pulled back, but not violently and the adults breathed a sigh of relief. It was good they had come.

The days before Christmas were full of talk, laughter and singing, memories and plans, cooking and eating. They opened presents Christmas Eve and felt stuffed with contentment. King's gift to Charles surprised them all. He had not even told Lehlia what he had chosen, had asked his secretary Mrs. Owens to order it. When she looked at him doubtfully, King said defensively, "The Boy likes small smooth things that he can make shapes with. The Scrabble tiles are perfect." And, he thought, just maybe the letters will come to mean something to him. "Don't argue, just get it."

He was right. Charles clung to the box, running his fingers across the pictured tiles. Theo reached over, opened the box, and poured the tiles out. Charles gasped, looked from

Theo to the tiles, grabbed a handful, then picked them up one-by-one, feeling their shape and smoothness. Greedily he turned them, moving them around, glancing worriedly at anyone who made a sound. Mrs. Neal said, "This Scrabble set is a Christmas gift from your Papa, Charles. He hopes you will like the little blocks." She looked at King and nodded, acknowledging the idea behind the gift. Charles threw an anxious look at his father, brushing a smooth tile against his cheek. And King self-consciously wiped a hand across his eyes. When Charles went off to bed still holding the boxed set close, Lehlia leaned against King, smiling to herself.

No one spoke for several minutes, thinking, hoping. "That was a brilliant gift, King," Jeanette said. "We haven't played Scrabble for years, Grandma. Do we still have our set? Let's get it out tomorrow."

The days before King went back to Montreal were busy visiting Philadelphia's historic spots, and browsing in the family's Woodstock Bookstore. Often, when the others went off being tourists, Mrs. Neal and Charles sat in on activities at The Academy. "Charles pays attention to whatever the other children are doing," she reported. "As yet he has not engaged in anything, but he does not avoid them. I am sure he understands much of what he sees. He has so much potential."

Charles, listening just outside the door almost grunted aloud; potential, she said he had potential. He has so much potential. How did he get potential? Could he believe this woman? He had looked in so many of Father's books. He crept off to bed, whispering the word over and over to himself.

Evenings the family talk always came around to memories - the past. "Do you remember my Aunt Felicity at all, King?" Constance asked one evening. "You were in her will for something, weren't you?"

"Yes, she left me some books, some letters and things. Made an issue of them not going to Pa Kingsley. I was summoned to Toronto for that. Never did really understand it. But I remember her best because she would answer questions."

King's laugh had a bitter tone. "That was the time I hated everyone."

"From what Maria Elena told me, you had good reason. Pa Kingsley had turned hateful to everyone, and he took it all out on you that Thanksgiving. She said that your father didn't have the courage to stand up for you. No wonder you hated everyone. You weren't more than four. How could you understand?"

"It was about a dog," King said remembering. "I found a picture of a beautiful red dog and a boy with red hair, and I asked Pa if I could have a dog like that. He just blew up!"

"That boy was my older brother, Little Kingsley," Constance said. "Papa was so bitter, Kingsley was his golden boy. Everyone loved Little Kingsley - he was the boy Papa wished he had been. I think Papa was never allowed to be a child. Grandma Margaret was a good woman but she was wrapped up in becoming "Canadian", as she called it – upper social class, really. So Papa Kingsley had to act like an upper class British man – not a little boy." Constance sighed, and there was a long silence.

"Little Kingsley died when he was eight, just before your father Charles was born, King Pa hated the world after that. He never got over it. Little Kingsley was so beautiful, and good.

Everyone just curled up inside for a while." Constance was silent for a long time. "Then Grandpa Theodore collapsed after Ernesto and Riata were killed in the Halifax explosion. And the final blow was when Mama Dorothy died in 1918, just before you were born. Papa felt that the world was turned against him. It had been a whole series of tragic things, not the dog at all really."

King felt strangely lighter. At least it had not been his fault. "I always wanted a dog." He broke off, thinking, if the boy and Mrs. Neal really connect, maybe...

Then he added, "I wonder if Charles would like a dog."

"I bet he would!" Theo had been listening intently. "Anybody would want a dog!"

That night as they prepared for bed, King said thoughtfully, "This has been good, Lehlia. I feel good about it. I'm glad we came. I do have to get back, see to things. But you stay. Mrs. Neal can learn more about the Academy's programme, see how Charles gets along."

"I think," he added thoughtfully, "I'll get Foster to come down, look into the Academy, get him together with Mrs. Neal. Do you think they'd work well together? Be able to help the boy?".

Lehlia smiled, thinking of the two - Mrs. Neal so solid and sure of herself. Mr. Foster, a fussy little man, but he makes me feel so hopeful. "I like him."

"They'd be a strange pair in a way, but they seem alike somehow. They both are positive. I think that is why I like them."

Lehlia smiled happily. King was his old self, making plans, talking about getting things done. But this was different. Now the plans included them all. She would suggest getting Dr. Foster to visit The Academy. If he and Mrs. Neal connected, maybe..... .

Tomorrow would be a new beginning.

ACKNOWLEDGMENTS

There are many people who have encouraged me and given me invaluable help and advice over the years while I was writing Redstone Manor.

Foremost among them are my Delta Kappa Gamma (DKG) friends who have applauded every effort and have honored me in many ways. I would like to name all hundred or so members who have become, over the past forty-five years, my friends, my Canadian family. Among them, three read and critiqued all or part of *Redstone Manor* (under a variety of titles.): Estelle Fainsilber, Catherine Sidorenko, and Dr. Jean Huntley Maynard. Each has given me helpful comments and advice. Rena Entus has also given Trojan service to our group, and has always been there when I needed help.

Jane Percy edited the manuscript to help me weed out typos and misspelled words. From many writing workshops at the McGill Institute for Lifelong Learning (MILL) and the Quebec Writers' Federation (QWF), I received many helpful critiques and suggestions.

I want to give special thanks to Judy Isherwood, who read the manuscript critically and made many valuable and much appreciated suggestions about style and line of story development.

Gilbert Laurin, a modest, but outstanding, local photographer gave me the picture of the wolf that adorns the cover of *The Wolfe Pack*, and created the image for the cover of *Redstone*

Manor. Many thanks, Gilbert.

Sean Huxley is the young friend I have been turning to with all my computer fumbles and glitches for forty years. He is an Apple guru and has helped me out of many problems.

Nora Hague, Archivist at The McCord Museum, spent several hours with me going over maps of Montreal in the late 19th century, and locating an effective photo of a Montreal mansion for the cover. Since she was born in one such mansion, and knows them all from experience as well as from her work at the museum, I received a wonderful history lesson as well as the all the maps and pictures I needed. Thank you Nora.

Finally, but very importantly, I thank Joanna DePoe, the young woman who prepared *Redstone Manor* for self-publication and created the website, www.mlburnsbooks.com. Her patience with a very old blind woman should go down in the records. My sincere appreciation Joanna.

MILDRED L. BURNS

I was born in Riverton, a small town in southern Iowa, a good many years ago. According to my mother, I was destined to be the sixth generation woman teacher in our family. I completed an undergraduate degree at the University of Nebraska in Lincoln, Nebraska in 1942.

I tried out a variety of jobs - soda jerk, sales clerk, Deputy County Treasurer, and Stock Control Manager in a department store. I have two children. My daughter Jeri Ohmart has worked in a program of Sustainable Agriculture in the Schools through The University of California at Davis. And my son Dr. Larry Jones is a professor of Econometrics at the University of Minnesota at Minneapolis.

Eventually I did become a teacher at Peter Lassen Junior High School in Sacramento, California and discovered that I liked teaching, and that I was considered a good teacher. After twelve years, I was granted a sabbatical leave and undertook a doctoral program at Stanford University. I completed the program in 1968, was awarded the PhD, and was offered a position as Assistant Professor at McGill University in Montreal to teach school administrative studies such as Planning, Finance, and Supervision of Instruction, along the way, becoming a Canadian citizen.

During my twenty-five years at McGill I worked with hundreds of students, some local and some from very distant countries. I was the major supervisor for twenty-five Masters and PhD thesis programs. Many of these students have remained good friends, becoming my 'Canadian family.'

Since retiring in 1995 I have whiled away my time with friends, and with writing a family memoir, *The Wolfe Pack*, and now this novel, *Redstone Manor*.

[1] In 1884, women were first allowed to enter McGill University, although in separate classrooms from male students. That year, Donald A. Smith gave McGill a $120,000 endowment grant "on condition that the standard education for women be the same as that for men for the ordinary degrees in Arts, that the degrees to be granted to women should be B.A., M.A., LL.D. which should be so granted to them by McGill University on the same conditions as to men."
In honor of Smith, McGill's female students were known for decades as Donaldas.

[2] In 1867, Henry Seth Taylor exhibited Canada's first automobile, the "steam buggy" at the Stanstead Fair. It resembled a car in appearance with four wheels (instead of the three wheels of the first Benz car). It had levers for steering, not a wheel, and was powered by a steam boiler. Reported by Mark Kearney and Randy Ray in "Whatever happened to...?"

[3] The Institute of Musical Art was founded in 1905 by Dr. Frank Damrosch, the godson of Franz Liszt. Dr. Damrosch was concerned about the number of American musicians and artists going abroad to study because the great artists of the day were found in Parris. The Institute became the Juilliard in 1924. When Augustus Juilliard, a wealthy merchant, died in 1919, he left a large bequest with which the trustees endowed the Juilliard School of Music.

[4] The Rubaiyat of Omar Khayyam
Rendered into English verse by Edward FitzGerald. Art Type Edition, The World's Popular Classics. Books, Inc. New York.

[5] Originally introduced by General Mills in 1941 and named Cheerioats, the name was changed in 1945 to Cheerios. Wikipedia.

[6] There was an actual case of a 'scam' based on a proposed

Montessori school in Montreal in the 1990s. (Reported in the Montreal Gazette, March 01, 1999). The Montessori system screens its prospective school operators very carefully. Anyone who is considering entering into a projected new Montessori school should check with the system.

[7] I have pre-dated the actual creation of the Lego Brick, the item by which the Lego Company is best known in North America. The Lego factory was founded in Denmark in the 1930s. Over the decades, it has created and produced thousands of wooden and plastic toys for children. Its most popular item, the Lego Brick was created in 1949.

www.ingramcontent.com/pod-product-compliance
Lightning Source LLC
Chambersburg PA
CBHW070635260626
47161CB00007B/2710